PRIMAL INSTINCTS

THE FERAL SENTENCE – BOOK 1
BEASTS OF PREY – BOOK 2
PRIMAL INSTINCTS – BOOK 3
REIGN OF BLOOD – BOOK 4
GAME OF DEATH – BOOK 5

Shade Owens
www.shadeowens.com

Edited by Nikki Busch
www.nikkibuschediting.com

RED RAVEN PUBLISHING

ISBN: 9798631704183

PART one

PROLOGUE

The bird squawked as if it were the happiest creature on Earth, its head pulled back and its beak aimed at the sky. It was the strangest-looking bird I'd ever seen—a brown-beige color with bright red feathers sticking straight out from the top of its beak, right in front of its eyes.

I watched as it stretched out its colorful wings in between the flowery branches, then closed my eyes and breathed in the dense scent of fresh earth and exotic flowers, feeling utterly calm. The sun had begun to rise, creating bright orange streaks on the forest floor. I followed the ropes of my hammock up to the branch overhead, where beads of condensation sat, almost teasingly. They looked cool and crisp and shiny enough to make you want to climb the tree and lick the branch.

But I was too tired—too relaxed to move a single muscle.

Maybe if I lay there without moving, reality would fade and I would find myself sprawled out on a beach somewhere soaking in my daily dose of vitamin D.

But then, someone's weight shifted nearby, and I opened my eyes. Morning had returned, and everyone started rising for another day of work. The lush greenery around me suddenly looked dry and withered and every smell I breathed in made me nauseous.

I wasn't in paradise—far from it. I was waking up in the middle of hell; waking up a prisoner to the Northers.

The pain in my hand started throbbing and my vision blurred. How long would this take to heal? Weeks? Months? I was no doctor, but from the looks of it, three of my fingers were broken. One way or another, Zsasz would eventually pay for what she'd done to me.

As I stared into the sky, through the thousands of multicolored leaves, the birds overhead became a nuisance and I contemplated my circumstances.

How long had I been here? I'd spent months being abused and tortured both physically and emotionally by the Northers, or as I'd recently learned—the Beasts. Wasn't it enough that they'd burned our Village to the ground? That they'd captured Murk, our leader, and held her prisoner to be beaten day in, day out? That they'd taken Franklin from our group to train her—or brainwash her—into being their perfect little soldier? And what about my friends, the Hunters? They would come back for me, I'd been told. Would they?

Would they even make it to me?

My thoughts drifted to Quinn and the dozens of women who came to me several nights ago. They'd stood tall with clenched fists, prepared to take a stand against the Northers.

But the truth was, nothing had changed. A few glances were shared every now and then, but no real plan had been set in motion. Maybe it was all for show. Maybe they weren't actually willing to fight back.

How was I supposed to go on like this?

I turned my head sideways when I heard Coin stretch. She always let out an exaggeratedly long moan in the morning, so I knew it was her.

I let out a long sigh. I was stuck here, surrounded by what could only be described as a living nightmare.

CHAPTER 1

Coin looked chipper today.

It wasn't like her to be chipper, ever. She always looked pissed off, on the verge of knocking someone's teeth out. And judging by the oral hygiene around here—or lack of, to be more accurate—that wouldn't have been a difficult thing to do.

She plucked berries from their stems with a smile on her dark face. Her lips seemed to move with her thoughts—one minute they were thin and flat, and the next, stretched so wide on her face that her golden tooth sparkled underneath the morning sun.

"Yo, chica," Arenas said, her head moving from side to side with fierce Latina attitude. "Why you being all weird and shit?"

Coin looked over, but her smile didn't fade. What did she possibly have to be so happy about in a place like this? In a hellish nightmare where we'd spent the last few months, or more—I'd lost count—being abused both physically and emotionally?

She shrugged, one of her eyes squinting more than the other over her puffy cheeks. "Just picturin' the house I'm gonna own when I turn thirty."

"Thirty?" Johnson said as if this was the only thing she'd heard. "How old are you?"

I didn't blame Johnson for getting defensive. She didn't look old, per se, but everyone in our group looked younger than her. Maybe this was bothering her, making her feel like she had less time left in life than the rest of us.

"What're you talking about?" Hammer cut in. She ran a hand through her short curly hair and tugged at her shirt, trying to get a breeze to slip through. "Your own house." It looked like she was about to scoff at Coin's delusion, but instead, she eyed me, lips sealed tight.

"Were you not there last night?" Coin said. "You saw what happened. These women..." She leaned forward, her flat, crop-topped stomach pressing against the pile of squash she held on her lap. "They wanna fight back. We're gettin' outta here."

"So, you mean a house made of bamboo and shit?" Arenas said. "Like a jungle house."

Coin shook her head, still stuck in her delusional state. "Naw, man. We're gonna get off this island. It's only a matter of time."

Poor Coin.

No one said anything but instead exchanged

glances.

I understood it—she was excited about Quinn being on our side and about all the women who'd come forward last night, prepared to stand up to the Beasts. I was excited about that too, but it didn't change all that much. It wasn't like we were getting out of here anytime soon. This was going to take a long time. We didn't know who to trust yet.

How were we supposed to hold meetings? Making any sort of attack plan was virtually impossible. There were hundreds of women inside the city. We didn't know which ones fed the Beasts information—and this *did* happen. The Beasts, though unnecessarily barbaric and cruel, weren't stupid. They had eyes and ears on the outside of their gate at all times.

We needed to be cautious about this.

I was surprised that Arenas and Johnson didn't chime in to pop Coin's rose-colored bubble. Instead of making some smart-ass remark about how we were going to spend the rest of our lives rotting on this island, they both cast their eyes down and went quiet.

"Well," Hammer said, breaking the silence, "I, for one, am gonna have a house with an acre of land, at least. Not too much, though. It'll remind me of this fucking place."

A few women chuckled, and Hammer

continued, "And every week, I'll ride out with my riding lawnmower and cut the grass. Then, my sexy wife will come out through the patio door with a cold glass of lemonade. That's how sweet she'll be—always wanting to take care of me."

Smiles spread out in our circle, and for a moment, it seemed like everyone forgot where we were.

"I second that," Johnson said. "But, with a man." She pointed a solid finger at the sky to make sure we didn't misunderstand anything, and everyone laughed. "He'll be tall, but not too tall, and he'll have pecs that I'll want to dig my teeth into." She bared her teeth and squeezed invisible pecs in front of her face.

"Yo," Arenas said, "you wanna talk about hot? This guy I was seein' before all this happened was six foot three, had abs of steel, and dark chocolate eyes you could get lost in." She sighed, obviously fantasizing about whoever this guy was. "And the perfect shadow, you know?" She brushed the back of her hand against her jawline. "The right amount that makes a guy look rough and badass."

Johnson, who now looked all excited, slid forward in the sand. "What about—you know?" and her eyes shot downward.

"Well, I didn't get that far, chica!" Arenas said. "But when he wore his favorite pair of blue jeans, I swear, that thing must've—"

"All right, we get it," Hammer said, wiping the air in front of her face as if Arenas's fantasy was distorting her own.

Arenas sighed and plopped her chin down into her palms. "God... what I'd do for a good pound—"

"All right, Arenas, clean the pile you have," I said, not wanting her to get into any descriptive details.

"Who made *you* boss?" Her bottom lip hung open revealing her teeth.

I slowly raised an eyebrow while hundreds of thoughts rushed through my mind. Not long ago, my first thought would have been, How can I best diffuse this situation? But as Arenas stared at me with that same carelessness she'd been exuding over the last few days, I found myself drawn to a thought I used to avoid having—the thought of violence.

After everything I'd done, was she seriously going to sit there and be a bitch? Trim had given up her life to allow me to lead, and now, some young, two-faced twat had the nerve to start something in front of everyone.

Not only was it demeaning, it was disrespectful.

"Trim did," Hammer cut in, her eyes darting toward my good hand. "Make her boss," she clarified.

I hadn't noticed, but I'd squeezed all the berries in my hand, and the bleeding juice probably looked like I'd torn someone's throat out.

Arenas pouted and shrugged one shoulder. "Didn't know her."

"Everyone knew Trim," Coin growled before I could get a word in.

"Knew *of* her," Arenas said. "But to be honest, no one liked her."

I didn't even have the time to react when Coin lunged over the pile of fruit and nuts between all of us and clocked Arenas in the jaw. A stock of plantains flew at my feet, and dozens of unshelled nuts rolled out into the dirt as Coin scrambled to get on top of Arenas.

"Get the fuck off me!" Arenas yelled, her arms flailing around in front of her face.

Coin swung another fist straight for Arenas's face; she grimaced upon impact, her beet-red skin looking like a ripe tomato under the sun.

"Stop it!" Hammer said, scrambling to grab Coin's legs.

But all that did was piss Coin off even more and she kicked backward, knocking Hammer in the chest.

"Hey!" someone shouted.

Coin brought a solid fist down again, and Arenas's entire head shook.

"Hey, hey, hey!"

It was Alice Number Two. She came scurrying over in a panic, her lanky arms frantically waving on either side of her. She grabbed Coin from behind with one hand around her throat and pulled back.

"Fuck off!" Coin shouted.

"Enough!" said Alice Number Two, and it was almost as if Coin only then realized what was going on. Her eyes went round and her anger dissipated as she fell into Alice Number Two's lap.

"What the fuck is wrong with you two?" Alice Number Two said. With her frizzy hair flattened on one side and her freckled cheeks rosy, she looked distraught. She slapped Coin on the back as a way of telling her to get the hell off her.

And Coin did exactly that—she rolled over to one side, shook her hand to relieve the pain in her knuckles, and glared at Arenas.

"Fucking bitch," Arenas said, rubbing the side of her face.

"Shouldn't have talked about Trim," Coin said. "You ain't known half the shit that woman did for us, so you keep your goddamn mouth shut about what you don't know."

A disturbing silence filled the air around us. In the distance, one of the elephants shook its head and the sound of its ears flapping filled the dirt-floored city. Women stopped moving about in the market tents and shacks, and a gust of wind blew hard, causing a flopping sound as it brushed through the city's hanging drapes and sheets of cotton.

"You're both idiots," said Alice Number Two.

She stood up, her chin pointed more toward the sky than the ground, and gazed down at both Coin and Arenas. It almost looked as though she didn't want to say what she was about to say but had no choice; it was the job she'd been assigned.

What the hell was going on?

And then, my stomach sank.

The chanting started out like a low grumble—a deep humming that couldn't be understood—until everyone's words meshed together and all we could hear throughout the city was, "Fight, fight, fight."

CHAPTER 2

"Are you seriously going to let this happen?" Hammer hissed.

"Fight!"

"Fight!"

"Fight!"

The voices carried so loudly across the city that everything began to feel surreal. Maybe this wasn't truly happening, and any moment now, I'd wake up in my hammock, prepared for another day of slavery. I wouldn't even mind it—I'd take slavery over having to watch two of my friends fight to the death.

But I didn't wake up, and the chanting continued.

Hammer stared at me as if waiting for me to take charge.

What was I supposed to do? Coin and Arenas had done this to themselves. They knew the rules—any form of altercation led to a death match. The only reason I'd gotten out of mine was that I'd somehow managed to kill the Norther—the Beast—hosting the match.

And after that, Rainer had made it clear that if anything like that ever happened again, we'd all pay for it. If there was one person I knew wasn't bluffing, it was Rainer. I could handle Zsasz's anger and violent outbursts, but Rainer, was something else. She looked like the kind of woman who'd sever three heads with the swing of her sword, all without batting an eyelash.

"That's Coin out there," Hammer said. She pulled at her fingers and paced back and forth.

"I get that," I said through clenched teeth. "I'm pissed off about this too, okay? What am I supposed to do? Rules are rules. If they don't fight, they both die. And if we get in the way, we'll probably all die."

I couldn't think.

Think, Brone, think.

But there wasn't an answer for this one. There was nothing I could do. I swallowed hard to keep the vomit from coming up.

"You okay, Brone?" I heard.

I turned around to find Quinn standing behind me with a handful of women around her. Her thick, flabby arms were crossed over her chest and her septum ring glistened under the sun. My heart was racing a mile a minute, but on the outside, I must have looked entirely heartless—too calm in a situation where one of my friends, if not both, was about to die.

"What happened?" she asked.

I shrugged. "A stupid fight."

Quinn let out a long breath and pinched the skin between her eyebrows. "Shit... Brone. I'm so sorry."

I swallowed hard. I wanted to scream or cry or punch someone. But I wasn't about to let my emotions get the best of me.

The cheering suddenly exploded around us and bodies moved closer toward the fighting arena—the sand pit located near the Northers' wooden gate. The smell of sour sweat invaded my nose, and I peered through a crack in between two heads in front of me to find Coin and Arenas staring at each other, both looking out of place.

This couldn't be happening.

How was this happening?

How were two young women—both with their entire lives ahead of them—being forced to fight to the death over some petty argument? This place was a nightmare. I couldn't wrap my head around it.

"Oh Lord, what is going on?" I heard.

I knew that voice. I turned around to find Georgia. She looked the same as she did the first day I met her—manicured nails, though they'd grown out quite a bit, and a snooty hop in her walk. That huge grin she'd had on her face for hours, though, had disappeared since I'd broken the news to her about her sentence being a lifelong thing.

"Is that—" she said, standing on her tiptoes to get a better view of the fight. "Oh." She let out a sigh and rolled her eyes. "A negro and a Mexican. I say do away with both."

I bit down so hard on my teeth that I heard something chip.

It isn't worth it. It isn't worth it. It isn't worth it.

The crowd exploded, and I was pushed to and fro as everyone cheered. I shoved back to get a view of what was going on only to find Arenas had climbed on top of Coin, bashing her fists down.

"Coin!" I shouted, but my voice cracked.

No, no, no.

This wasn't happening. I couldn't lose Coin. In a sick way, the only reason I hadn't lost my mind was because I thought Coin was going to win. I didn't want Arenas to die, but if I'd had to choose...

Georgia threw her arms in the air and clapped over her head. Her eyes rolled my way, and when she realized who I was, her lips turned upside down like she'd eaten a piece of turd.

"What're you so sad about?" she sneered, obviously still bitter about what I'd said. "That little Mexican is doing you a favor."

I couldn't hold it in anymore.

I shoved everyone out of my way—everyone blocking me from getting to Georgia—and tackled her to the ground. The cheering around Arenas and Coin suddenly broke, almost in confusion, and the crowd began to split apart, not knowing which fight to watch.

I grabbed her by the throat and shook her, her head bouncing back and forth, then shook so hard her head smashed into the ground beneath her. She resembled one of those rubber stress toys— the kinds with popping eyeballs.

But it wasn't enough.

There was so much anger in me that I wanted to kill her. I didn't care anymore—I'd add another life to the list. I closed my good fist and smashed it hard against her nose. A loud crack split underneath my knuckles, and blood came pouring out of her nostrils.

She yelled, but I didn't care.

I hit her again and again and again until I was brought back to my incident with Hammer. The image flashed in my mind so vividly that as I looked down at my victim's face, all I saw was Hammer. Instead of swinging down again, I held my fist midair. It shook, and my teeth clattered. But then Georgia came back into view, looking like a squished tomato, and although I wanted to hit her again, I realized she'd stopped moving.

I'd blacked out again.

"What is this?" someone growled.

Footsteps scattered away from me and I looked up to see one of the Northers moving toward me and the bloody scene I'd created. She swung her arms at her sides in an exaggerated motion and looked at me like a raging gorilla—wide nostrils over a mouth and chin forming an angry pout.

She had long black hair, though it looked more like hanging wires sticking out of her head, and her skin looked like she'd sat in the sun for far too many hours—leathery and worn.

And then another Norther came rushing toward us from the main gate, her footsteps heavy in the sand. She stomped like she weighed three hundred pounds and when she stopped running, she placed her filthy hands on her waist and smiled down at me. She was much taller than the one who looked like a gorilla and had two black-dotted markings on her face that appeared to be permanent ink. They ran across her cheeks and up toward her temples.

"Two fights?" said the taller of the two. "In one day?"

She looked amused, almost as if this were the most exciting day she'd had in a long time.

"It's the troublemaker," snarled the gorilla-looking Beast.

The taller one didn't seem to care who I was, but rather, that I'd generated some excitement for the day.

"Finish your fight," yelled the taller one, turning her attention toward Coin and Arenas.

I'd been so focused beating down on Georgia

that I'd completely forgotten about Coin and Arenas. I sat up, wiped the back of my hand against my sweaty forehead, feeling a layer of warm blood coat my skin, and stood up.

Arenas wasn't on top of Coin anymore, and it didn't look like she was trying to attack her, either. They both stood looking at me, as lost as everyone else.

"Fight!" shouted the tall Beast.

Arenas's eyes shot in my direction, then at Coin, and she hesitated. Coin closed her fists, opened them, then closed them again. She didn't know what to do, either. The crowd had stopped chanting, and no one knew in which direction to look.

"You!" the tall Beast shouted at me, realizing that her command wasn't being obeyed. "Finish what you started."

I glanced down at Georgia, whose bloody face was already swelling. She lay unconscious with her lips parted and her cheek resting in the sand. Although she was a racist piece of shit, I didn't have it in me to finish her off.

But then, as I thought of Rainer, I realized that if I didn't do this, Rainer wouldn't be forgiving this time around.

How hard would it be? To take an innocent life? Was it worth it? Was my life worth more than hers?

I shook my head and squinted.

What the hell had I become?

Why was I even considering killing this woman? For what? To save my skin? I wasn't a murderer. At least not a cold-blooded murderer. I'd taken a life to protect myself before, but this... this was different. This woman was lying unconscious and unaware of what was going on. She hadn't asked for this—I was the one who attacked her.

Then, a third Beast stepped in, obviously curious about why the entire city had gathered near the gate. She was unusually frail-looking for a Beast, with scrawny, gray-skinned arms and bags under her eyes that made her look like she was on her way to the other side, or like she'd been bitten by a zombie. Below her chin hung a half-skull mask, which meant she'd recently been out beyond the city limits.

"What's going on?" she croaked.

"Someone wants to die," said that gorilla-Beast. She tore a bone-carved blade from her right boot and took a step toward me, but what happened next was something I couldn't have anticipated.

Something hard smashed me in my ribs, though not hard enough to send me to my knees. I turned toward my attacker to find Quinn standing tall with her arms crossed over her chest and a smirk on her bright red lips.

What the hell was she doing?

Then, one of her followers—a middle-aged

woman with loose, leathery skin and rounded shoulders—swung a tight-knuckled fist straight at Quinn's face.

My eyes went huge, but Quinn didn't swing back. Instead, she winked at me, then turned around and punched another woman in the face. It took a few more punches among random women for me to understand what was going on.

They were starting fights—all of them. The sound of bone on bone and skin against skin spread through the city as the Beasts stood there perplexed, looking like a group of tourists without a map.

CHAPTER 3

"Get back to your posts!" Zsasz roared, her deep voice rumbling across the city.

Women scattered away from the fighting ring, where Coin and Arenas stood with smiles on their faces.

We'd done it—I couldn't believe it. Outsmarted the Beasts and rendered them powerless. I drew in a deep breath, my chest heaving, my shoulders drawn back.

We truly were stronger as a group.

I glanced back at Quinn, who winked at me, her right cheek pink and inflamed. She didn't seem to mind. In fact, none of the women seemed to mind that they'd been hit one way or another. In the end, it was for a greater cause.

"Now!" Zsasz shouted, and a young woman beside her—a Peasant—moved past Zsasz with a cocky smirk on her face and a smile that said, *We're untouchable.* A long ponytail hung from the top of her head all the way down to her lower back, and it swayed from left to right as she walked.

But she didn't make it very far. In one quick

motion, Zsasz reached out a scarred hand for the woman's ponytail and tugged it hard. The woman's arms flew in the air as she tripped backward, landing flat against Zsasz's chest.

And then, it was almost as if the magic around us had been vanquished by a powerful force. Smiles turned to grimaces and anxiety filled the space around us.

We weren't untouchable—we were far from untouchable.

Zsasz wrapped her mangled forearm around the woman's jugular, stretched her hideous zebra-striped lips into a smile, and pressed her cheek against the woman's face. This woman, someone I'd never noticed in the crowds before, struggled to breathe underneath Zsasz's clutch. That cocky smile of hers had disappeared instantly and she squirmed attempting to free herself.

But Zsasz didn't let go.

Both of their faces reddened—the woman, because she couldn't breathe, and Zsasz, because she was either enraged or struggling to keep hold of the woman. Squiggly blue veins appeared on Zsasz's temples, making her look even more psychotic with that wide grin of hers.

"You think you're all so smart," she spewed, and the woman flinched as Zsasz's jaw moved up and down against the Peasant's face. "You think banding together is going to protect you?" She laughed this time, and instead of tightening her grip on the woman, she let her go but held onto her ponytail, using it as a leash.

The woman reached for her hair, but Zsasz tugged on it, her wild eyes darting between all of us.

"You haven't learned anything, have you?" she said.

Her lips curved upside down, so much so that she began to look demonic.

The woman with the long ponytail tried one more time to get out of Zsasz's hold, but Zsasz pulled back on her ponytail again, only this time, when the woman landed against her chest, Zsasz didn't wrap her arm around her throat. Instead, a blade appeared, and in one quick slice, Zsasz slid its sharp edge through the woman's throat.

Her eyes rolled in the back of her head and dark blood poured out of the gash.

Screams erupted around me and one woman came charging straight for Zsasz with both fists held high by her face. She didn't even get the chance to hit Zsasz when Zsasz pushed the dead woman's body to the ground and stabbed her attacker in the stomach. This woman—the one who'd come charging to defend her dead friend, dropped both arms on either side and stared at Zsasz.

Zsasz smiled at her, then tore the knife out. The

woman collapsed to her knees with her hand clutched over her bloody stab wound. She crawled to her friend, slurred words coming out of her slobbery mouth, then grabbed her friend's pale face. "Please, Kay, please, come on. Wake up. Kay, wake up."

She did this for a few more seconds until her words became incomprehensible and she lay her head on her friend's shoulder. The next thing I knew, neither one of them was moving, and both lay there lifeless, their eyes wide open.

"Don't you fucking underestimate me!" Zsasz snapped. With shoulders hunched forward, she looked like a monster out of a horror movie—unkempt hair, blotchy skin, and blood dripping from her hand. She breathed in and out fast, but it sounded raspy and strained. "You think sticking together will save you?" She burst out laughing, then reached her hand up and licked the blood sliding down her forearm. "I will fucking kill every single one of you if I have to." Then, in one final outburst, she shouted, "Don't you *ever* disobey me again!" and saliva came splashing out into the crowd.

A heavy silence filled the city as everyone stared in horror.

My heart raced and my throat became sticky. I'd never seen her like this before. Of course she was crazy—but this was a whole new side of Zsasz I wished I hadn't seen. Was she seriously willing to kill as many women as necessary to teach us a lesson? Would she put herself and the other Beasts in a position of hardship by destroying the very people who kept them alive?

Her bloodshot eyes rolled my way and my stomach sank. But she didn't say anything. Instead, her gaze continued to explore the crowd as if searching for someone. Was she searching for the person responsible for all of this?

"It was the troublemaker," said the gorilla-looking Beast, her bright eyes finding mine.

The bumpy skin on Zsasz's ugly face stretched and she glared at me, a mixture of amusement and loathing in her eyes. "You."

I didn't even have the time to contemplate trying to run. A cold hand suddenly grabbed me by the back of my neck, and someone's hot breath blasted down against the top of my head.

"Got her," said the Beast behind me.

Zsasz walked toward me, her steps slow and calculated.

But then, someone else's voice carried through the crowd.

"It wasn't her."

Who in their right mind would come to my defense? My eyes followed the voice, but... How was that even possible? Why would *she* come to *my* defense? It was the lanky-looking Beast—the one with dark bags underneath her eyes and unusually pale skin.

Zsasz swung around. "What'd you mean?"

"She didn't start it," the Beast said. Her eyes rolled toward me, then back at Zsasz. Was she an idiot? It was me—I was the one who'd jumped on Georgia. But there was no anger in her eyes; there was no hatred. Was she defending me? Why on Earth would a Beast try to protect a Peasant? And she wasn't a trained Peasant, either. The dark digit tattoo on the inside of her wrist said as much.

She was an Orphan—one of the Russian children raised on this island.

"Then who did?" Zsasz asked. She was obviously annoyed by the contradictory information she was receiving.

"Yes it was!" shouted the gorilla-Beast.

But the tall, zombie-looking one shook her head. "No, Vluri, I don't think it was. A few of them started it at the same time. We can't punish one for the actions of many. You heard Rainer... She's a merciful leader. And by the looks of it, you've already punished them." She cast her eyes down at the two dead bodies lying in the dirt.

"You also heard Rainer say that if this happens again..." said the gorilla-Beast.

But the tall one shifted her gaze on her, which seemed to quiet her. "They didn't kill one of our own. There's no reason to keep slaughtering them."

Zsasz's wild eyes searched the other Beasts, but they shrugged and looked away, not wanting to counter the tall one's response. Were they scared of her?

What was going on?

Zsasz let out a frustrated grunt and turned away, brushing past the tall one, who I only then noticed was even taller than Zsasz. She stared at me a bit longer than necessary, making me uncomfortable. Her face was so expressionless, it was like staring into the eyes of a stone statue—I couldn't even begin to guess what she was thinking.

"Come on," I heard, and someone tugged on my arm.

It was Quinn. She held my wrist and shoved her way through the dense crowd. Whispers erupted around us, and I heard Georgia's voice. "Oh Lord... What on Earth..."

I swung my head around, but I couldn't see her. She was too short, but based on her tone, she was disoriented and hadn't the slightest idea what had happened. The pain in her face was probably setting in, and soon, she'd look down at all the blood around the collar of her shirt and have a panic attack, wondering if she was now disfigured. Then, she'd keep panicking when she realized that Kormace Island didn't have mirrors.

"I can't—" I tried. "I can't believe you."

I couldn't think. What had happened?

"What'd you expect?" Quinn said. "We're in this together, Brone." Her rose-cheeked face came into focus and I stared at the ring dangling from her nose.

I wanted to thank her, but I couldn't. I felt like I was floating in the air. Maybe it was the adrenaline, or maybe it was the realization that I'd escaped death so many times I was beginning to taste it. Soon, and very soon, my time would be up. I'd pushed my luck time and time again. Why had those two women died instead of me? I was the reason this whole fight broke out. Those women were only trying to protect me, and I'd gotten two of them killed.

"Meet me at the hammocks at supper," Quinn said, and her voice sounded like it had come from inside a long metallic tunnel.

I nodded, or at least, I thought I did.

Something loud suddenly snapped beside me and I flinched.

"Back to your post!" shouted Alice Number Two. She clapped her hands again, and this time, right by my ear. "You too, Brone."

CHAPTER 4

Arenas was quieter than usual—far more quiet than usual.

Ever since the fight, she hadn't said a word. She'd glanced up at me a few times, almost apologetically but looked away and went on scrubbing dirt off coconas—yellow, bell pepper-textured fruit that didn't much taste like fruit.

In the old world, I wouldn't have known anything about it, but I knew they were called coconas because it had started a whole argument the other day.

"Coconuts?" Arenas had said.

"Coconas!" Coin had shouted.

Arenas had cocked an eyebrow, thinking Coin didn't know what she was talking about and didn't know how to say *coconut*.

"Co-co-nah," Johnson joined in. Maybe she'd recently learned what it was, too, but didn't seem to have any trouble understanding.

Out of frustration, Arenas had flicked her wrists in the air as if to say, *Whatever*, and in the same motion accidentally propelled slime from inside a passion fruit onto my chest.

The whole gang had laughed at me.

Today, though, there was nothing to laugh about. We'd watched the violent slaughter of two more women, and no one seemed to have anything to say about that. Everyone was too afraid to talk, especially Arenas, who I assumed felt guilty for having talked back to me. Sure, Coin was the one who'd attacked her, but Arenas was the one who'd started the argument.

Or, maybe... maybe Arenas felt guilty for having jumped Coin in the fighting ring. She'd jumped at her with every intention of killing her all because *rules were rules.*

The afternoon seemed to drag on forever, and all I could think about was meeting Quinn by the hammocks at suppertime. What did she want to talk about? Were we going to devise a plan to fight back against those horrible Beasts?

That was what I needed.

A plan.

"How did she look?"

I turned my face toward the voice. It was that old Russian woman, the one who'd cared for the Orphans before their plane crashed on Kormace Island's shore. I wondered what that felt like— losing the children you cared for to a monster like Rainer. That was precisely what had happened. Rainer had taken those young girls in her care, only to raise them to be soulless soldiers.

The woman's long chin pointed left and right as she licked her slobbery lips.

What was she talking about? How did *who* look?

"My sweet Iskra," she said, the R rolling thickly off her tongue. It sounded more like she was reminiscing rather than actually telling us *her* name, whoever *she* was.

"What're you talking about?" Johnson asked, glaring at the old woman.

The woman's gray eyes, which sat deep beneath two protruding brow bones, rolled toward Johnson, then toward me. "My Iskra," she repeated. "I thought I saw her." She pointed a bony-knuckled finger in my direction. "Near you."

"I don't know who you're talking about," I said, careful not to come across as rude. This woman had shared with us incredibly valuable information, and though I was hurting in too many ways to count and contemplating cutting off my own hand, I had to be cautious if I wanted to stay on her good side.

We needed her.

"Who's Iskra?" Hammer asked, coming across as the gentle one.

The old woman pressed a water-wrinkled hand on her lumpy chest and closed her eyes. "My sweetest girl. She vas always the quietest... Such a shy little girl. After de accident, she stayed with me for a long time, even as her friends followed Rainer." She smiled to herself, a half-toothed smile at the center of tired skin, which was the most beautiful thing I'd seen in a long time. "She still visits me some days... Visits old Olga. When dey aren't around. De others." Her eyes shifted, and she glanced in the general direction of the gates as if afraid to be caught talking about her dearest Iskra.

I leaned forward with my elbows digging into my knees. "What does she look like, Olga?"

Her face lit up like she'd been asked to talk about the magic of Christmas. "My Iskra?" She shook her head and excitedly wiggled her fingers in the air. "Oh, she is beautiful. Very tall, like model. Dark hair, big blue eyes."

"Taller than most?" I asked.

Grinning, Olga nodded with two hands clasped together over her chest.

Could it be possible? That one of the Northers— one of the Beasts—wasn't as bad as the others?

I wanted to ask more questions, but something sharp poked me in the back and I stiffened. I didn't even have to look behind me to see what was going on; it was happening in front of me, too. A dozen women circled us, their eyes narrowed, their hands clenched in fists.

I didn't know what was pressing into my back, but it felt like a shiv. Coin glowered, as did everyone else, and I realized they were also being threatened at knifepoint.

But the city kept moving—women continued to work their posts; the sound of metal hitting metal echoed nearby, as did the sound of wood being chopped into fine pieces. It was far too noisy in the city for anyone to notice an out-of-the-ordinary event.

And right now, we looked like a bunch of women gathered in a circle.

"Keep doing the shit you are doing, and you will not live to see another day," said the one behind me. She had a thick accent I couldn't distinguish— a blend between African and Middle Eastern. Her breath smelled like a garbage bag left outdoors for months. She pressed her hot, sticky face against mine. "You're risking all of our lives."

She wasn't a Beast—that much I knew. And neither were her followers, the ones circling my women. They all had skin as black as the night, thick lips, and hollow earrings that formed big holes in their ears. Across the bridges of their noses were small pieces of wood pierced through their skin, right between their eyes, the way a barbell sits under the skin of an eyebrow. They made me think an African tribe had somehow landed here on Kormace Island. But, at the same time, they looked native to the land with white-henna-tattooed faces and leafy clothing.

"I'm not trying to risk anyone's lives," I said through clenched teeth.

"We don't care what you are trying to do," she said. "Keep us out of it." She gave me a hard nudge and my head rocked back and forth.

Her followers did the same thing, digging their elbows into the necks of my women as they stood up. Coin winced and looked at me, but I didn't say anything. It wasn't worth getting into a fight—not with these women. We were outnumbered, and I'd caused enough trouble for one day.

I spun around in time to catch the leader looking back at me over her shoulder. I could barely see her features because her skin was so dark, but what stood out most were the white markings on her face. They looked like tattoos, or paint, only they resembled speckles of snow sprinkled across her skin. It spread down her neck and onto her shoulders as if she'd dived headfirst into a snowbank. Her followers had a few markings on their faces too, but nothing like hers.

Where was she going, anyway? I'd never noticed her before. I watched as she disappeared through the merchant tents, her fuzzy, dreadlocked hair tied back in a ponytail and hanging in between her muscular shoulder blades.

Great.

Johnson leaned forward, her freckles almost invisible after having stared at that woman... At that Snow Face.

"Who the hell were they?" she asked, her eyes darting at them.

I shook my head. "No clue. I've never noticed them before."

"Me neither," Coin chimed in.

Hammer rubbed her chin pensively but seemed unable to pinpoint where she'd seen this woman and her tribe, so she shook her head and shrugged a shoulder.

Arenas sat quietly, still staring at the ground, and Tegan... Well, she started blabbing away about snowstorms and how they always looked like dandruff falling from the sky.

"Pssst."

Our heads followed the voice to a middle-aged woman who sat beside Olga. Cross-legged, she planted seeds in what appeared to be a newly built garden bed. She inched toward us like a crab, still in a seated position, and rested her elbows on her knees, all while Olga sat there chewing on her bottom lip and playing with her fingernails as if reality were nothing but a blurry dream.

"That was Storm," the woman said in a sharp whisper.

I slapped a hand over my mouth, but the laughter came spilling out anyway. Seriously? Some big bad tribe leader had gone ahead and named herself after a character?

Then again, she probably hadn't taken the name from the comic book. She didn't look like someone who'd grown up in Western civilization. More likely, she'd chosen it to sound fierce. I'd stick with Snow Face—it took away from the intimidation factor she wanted so badly.

The others joined in on the laughter, but the woman didn't seem impressed. Her wrinkled eyelids dropped, and her lips flattened as straight as a plastic pen.

Coin's mouth stretched wide into a grin. "She got any superpowers?"

The woman who sat cross-legged raised an eyebrow.

"Hey..." Johnson joined in. "Is she a mutant?"

Clearly not in the mood for jokes nor having any knowledge of comic books, the woman flung a hand in the air and turned around in a huff.

"No, wait," I said. "Who is she?"

The woman rolled angry eyes in my direction. She reminded me of an old grump who always frowned, no matter the situation—the kind of person who was seemingly allergic to any form of humor.

But why was I laughing, anyway? I'd just been threatened at knifepoint.

Maybe I was getting tired of being threatened. Maybe the idea of dying felt surreal now. Maybe having survived the most awful of situations imaginable, I couldn't even conceive of anything worse than what I'd already endured.

I was becoming arrogant and beginning to feel unstoppable.

Or, perhaps, having cheated death so many times, I'd lost sense of reality and grown numb.

Either way, when I thought of Lydia, I thought of someone else. I wasn't *me* anymore. I was someone else. And though I'd fought so hard not to turn into something I hated, I hadn't been able to stop it.

"No one knows exactly," the woman said. "She's been here longer than most of us. Knows the ropes. Keeps her head low."

"If she keeps her head low, then why's she threatening us?" I asked.

"Same reason that group of women over there is staring at you." The woman pointed a digging tool toward the merchant tents.

Four women stood with their arms crossed over their chests and their heads lowered, shadows masking the color of their eyes. One of them leaned in and said something to the others, and they shifted in their stances but didn't break eye contact.

The woman turned around, stabbed her tool into the dirt, then looked back at me. "Looks like you're making yourself some new enemies, my dear."

CHAPTER 5

I paced back and forth, slipping through the hammocks and brushing my fingers along the tree trunks.

"Whoa, easy," Quinn said.

"Easy?" I blurted. "Everyone's turning on me." But I stopped myself short when I caught Quinn's bright eyes narrow, and behind her, a handful of women watching me like caged animals in an exotic zoo. "Well, not *everyone*," I said.

"And keep your voice down," she said. "You're attracting attention."

Two young women, a dozen or so hammocks away from us, were sitting together at the base of a tree inspecting something in their hands. But every few seconds, they looked up at me, and I couldn't tell if they were curious or annoyed.

Either way, Quinn was right—I had to be careful what I talked about and who heard it. I looked at her and sighed, and for some reason, I immediately felt better. Quinn reminded me of someone you'd find coaching a drama class or a sports team. It looked like leadership came so naturally to her—

like she always knew what to do and when to do it.

I, on the other hand, felt like I was drowning.

I wasn't a leader, at least not naturally.

She placed two strong hands on the sides of my shoulders and stared at me until I calmed down. Quinn didn't treat me differently despite everything that had happened over the last few weeks; she wasn't afraid of me, and I needed that.

"Okay, okay," I breathed.

She smiled, then let me go. "I wanted to talk to you about last night."

Had I had a sense of humor left, I'd have probably said, "Last night was great, Quinn, but it was a one-time thing."

"I have fourteen women we can count on," she continued.

"Count on how?"

She looked around and signaled me to follow her. We passed through hanging vines, cotton sheets, pinned tents, and another row of hammocks until we were nearing the edge of the city. Deep into the forest, through the multitude of narrow tree trunks stood a Norther with a bow in her hand, poised to shoot anyone who tried to run.

They probably had several of them lined up around here in the evening—it was where all the women gathered to sleep.

She brought me underneath a tall palm tree that curved so much it looked like a giant hook. Peering around to make sure no one was watching, she crouched and pushed aside a pile of crisp leaves. A shiny beetle came scurrying out, but she ignored it and reached for what looked like string bracelets.

"What is that?" I asked.

She plucked a handful of them, pushed the pile of leaves over the remainder, and stood up.

"Our communication," she said.

"Communication?"

"You said it yourself, Brone. People here aren't happy with you. Some of them would rather live a shitty life than lose it. But others, like me, want to get the fuck out of here."

She slid one of the bracelets around my wrist. One strand was beige, and the other red, and they twirled around one another. She handed me the rest of them, a total of five, and took a step back.

"It symbolizes unity." She raised a fist in the air. The same bracelet encircled her wrist, and as her forearm pointed straight up, it slid down a bit. "When you see someone wearing this," she added, "it means they're on our side. I've already given fourteen of them to my girls. We can trust them, Brone." She bowed her head and her gaze remained fixated on me a bit longer than necessary. "With our lives."

I scoffed, though I hadn't meant to.

"What's so funny?"

"You can't trust anyone with your life," I said.

She crossed her thick arms over her chest as if I'd called her mother ugly.

"What?" I said, returning the big-eyed look she was giving me. "It's true. Everyone only cares about themselves in the end. Humans are selfish by nature."

"Speak for yourself, Brone. I've been with these women for years. They're family. If you don't have that with your women, well, then I feel sorry for you. And if that's the case, you shouldn't be giving them those bracelets."

I couldn't even respond to that. The truth was, I did have that—with the Hunters and with Ellie. I hadn't known them for years, but I'd begun to think of them as family. I swallowed hard, suddenly realizing that I'd given myself up for my friends—I'd thrown Rocket, Ellie, Fisher, and Proxy into the river to save them from the Northers.

If that wasn't love, I wasn't sure what was.

And now I had Coin, Hammer, and Johnson, who I truly cared about. Arenas was slowly making her way onto my list of people, but she had a way to go.

"You *do* have someone," she said, tilting her head forward until I made eye contact.

"Yeah."

"Then use that," she said. "That love you feel. That's enough to keep you going when you want to give up."

I took in a deep breath, trying hard not to allow emotion to resurface.

"What's your story, Quinn?" I finally asked.

She wiggled her bracelet, took a step back, and crossed her arms over her round belly.

"I'm a murderer, obviously," she said plainly. "Killed my sister's ex-boyfriend for laying a hand on her. Don't know what happened, to be honest." She looked all around like she was watching a holographic film being projected into the leaves overhead. "One second I was yelling at him, the next, bashing his face in, and then I had a frying pan with teeth stuck to it and he didn't have much face left."

"Holy shit," I breathed, my jaw hanging open.

"What's yours?" she said nonchalantly.

"That's not what I meant when I said your *story*," I said. "But I'm happy to know I'm not the only one who used a frying pan to kill someone."

She let out a loud choppy laugh and it trailed off into the market. I hadn't meant to be funny, but it felt good to make someone laugh.

"I meant, what's your story on the island?" I continued. "How'd the North—how'd the Beasts catch you? And are you all from the same tribe? Same gang? Did they catch you all at the same time?"

She bowed her head grimly, uncrossed her arms, and interlocked her fingers in front of her belly. I stared at her arms, noting the colorful ink sleeves down both. But the closer I looked, the more I realized how ugly the ink was—it looked like a blotchy mess done in someone's basement.

Maybe she'd come from a rough life.

"I can't even tell you how long I've been here. Fifteen years, if I were to guess."

"But what about—" I cut her off, pointing at her hair. It was a washed-out pink mixed in with bleached blond. It looked like she'd been dropped on the island a few months ago.

She grinned from ear to ear, revealing stained yellow teeth. "Had a little fun with my girls awhile back. We played around with lemon and fruit juices."

"So if you've been here for fifteen years, where've you been hiding out?"

"We weren't hiding," she said. "We were living our life south of here. A small gang, but it was nice, you know? Everyone took care of each other and worked together to keep shit going. We were all dumped here together from Swanson Juvenile Facility."

"Juvenile?" I cut in. I wasn't all that surprised to hear it, but it still upset me every time. How the hell was the government getting away with this? "How old were you?"

"Don't let the name fool you," she said, pointing a finger in my face. "We were the country's most well-known juvenile center. Kids killed each other every other week in that place. I was fifteen at the time—"

"Fifteen?" I cut in. "Who sent you here?"

"Jesus, Brone. What's with the interrogation?"

"Just answer me."

She cocked an eyebrow, then reached for her septum ring and played with it. "The government. Who else?"

"Which government?"

She pulled back and placed two hands on her hips, obviously getting annoyed with my questioning. "Canadian, why?"

CHAPTER 6

"So it's true," Coin said, clicking her fingers in the air. "Man, I knew it!"

"Keep it down," I said, my eyes rolling toward a group of women around a campfire. "We've already attracted way too much attention these last few days."

The sun had begun to set, and women gathered near the sleeping area—some ate their supper's leftovers, others gabbed away after a long day of work. The air was dense and humid, more humid than most evenings, which attracted big-winged bugs around us.

A gust of wind rustled the leaves overhead, turning them upside down.

"Looks like a storm's coming," Johnson said, glancing at the greenery above us.

"How do you know?" Hammer asked.

Johnson, her frizzy-haired head still tilted back, took a deep breath and blew it out. "My mom used to say that was how you know a storm's coming. See that?" She pointed straight up at the nearest tree. "How the leaves are turned upside down?"

"Man, no one cares," Coin cut in. "Brone, talk to us." She slid forward in her hammock, her shoulders rounded and her eyes big. "Did she say anything else? Is the Canadian government involved, too?"

Hammer scoffed. "I doubt it. They probably paid the states to use their island as a one-time thing. Canada's way too liberal to pull something like this. What'd you say the name of the facility was? Swanson?"

I nodded.

She slapped Johnson on the shoulder seeing as she was the only one sitting at arm's length, and Johnson gave her a dirty look. "I saw that on TV— the Swanson fire."

"What're you talking about?" Coin asked.

"In 2070," Hammer continued. "I remember the year because it's the year I got sent to this hellhole. It was February, and it was all over the news. How haven't any of you heard about it?"

Everyone stared at her, so she kept going. "Apparently, the whole facility went up in flames and no one survived."

I gawked at her. "Um, well, that's bullshit. A bunch of them are here."

"Must've been a cover story," Johnson said, rubbing the arm Hammer had slapped.

"I feel like we're in a fuckin' TV show," Coin said. "Man, why the hell would they ship a bunch of juvenile convicts here, then burn the damn place up and make it look like an accident? If they wanted to get rid of them that bad, why didn't they actually *burn* them?"

I shook my head. "I don't know. I have no idea what's going on. For some reason, they wanted the bodies here, on the island."

"Don't make no sense," Coin muttered, rubbing her hands through her fuzzy hair.

I let out a long breath, then pointed at the bracelet around her wrist. "So, are we clear on the bracelets?"

Everyone nodded.

"Don't tell anyone about them, and if they ask about them, you tell them it's the latest style. If they ask for one... send them to Quinn. She'll sell them blue ones."

They all nodded again, but then Coin furrowed her brows and glared up at Arenas. "How do you know we can even trust each other?"

"Back off," Arenas said, which was the first time she'd spoken since standing face-to-face with Coin in the fighting ring.

"Are you fuck—" Coin started, but she lowered her voice when she caught my eyes. "Girl, you didn't even hesitate in that ring. You came at me like you didn't even know me!"

"Yeah, and you just stood there," Arenas said. "No wonder Murk never chose you to be a

Battlewoman. I'm sorry, okay? You think I wanted to hurt you? You think I wanted to fight?" She moved her head from back and forth, her bold attitude resurfacing. "Chica, it was a life-or-death situation, and if I have to choose between me and someone else, I'll always choose me." She jabbed a finger into her chest, breathing hard, her small shoulders bouncing up and down. It was apparent she'd been holding this in for quite some time.

"Hate to take sides, here," Johnson said, "but the girl's right."

Coin's hateful glare rolled toward Johnson, who raised two hands and added, "Like I said, I'm not taking sides. But you guys were put in a situation where only one person comes out alive. If you want to live, morals are out."

"You've never been in that situation," I said, "so how would you know?"

"Look, guys," Hammer cut in. "It's over, okay? You're both still alive thanks to Brone. So how about we all shut up and move forward?"

To think that a year ago, Hammer had jumped me in the forest and threatened me at knifepoint was all too surreal. She wasn't that woman anymore—she'd changed so much, both physically and emotionally, that I didn't even recognize her anymore. Anytime tension started to build, she'd try to defuse it.

I was lucky to have her.

"So, about these bracelets," she added. "What's the purpose? Solidarity?"

"Something like that," I said.

"I hate to say it, Brone, but that's not much of a plan," she said.

"It's not a plan," I said. "It's the start of a movement. We can't start fighting back without knowing how many of us *want* to fight back. It'll get us killed. We need a symbol—something that lets us know who's with us and who isn't. When the time's right, we'll take a stand."

I wasn't sure when the time would be right, but all I kept thinking about was what that woman had told me from behind her prison bars. It had sounded like she'd been reciting lines from a poem—like she'd memorized every word for me.

"We're alive. Fisher made it. We're coming for you."

When were they coming? And who were *they*, exactly? I hoped to God that the Hunters weren't stupid enough to come on their own. They needed reinforcements—more Battlewomen if they hoped to stand a chance against the Northers. Had they found more women to join their society? Had they received new drops? There was so much uncertainty it made me sick to my stomach.

I couldn't bear the thought of my friends coming to our rescue only to get themselves killed.

They needed to be prepared, and we needed to

be ready to help them help us.

"Try to keep your heads low for the next little while," I said, my stare lingering on Coin and Arenas a little more than the others. "That means no fighting."

Arenas flicked two fingers in the air as if to say, *You got it,* and Coin gave me her usual nod.

But the sound that followed next was the last thing I'd have expected to hear.

"W-w-why don't we r-r-run?" said Tegan.

Everyone's mouths hung open as they turned their attention to Tegan. Her arms were wrapped around her legs, her bony knees pressed up against her chest. Her shaggy brown hair hung over most of her face and swayed from this way and that every time she jerked her head to move the hair out of her eyes.

She didn't look up, though. Instead, she stared at her curling toenails and scratched at the skin of her bare feet. "W-w-why fight? If we all r-r-run at the... the same... the same time."

I looked at Hammer, then at Coin. Was Tegan onto something? Yesterday, that was precisely what I'd intended to do—to run. What if Tegan was right? What if we all ran together? Dozens of us. How on Earth would the Northers catch us all?

"What about those who don't follow?" Johnson said. "We leave them behind?"

"We c-c-c-ome back," Tegan said. "With the H-

H-Hunters."

Why hadn't I thought of this? It was much more realistic to escape, gather strength, and attack the Northers from the outside than it was to attempt to fight back from within. I wanted to throw my arms around Tegan, but I could tell from her body language that she didn't want anyone near her.

"Tegan's onto something," I said, my voice turning into a whisper. "Think about it. If there are dozens of us running in the same direction, it'll be impossible for them to catch us all. There are what? A dozen Northers spread out around the city's perimeter?"

"Thirty-two," Sumi said.

I swung around to spot Sumi standing behind me, arms crossed over her flat chest, and her large hood pulled forward, making the burn scars on her face and head less visible.

Her dark eyes darted back and forth. "And I'd suggest you find somewhere else to talk about this." She then playfully pinched the red and beige bracelet around her wrist and offered us a crooked, lipless smile.

CHAPTER 7

Alice Number Two came storming toward us, a blanket over her head and her legs covered in mud. She was yelling something with her mouth wide open and one arm waving out from underneath the blanket, but the heavy rain and strong gusts of wind masked her sounds entirely.

It was like watching a television show on mute.

When she finally reached us, she tore the blanket off her head, which hadn't helped her stay dry, and gave us an impatient, unimpressed stance—both hands on her hips and her weight shifted onto one leg.

"Get your asses out there," she ordered.

"Are you kidding?" Arenas said, and a loud clap of thunder erupted in the sky. She then made her eyes go big as if to say, *My point exactly.*

"I don't care if it's raining," said Alice Number Two. "Get out there and do your job."

"I think it's being done for us," Johnson said, and Coin burst out laughing.

"Girl's got a point." Coin waved a finger toward our station. "All that water's cleanin' everythin' for us."

"That water," sneered Alice Number Two, "*ain't* prepping meals for everyone."

"No one else is working," Johnson said. "And we barely got any sleep all night." She shivered and wrapped her arms around herself.

It had rained most of the night, and every few hours, flashes of lightning illuminated the sky above us before the thunder kicked in, shaking the trees around us.

I was cold, wet, and exhausted. The last thing we needed right now was to get even wetter and colder. She was being ridiculous.

"No one else has a job as important as you," she said. "People need to eat."

"They can eat fuckin' bananas today!" Coin growled.

Alice Number Two took a long, exaggerated breath through flared nostrils. "Unless you want Zsasz involved right now, I suggest you get off your asses and get to work."

Everyone turned my way, expecting me to take a stand.

Pick your battles, I thought to myself. I contemplated telling her to piss off, but she'd already threatened to get the Northers involved. The last thing we needed right now was more heat. So instead, I got up and signaled everyone to follow me, which they did but while grunting and moaning.

The moment we stepped out from underneath the safety of overhead trees, the water came pouring down on us as if being dumped by the bucket.

"This is bullshit!" Coin shouted, water splashing off her lips.

I looked back at her, glaring to keep water from getting into my eyes. "I know, I'm sorry," I shouted. "But like I said, we need to keep our heads low."

A few other women came trudging out from the sleeping area, their bare feet slipping and sliding in brown gunk. Along with them came Olga, the old Russian woman. She was old and frail, and Alice Number Two should have let her stay in the forest. But Olga and those with her were the other half of the Food Station, so they needed to be out here. They looked as annoyed as we were.

Aside from the rain coming down hard, no other sound came from the city. Instead, everyone remained safe within the sleeping area, covered by thousands of leaves and angled tree trunks. We, on the other hand, shivered as we moved to our post.

I clenched my teeth, imagining where the Northers were right about now. They'd probably gathered inside their fancy wooden cabins to stay warm and dry.

Something suddenly splashed behind me, and I turned around to spot Tegan lying in the mud, her entire face glistening and her limbs frantically moving around to gain traction. She looked like a fish flapping in water.

Poor Tegan.

Hammer rushed to her side and grabbed her underneath the armpits.

"I got you," she said, pulling her up.

Why was Alice Number Two doing this? Why couldn't she have waited for the storm to settle?

Arenas was the first to approach our daily workload—a massive pile of fruits, vegetables, and nuts that had begun rolling overtop one another due to the rain. Shells and skins glistened, and the sand all around them turned into a mud pit.

This job was like a never-ending cycle—like working on an assembly line. No matter how hard we worked, food kept getting dropped in the mud. But we kept cleaning, cutting, peeling, and sorting. Maybe eventually, we'd finish the pile since no one was out gathering resources to add to it.

Arenas almost fell coming back with two coconuts in her hands. I had no idea how she planned on cracking them open in this rain.

The rain persisted up until around lunchtime, and by then, we were all quivering and feeling sick. But Alice Number Two didn't care. She told us to shut our mouths and keep working, so that's what we did.

It wasn't long before I realized that keeping my

mouth shut was a lot harder than speaking up. When the rain finally stopped, the city returned to normal and it became even harder for me to stay quiet. Every few minutes, we were either being harassed by Alice Number Two or by hateful Peasants walking by, shouting insults, or telling us to go back to wherever we came from.

And every time this happened, I closed my eyes, took in a long breath, and slowly let it out. Everyone stared at me, expecting me to finally snap, but I didn't. I'd meant what I'd said to all my women—we had to keep our heads low. There was a bigger goal in mind here, and I wouldn't allow my emotions or my pride to get in the way of that.

The evening went by as it did most nights, only, without a fight this time—without my getting us into trouble. I was quiet, for the most part, aside from a few groups of women who laughed out loud with fingers pointed in our direction.

What was wrong with them? Why were they treating me like the enemy when the real enemies were living a somewhat luxurious life behind that giant wooden gate, spending their days eating, sleeping, and training Fighters. In the meantime, we were out here, suffering from exhaustion, hunger, and cold, all to ensure the Beasts had a comfortable life.

These women had been brainwashed into believing this was the safest life for them—under the protection of the Northers.

I stared at the sky that evening, watching as it darkened from a powder blue to a midnight blue filled without thousands upon thousands of stars. I couldn't see them all from here, but every few meters, I caught a crack between a multitude of leaves and the stars I did manage to see looked like little diamonds floating in the sky.

Maybe one day, I'd get to appreciate the sky again.

We had to get out of here.

I turned over in my hammock, still cold from being forced to work in such horrible conditions that day, and all I kept thinking about was Ellie and the warmth of her body against mine. Picturing her there kept me warm a bit.

She was okay, I kept telling myself. I'd get out of this nightmare of a prison and find my way back to her. I closed my eyes, the sound of whispers fluttering around me. It wasn't something I enjoyed, but it was something I'd gotten used to—there were always women chitchatting even after everyone was settled in their sleeping arrangements.

Some lay in the dirt, others on sheets of cotton, while my women and I, along with Quinn and hers, lay in hammocks Quinn had constructed and allowed us to use. It was far more comfortable than the ground and much less cold.

So I held on to this speck of positivity amid a sea of negatives and slowly, the voices began to fade away. I wasn't sure how long I lay there, listening to beetles, frogs, and insects I'd probably never see on this island until I disappeared from reality for only a few hours—long enough to get away from the anger, hatred, and despair.

CHAPTER 8

I felt like a robot—like a piece of machinery built for production and nothing else.

The days began to bleed into one another, and my exhaustion was getting the best of me. Every night, I spent hours staring into nothingness, waiting for the voices to subside, and by the time I fell asleep, it seemed as though morning had just arrived.

After a few weeks of repetition, the bracelet around my wrist lost meaning.

Everything lost meaning.

No one looked at me as their savior or hero anymore. I wasn't some rebel who'd stormed into the Northers' city to save these women. I was a nuisance who'd gotten people killed. As for the women who did stand at my side, I felt sorry for them. I wasn't doing anything to console them out of fear of getting someone else killed.

A clammy hand grabbed me by the forearm one morning, and I cracked my eyes open.

"D-d-did you th-th-think about it?" Tegan said.

I wiped gunk from my eyes and mouth, sat

upright, and stared at her with tired eyes. "Think about what?" I whispered.

Women were still asleep, and a morning fog covered the forest floor.

Tegan raised a hand beside her mouth as if this would somehow keep her words safe.

"Running," she mouthed.

Running, I thought.

No, I hadn't thought about it.

Why hadn't I thought about it?

What was wrong with me?

I was losing my mind.

Hadn't Tegan brought this up a few days ago? Or had it been a few months? I rubbed my forehead, creating little pieces of oil and dirt underneath my fingertips. When had I last cleaned myself?

God, I missed the Waterfall. I missed being able to dive headfirst into water, the salty warmness caressing every inch of my body. Here, no one showered. At least not the Peasants. Once per week, we were given the privilege of using the community water buckets to clean our skin.

In other words, the Northers placed a dozen big cauldrons of water near the wooden gates and allowed us, the Peasants, to circle them like vultures. The few times I attempted to use it, the water was brown by the time I got there. Other times, they were empty. Oftentimes, some Peasants dumped the entire bucket on themselves, leaving nothing for the others.

"B-B-Brone?"

I looked down, realizing that Tegan was still standing inches away from me. The freckles on her face looked like they'd tripled underneath all the filth. I couldn't tell her skin apart from the dirt.

"D-d-did you... D-d-d you th-th-think ab-b-b—"

"No," I snapped, not wanting to hear any more of her stuttering. She cowered back like a helpless, beaten dog, and I cleared my throat. "I'm sorry. It's a great idea, Tegan. Let's chat about this later, okay? When it's"—I looked around to make sure no one was listening—"more private."

She smiled at me, which was something I hadn't seen her do since I got here. In fact, I realized then that I could see the entirety of her face without her hair draping over it.

She twirled on her feet, but I quickly reached out and grabbed her arm. She flinched and pulled away but seemed to calm down when she realized it was only me.

"It's nice to have you back," I said.

She nodded fast and scratched the side of her head, obviously not yet comfortable enough to talk about anything she'd gone through.

The moment she disappeared from the sleeping area, I sat upright and stretched my neck.

Why *hadn't* I thought about it? Although a bit

risky, running away seemed like our best option, especially if orchestrated correctly. And especially since the Hunters, my people, still hadn't come for us. We couldn't sit around and wait, either.

Besides, a few Northers wouldn't have the means to stop dozens upon dozens of women running out from the city.

"Ahhhh, fuck," Hammer growled.

I turned sideways to find her lying in the dirt beside my hammock. She held a white-fingered hand against her cheek, and squinted her eyes so tightly they looked like little caterpillars.

"What's wrong? You okay?" I asked.

"My... My f...ing tooth," she mumbled.

Hammer wasn't the first woman to complain about a sore tooth, and she sure as hell wouldn't be the last. In the Village, we'd been careful about oral hygiene for the most part—chewing on peppermint leaves, using wood to scrape away plaque, and even creating little brushes out of weird, dry plants found in Tegan's shop.

But here, none of that mattered.

We had no rights, and hygiene didn't matter to the Northers.

I licked the front of my teeth, feeling a thick, grimy layer against the tip of my tongue. My breath, too, was something I'd learned to ignore. Mornings were the worst—sometimes, almost enough to make me gag.

But it was part of the package—part of the cruelty we were being forced to endure.

"Yo, what's up with your girl?" someone asked.

I looked up to find one of Quinn's women standing in front of me, her hands on her waist. She had wiry blond hair like a helmet made of hay. I didn't know her name, but she wore one of our bracelets around her wrist. I had to trust this meant something.

"It's... S'my tooth," Hammer mumbled again.

"See that?" the woman asked, pointing through the trees and straight into the market.

Hammer followed her finger, as did I, though I had no idea what she was pointing at.

"The shack on the right," she added. "It has a cloth roof with a hole in it. See it? And right beside it"—she jabbed her finger in the air as if trying to touch it—"is a sign. It looks like a three-year-old scribbled something on it, but it's supposed to be a tooth."

I almost scoffed, but I wasn't even in the mood to fake laugh. "Let me guess... the town's dentist?"

The woman nodded. "Not much of a dentist, but she'll rip it out for you."

Hammer's eyes went huge and she pulled her face back until the back of her head hit the tree behind her.

"You don't have much of an option around here," the woman continued. She then pulled her right cheek away from her teeth, revealing several black holes. "You'll have more problems if you let that cavity get out of control."

Hammer's eyes were still popping out of her head.

I didn't blame her. Who the hell wanted some uneducated woman to pull out their teeth? And without proper equipment, it would hurt way too much.

The woman must have noticed the horrified look on my face, too. She laughed and said, "Ya won't feel it. She's good friends with Mashi. She's got all you need to numb that shit."

I remembered that name—Mashi. Sumi had told me about her. She was the one who snuck drugs into the city while gathering resources.

Hammer, not looking any more convinced than earlier, stared at the woman like she was insane.

"Hammer," I said, "it'll be fine. Didn't we have someone in the Village who used to do that?"

She swung her head my way. "Lilac? S-she... She was t-the swe...st thing. Ev...everyone trusted her."

The woman gave Hammer a solid smack on the shoulder. "Don't worry. Ripper'll take good care of you."

"Ri—" Hammer tried, but the woman started laughing and walked away. Hammer's big eyes rolled my way and although anyone else's jaw would have dropped at this point, her teeth remained clenched together tight, like she was afraid that if she breathed, her teeth would fall out.

"I'm sure she's only messing with you," I said, though truthfully, I wasn't entirely sure. "Come on, let's go before Alice Number Two starts yelling at us to get to work."

CHAPTER 9

The sign overhead looked like someone had tried to carve a troll or a disfigured goblin. How the hell was that intended to be a tooth? It looked old, too. With a doughy-looking texture and stained edges, the wood looked as though it had endured hundreds upon hundreds of storms.

The building had no walls per se, other than cotton sheets that hung from loose hooks on wooden poles. There was, however, an entryway built of wood that resembled a doorframe. It almost looked like this alone was what supported the entire structure.

Hammer glanced sideways at me one more time before we bowed our heads to fit through the entryway, suddenly wishing we hadn't.

* * *

"Mom, do we have to come here?" I asked, staring at the building's front door.

I was due for a dental checkup, and being that our usual clinic had caught fire a few weeks ago, my mom decided to take me to this new place, 99 Dental. It was the cheapest place in town. At ten years old, I didn't have much say.

It looked incredibly cheap, too. Maybe that was why it was called 99 Dental.

The windows were all foggy, but not foggy on the inside due to the weather—rather, a buildup of condensation either from the inside of the building or in the windows themselves. The front door, something that looked more like a white slab of wood than anything else, had peeling paint all over the place, revealing big brown patches.

"Come on, sweetheart, let's go inside," my mom said, reaching for my hand.

I was so disgusted, I almost pulled away. But I knew it wasn't her fault, so I didn't. Working night shifts in a hardware store wasn't exactly the best-paying job, and because of her fibromyalgia, she constantly missed some of those shifts, which cut her pay in half.

I'd gotten pretty used to being poor.

A little bell rang over my head as I walked in, and the woman behind the reception desk looked up at us, her bright eyes hovering over the crusty-looking counter.

"Hi there," she said, almost too happily. It was like she was forcing it, knowing that if she didn't, we'd walk out.

My mom walked up to the counter, eyeballed the woman's name tag and said, "Hi... Josephine. I booked an appointment for my daughter Lydia."

She stretched over the counter like she was trying to read right off Josephine's paper. "Lydia Brone."

"Ah, yes," Josephine said. Her perfectly straight teeth looked like they'd been bleached twice a week for an entire year. "Please, have a seat."

We sat down on green leather chairs—the only two at the back wall that didn't have long cracks in them. Even the television overhead was old—a regular flat-screen TV from my mom's time. No one carried these anymore, and you never saw them in public spaces. The cool thing was to have the holographic televisions: two small speaker bars distanced from one another that projected a screen inches away from the wall.

I was five years old when they first came out, and my mom wanted nothing to do with them. At first, you had to buy some special paint to put on the wall behind it to ensure the image quality shone through, but over the years, they'd developed better technology, allowing the screen to be viewed anyplace, anytime, and under any condition.

This place was obviously too poor to afford a TV like that. But then again, so were we.

It seemed like we waited hours in that place, and every minute of it, my stomach churned. What would the dentist be like? Would he or she cause me pain? This place was so filthy. What if I caught an infection?

I stared at the children's books on the coffee table, wondering how many germs were crawling all over them. I hated school for that—teaching all of us the importance of hygiene and the effects of bacteria. I was only ten years old and I hated opening doors in public without a napkin. My mom seemed pretty happy about this, though. She'd said something along the lines of "It's about time people become aware."

Aware, or paranoid?

She kept insisting it was awareness.

"Brone?" came a sweet woman's voice. "Lydia Brone?"

I looked up and caught the eyes of a tall, thin black woman. She had silky-looking hair that hung over her shoulders and a smile on her face that instantly made me feel better. I was strangely at home here, and every preconceived notion I had about that dental clinic disappeared.

"I'm Dr. Lina," she said, her hand holding a wooden door open. "Come on in."

* * *

"Mmm," the woman grunted.

She was no Dr. Lina—in fact, she wasn't a doctor at all. She looked like she'd once lived on the streets of New York City: ragged clothes, dirt-covered skin, a hump on her back, and gray hair that almost looked black because it was so dirty.

Impatiently, she waved a wrinkled hand without

looking at us when she realized we weren't coming in.

I took a step forward and looked around. A bed sat at the very center of the shack. It was more of a wooden plank elevated by uneven posts. There were no cushions, no hay... only a solid bed that lay on an angle, probably to allow her a better look inside one's mouth. It looked wet, too, or water damaged, probably because there was no roof.

Sunlight came blasting in, creating a white patch at the top of the woman's head. She finally turned around on her stool, eyed us both up and down, and said, "What'd ya need?"

Her upper lip curled over her teeth, revealing black holes everywhere.

I suddenly wished I was back at 99 Dental.

This place looked like a nightmare. And what tools did she use? I peered over her shoulder, where a tray made of bone held a few metallic tools. They looked like pliers and knives.

I swallowed hard, relieved that I wasn't the one who needed dental work.

"Uh... M'tooth," Hammer said, slapping a hand over her cheek again.

"C'mere, then. Lemme look at ya."

Hammer reluctantly stepped forward looking like a shy kid on the verge of giving a classroom presentation.

"On the bed," the woman said.

Hammer pulled herself up—something she'd probably been unable to do when she'd had the extra fat around her waistline—and lay on her back.

The woman slid her stool closer and leaned forward, the hump between her shoulders making her look crippled. She stuck her fingers inside Hammer's mouth and pulled her cheeks apart.

"Ahhhh, right there, then?" she asked, and Hammer kicked the air and let out a long moan.

"S'all swollen and 'fected," the woman said, her eyeball almost in Hammer's mouth. "Looks like an abscess."

She pulled her fingers out and slapped her knees. "Gotta take 'er out."

Hammer's eyes shot at me and at the dentist woman. "Like... pull?"

"Er, yeah!" the woman said. She reached over Hammer, let out a short grunt, and plucked a pair of metal-looking pliers from her bone tray.

"W-What about t-the pain?" Hammer asked in a panic.

The woman didn't say anything. Instead, she smiled—or at least, I think she did—and pulled from her pocket what appeared to be a pouch made of either animal skin or liver. It was sealed tight with dozens of stitches at the top.

She poked her nails at the string until the bag finally opened up. Then, she licked her finger, stuck it into the pouch, and pulled it back out. It was covered with white powder over the spot she'd licked.

"W-what is that?"

"Don't ya worry," she said. "It'll numb ya right up." She shoved her finger inside Hammer's mouth, and as Hammer kicked the air, I turned away. I couldn't stand around and watch this crazy woman pull a tooth out of her mouth.

"I'll be at our station..." I said, feeling queasy.

Hammer moaned loudly, and although it had made no sense, it had probably been something along the lines of, "No, don't leave me!"

Hammer was tougher than she gave herself credit for.

She'd be fine.

I walked out just in time. The next thing I heard was Hammer yelling. I should have been a good friend and stayed with her, but when it came to teeth... I couldn't do it. It was my weakness. I'd grown accustomed to watching people heal stab wounds and infected cuts, but I wouldn't stand there and watch someone rip out a tooth.

"Yo, Brone," I heard, followed by heavy footsteps.

I turned around to find Coin jogging toward me. "Headin' to the Food Station?"

I nodded.

She parted her lips to say something else, but a

loud trumpet sound resonated throughout the city.

CHAPTER 10

"Out of the way!" Zsasz spat, stomping her way through the city grounds.

Rebel, her ugly, choppy-haired sidekick, followed close behind almost as if being dragged by a leash. Then, a dozen more Norther-looking women came blasting out of the wooden gates. They wore masks on their faces—half skulls that hung below their eyes—but there was something off about them.

They didn't look like Orphans or Originals—they looked much frailer and less armored. And, unlike the Orphans and Originals, they didn't have padded fur on their shoulders or metallic weapons. They carried wooden sticks, bows, and hammer-like weapons built of stone and rope.

Zsasz whistled, and the dozen armed women marched forward, staring straight ahead as if they'd been programmed to obey any order given to them. They were so rigid they almost looked like robots covered in flesh.

"What's going on?" Coin mumbled, leaning in toward me.

Hammer came out of the Dentist's shack with one hand pressing hard into her cheek. She scowled at me but didn't say anything.

"I'm not the one who told you to go see..." But I fell short, uncertain of the dentist's name.

"Rip... Ripper," Hammer said.

My jaw hung open, and though mortified, I couldn't help but smile. "You're kidding me," I said. "I thought that was just a joke that Quinn's girl told you."

Hammer shook her head, her hateful glare still fixated on me.

I was about to point out that again, this wasn't my decision. I hadn't given her an abscess, and I sure as hell hadn't forced her to walk in there.

"Wh-what's this?" Hammer asked, staring straight ahead at the crowd that had now formed around the women dressed in primitive armor.

I shrugged. "No idea."

"Argalis!" Zsasz shouted, jabbing a spear into the air.

Her figure, which was much larger than everyone else's, made her look like a monster. Her shoulders were drawn back, dark fur standing out in every direction, and her skull mask hung under her chin, held by what I could only assume was a string around her neck.

"That Russian?" Coin asked.

"Doesn't sound like it," I said.

"It's not Russian," I heard, and I swung around to find Sumi standing beside me.

Today, I could see the beautiful half of her face from underneath her hood. She'd pulled her black hair over the pink burn scars. Her dark eye narrowed in the shadow of her hood.

"I don't know what it is," she continued. "It's like they have their own language for only certain words. I don't think they've developed an entire language, but whatever it is, they can use it to communicate."

Coin planted two hands on her waist and scoffed. "Are you shittin' me? You're sayin' these crazy bitches found a way to communicate without anyone else bein' able to understand?"

"Exactly," Sumi said.

"Well th-that sucks," Hammer said.

"What's goin' on, chicas?" came Arenas's voice. She craned her neck, her eyes reaching over my right shoulder, and stared at the crowd of women. "Oh, shit..."

"Yeah," I said. "Doesn't look good."

"You think they're goin' out to fight?" Arenas asked.

Coin and I exchanged a glance, but she spoke first. "Looks that way."

"Yeah," Arenas said, "and who're they goin' after this time?"

Then, Johnson popped up beside me, her frizzy

hair looking yellow underneath the morning sun and her freckles making her face look brown. "What's going on?"

"They're goin' out to fight, we're guessin'," Coin said.

"Fight who?" Johnson asked.

"Get your asses to work!"

I turned around to find Alice Number Two standing with her legs at shoulder's width, her eyes bulging out of her skull, and her bony arms crossed over her flat chest. It looked like she'd lost even more weight these last few weeks—so much so that her wrist bones were popping out.

"We're goin', we're goin'," Coin said, but she didn't budge.

"You think they're going after our people?" Johnson asked. She cast her eyes down and bit her lips. "Well, what's left of them..."

"You think they know about the Co—" Coin started, but she cut herself short when she caught my glare.

The Cove was the only thing keeping the Hunters and a few survivors safe. How could the Northers possibly know about that? They couldn't, could they? How on Earth could they have gotten that information? The only people who knew about the Cove were us—the ones standing right here, and...

Then my stomach sank.

As the crowd moved forward and the army marched, Zsasz shot me her usual hateful, scarred smile. The stripes stretched into wide cuts, revealing a darker shade of pink inside each scar.

But she wasn't the one who scared me—not this time.

What caught my attention was the first woman standing at the front of the line. She wore padded armor that appeared to be made of turtle shells glued together, tall boots made of leather, and a half-skull mask that was chipped at its jawline, revealing her skin underneath. Her thin, tattooed arms were bare and covered in dirt and bruises, but she swung them back and forth as if they were the strongest set of arms on Earth.

And although she looked dangerous, that wasn't what frightened me. It was those eyes... I swallowed hard as they rolled my way above her skull mask. I'd have recognized them anywhere.

Franklin.

But she wasn't looking at me like an old friend. In fact, she wasn't even looking at *me*—she was looking through me like she'd never seen me before.

CHAPTER 11

"We need to leave tonight," I said, staring at the sand at my feet. So many thoughts rushed through my mind that all I wanted to do was get up right then and run—I'd take my chances with the guards around the city's perimeter.

Hammer tossed a coconut shell onto the pile beside her, scanned her surroundings, then said, "You're sure?"

I nodded. If I was right... If God forbid the Northers had managed to pull information out of Franklin, then they were on their way to the Cove, probably being led by Franklin. Though she didn't know where it was specifically, she knew the general direction. And it wouldn't be hard to find a Cove off a shoreline. All they had to do was walk toward the beach.

I couldn't let that happen. I had to get to the Hunters, to my friends, before they were attacked... Before they were killed.

"Brone?"

I'd been staring at the ground, probably looking like a serial killer with wide eyes and a clenched jaw.

"You guys remember what Tegan said?" I suddenly realized Tegan wasn't even with us. "Where is she, anyway?"

Arenas shrugged. "Girl's been throwin' up all morning."

"Better than out the other way," Hammer said. Her cheek was swollen on one side, but it looked like she was getting used to the pain. In fact, it kind of looked like she was high. She suddenly let out a broken laugh, and a goblet of blood spat out in front of us. "You guys remember the Cliff?"

Who *didn't* remember the Cliff? How could anyone forget that foul-smelling place? Besides, I didn't like to think about that place. All it did was remind of me of when Hammer, whose identity I didn't know at the time, had forced me to give her some of my pearls on a weekly basis.

It was my money, but I'd been forced to go bury some of it at the Cliff for her to collect.

So yes, I remembered the Cliff.

She must not have noticed my irritation, because she kept laughing and said, "One time, it got so bad that when I was done, some woman slipped right in it."

"Fuck, Ham," Coin said, smacking her on the shoulder. "We didn't need to know that."

Hammer threw her head back and kept laughing.

It wasn't *that* funny. At least not to me and not now.

"Tegan," I said, trying to bring everyone back to our conversation.

Everyone but Hammer, who was now wiping tears from her eyes, nodded.

"About running," I added, but I could tell they knew what I was talking about. "I think we should go tonight when it gets dark."

"Why tonight?" Coin asked.

"They'll be distracted. Some of the Northers have already left with their trained Fighters."

"You guys saw her too... Right?" Johnson asked.

I side-glanced her but didn't answer.

Everyone had seen Franklin, but no one had said anything. Besides, she was as good as dead now. She'd said it herself—she'd been diagnosed with pancreatic cancer before coming to the island. It was only a matter of time before she died.

The sick part in all of it was that for a moment, I hoped she'd die before reaching the Cove. I didn't want any harm to come to her, but if it was a matter of choosing between someone who was already dying and my friends' lives, I'd pick my friends.

I looked up at the others, wondering if any of them were having the same morbid thought as me. I wouldn't voice it, though. I didn't want them to see me as heartless. But that's exactly how I felt—

heartless. As my mind processed these thoughts, I had no guilt. Why didn't I? Was it because I'd learned to think with my head and not my heart?

The reality was... Franklin was already gone.

Did it make me a bad person for wanting her gone sooner? Maybe. But I didn't have time to start self-reflecting and I especially didn't have the energy to start dwelling on my *feelings*.

Johnson leaned forward and dug her elbows into her thighs. "So, what's the plan?"

"Yeah," Arenas said. "I mean, you gonna leave some good women behind? I get that they ain't all wearing these bracelets, but that doesn't mean that given the chance, they wouldn't run, too."

I stared at Arenas.

"What?" she said, making her dark eyes go big.

"Nothing," I said. "You're completely right."

"Maybe," Coin said, "but we can't trust all these bitches to pack up and leave with us."

"They're not bitches," Hammer said, the smile on her face suddenly gone. "These women are human beings. Have some respect, man."

Coin almost burst out laughing, but when she realized Hammer wasn't joking, she straightened her posture and rolled her shoulders back. "Just a sayin'," she said.

"I agree with Arenas," Hammer said. "We can't leave them behind. God knows what'll happen to them when the Beasts realize we've all left."

I tapped my fingers on my knees, bit my lip, and looked around. How the hell were we going to do this? I didn't want to leave anyone behind, but the truth was, we couldn't trust them. The whole point in having our bracelets was to identify which women stood with us—which ones we could trust to be on our side.

"If they don't have a bracelet, they're not coming," I said coldly.

Everyone drew back.

"I'm not trying to be coldhearted," I said, "but the whole reason we're doing this right now is to get to the Cove before *they* do. We can come back for the others when we're ready to fight. I get it, guys. I wish I could convince everyone to grab their things and run. But the truth is, a lot of these women are comfortable here. As sick as it sounds, it's all they know. They're not gonna run. And they sure as hell won't let us run if they find out about it. Look at Snow Face, for example."

Hammer scoffed and rolled her eyes. "Don't you mean the almighty *Storm*?"

"That's not the point," I said, not in the mood for Hammer's jokes. "You guys heard her. She already warned us not to ruin things for her. So we have one shot at this, and we have to get it right."

"All right," Coin said, slapping her hands together. "So when're we leavin'?"

"After supper," I said. "As soon as the sun starts

to set."

"What?" Johnson blurted. "Why wouldn't we leave when it's dark?"

I glanced sideways at her. "Because I have a plan."

CHAPTER 12

When the sunlight hits the pointed tip of Rainer's front gates, we run east.

I watched as several women throughout the city leaned into each other, whispering and pointing toward the tall wooden gates. The one receiving the message always nodded and then went on to find someone else wearing a bracelet.

Of course, those not wearing the bracelet kept looking back, most likely wondering what they'd missed.

"I still don't get it, Brone," Quinn said, shoving a piece of bright red meat into her mouth. It smelled salty and sweet, and the fat dripping from the corners of her mouth was enough to make my stomach growl, even though I'd already eaten.

A handful of women had gone out hunting that day. They'd brought back wooden crates of fish and a dead boar. Those women—the ones who did the hunting—never spoke to anyone. It was a shame, really, since they carried weapons. If there was a group of women I wanted on our side, it was them. But they reminded me of Smith—the blacksmith chained at the ankle all day long. She had one job and one job only: she was responsible for providing weapons to the Northers.

These hunters looked like they'd been trained, or brainwashed, into existing solely to provide protein to the Northers. Most of the time, no one even shared the meat with us. We were left with fruits, vegetables, nuts, eggs, and fish, while the Northers sat in the comfort of their ten-foot gates, filling the air with laughter. And it wasn't a pleasant laugh, either—it wasn't the kind of laugh that makes you want to laugh along. It was almost sinister, and if I had to guess, they were being entertained by women fighting each other.

Quinn swallowed her last bite of meat. "Why not go when the sun's completely set?"

"Because these women aren't trained to survive in the jungle at night. They'll trip all over themselves."

"So, what?" Quinn said. "We cross the village in broad daylight and—"

"It won't be *broad* daylight," I said. "See that?" I pointed straight toward the Northers' base. "I've been in there. On my way out, the sun was setting. The nice thing about the sun"—I smirked up at her—"is that it can be blinding if you don't have sunglasses."

"You think they won't see us?"

"Not saying they won't, but I don't think they'll

realize what's going on until it's too late. Besides, if we leave after nightfall, we'll be heard before we even make it out of the city. Right before sunset, women are still roaming the city, buying items from the market, and having loud conversations."

Quinn rubbed her chin, tapped her cheek, then made her way to her septum piercing.

She pointed a finger at me. "You're smart, Brone."

I didn't feel smart, but I'd take the compliment. "Has everyone been t—"

But then someone caught my attention. She walked behind Quinn, her gaze aimed in my direction and her two-tone hair hanging over half her face. She playfully pulled at the rope string around her wrist, and although it looked like she was waiting to talk to us, she didn't say anything.

"Holland," I said.

I knew I'd sounded cold, but I didn't care. Even though she'd begged for my forgiveness, she'd never have it. And out of all the women on this island, she was the last person I'd trust. So why had Quinn given her a bracelet? I glanced at Quinn, who didn't say anything, then back at Holland.

"H-hey," she said. "I heard about the... you know."

I stared at her.

I could tell she hated herself for what she'd done—for being responsible for the loss of hundreds of lives—but at the same time, I wasn't certain it was genuine. When we'd first found her near the Village, she'd looked like a new arrival clad in blue jeans and with bleached-blond hair. But the entire time, she'd been working for the Northers.

So why were we trusting her now?

"Is there anything I can do to help?" she asked, looking at her feet. She pulled at the bracelet again and bit her bottom lip. With light eyes, a strong jawline, and a petite frame, Holland wasn't an ugly girl by any means. In fact, she'd probably have landed a modeling contract in the real world. But after everything she'd done, she was one of the ugliest women I could stand to look at.

I ground my teeth, carefully weighing my next words. I wanted to tell her to go fuck herself, but there was no point. I opened my mouth, prepared to tell her there was nothing she could do, when I realized there *was* something she could do.

"Yeah, actually," I said, and her eyes rolled up at me. "Go see Hammer at the Food Station."

"Food station?" Quinn asked. "Our shifts are up."

I smirked. "Yeah, well, she's still working"—I formed two air quotes with my fingers—"hard over there. I asked her to carve out a few weapons."

Quinn's face stretched, revealing a big yellow smile, and she smacked me on the shoulder. "Good thinking, Brone."

"What if she gets caught?" Holland asked. She

stepped closer when a few women started spreading away from the market and out into the city. "You do know what they do to women if they catch them with a weapon, right? Smith's the only one allowed to—"

"Why would they catch her, Holland?" I said, though it came out as an accusation.

She quickly shook her head. "I-I don't know. They just know things. They see things. Especially the ones on the elephants."

I stared toward the market, spotting only one elephant rider out and about today. The other one must have been resting behind the wooden gates. The elephant walked slowly, looking like a giant piece of crisp clay in the heat of the sun.

Poor thing.

The woman on top didn't look any better either. Her face and shoulders looked like burned leather, and although she was far away, I could see sweat shining on her forehead. She wiped it every few minutes, prodded at the elephant, and made her way around the market.

"Hammer's not stupid," I said. "She knows how to hide what she's doing."

Why was I even telling her this? What if she ran off to the Northers to tell them everything we were planning? But there was something in her eyes that told me she felt so guilty, she'd do about anything to gain my trust.

"I know you don't trust me, Brone," she said as if reading my mind. "But I want out of here as bad as you do... You have no idea the things... the things they've—" But she turned her head and bit hard on her lip. "They had my sister, Brone. They had her and they said unless I—"

"Where's your sister now?" I asked.

But she didn't answer. Instead, she shook her head and wiped tears from her eyes.

"Look," Quinn interrupted. "I think we can all agree that they're complete savages and that we all want out of here."

Quinn was right. Holland would have had to be downright psychotic to help the Northers after everything they'd done—especially if what she was saying was true; if the Northers had threatened her with her sister's life, only to then kill her.

"There's nothing here for me anymore," Holland said.

I gave her a brief nod. "Okay, then. Go see Hammer and get yourself a shiv. If you're on our side like you say you are, you'll be prepared to kill anyone who gets in our way when we start running."

CHAPTER 13

An eerie tension filled the air inside the city; the kind that follows a catastrophic event on a rainy day.

Women gathered closer and closer to the eastern edge, prepared to follow my instructions. But what bothered me most was that numerous women without bracelets stood prepared, their gazes scanning the city in search of me.

There was nothing I could do about that. These bracelets didn't divide us from our slaved society. They were intended to create a sense of union—not separate us. If these women had learned of the plan and wanted to run, I couldn't stop them.

In fact, our odds of surviving increased with every woman who joined the escape, so long as they didn't get in my way.

"What are these women doing?" I heard.

I turned sideways to find Storm, or Snow Face, standing beside me with her white-freckled arms crossed over her chest. I still didn't understand what kind of a person tattooed white speckles all over themselves, but it wasn't my place to judge.

"I don't know," I said. "Throwing a party."

The next thing I knew, her hand was wrapped around my throat and one of her followers stood behind me with something sharp jabbing me in the back.

"You think you are funny?" Snow Face said, her putrid breath slipping into my nostrils and mouth.

I didn't say anything.

Her dark, hateful eyes turned into little slits. "If you are planning anything—"

"Back the fuck off, Dandruff."

Snow Face's grimace turned into a malevolent smile—the kind of cliché smile that says, *You may have won this battle, but you didn't win the war.*

Behind every one of Snow Face's followers stood two of Quinn's women—young adults with tattoos, piercings, and rope around their wrists and ankles. They stood close to Snow Face's women with their chests pressed up against the other women's backs.

Snow Face gave a quick jerk of her head, and her women backed down. Their eyes, however, didn't leave mine. It was as if they were trying to threaten me to sleep with my eyes open.

But I wouldn't be sleeping here tonight.

"Thanks," I said, and Quinn gave me a sturdy slap on the back.

"Don't mention it."

"You guys ready for this?" I asked.

The women nodded. I felt bad for them. They didn't seem much older than me, and their fearless attitude made them look exactly like a group of girls who'd spent several years growing up in juvenile prison, which, according to Quinn, they had.

I looked over my shoulder, toward Rainer's wooden gates. It wouldn't be long now, and together, we would all run.

The sound of wood clanking against wood drew nearer and nearer until I realized it was Hammer making her way to me with a bag in her hands. She grinned from ear to ear, her puffy cheeks forming little balls under her eyes when they'd have formed big balloons only a few months ago. Beside her stood Holland, looking angry, almost, but I could tell she was nervous.

"Get armed, ladies," Hammer said.

I grabbed her arm and pulled her around a hanging sheet of cotton.

"Did anyone see you?" I said.

She cocked an eyebrow as if to say, *What am I? An amateur?*

"Where's everyone else?" I asked. "And Tegan? What about Sumi?"

"Relax, Brone," she said. "They're coming."

Quinn was the first to reach into the bag. She plucked from it an unevenly carved piece of wood that reminded me more of a miniature stake one

97

would use to kill a vampire.

"We still on?" came Coin's voice. She crouched beside me with Johnson to her left, her face hovering over the bag of weapons.

"Yeah," Quinn said.

At the sound of her voice, I stretched my neck back and looked up at her. For the first time, she didn't look like someone who ran the place—her confidence was gone, and her forehead was shiny, beads of sweat dripping along her long-haired brow.

"You okay?" I asked.

She nodded, cleared her throat, and said, "Whatever happens, guys, keep running."

"Why?" Johnson said. "Is something *going* to happen?"

"We don't know," I cut in. I rubbed my finger along the tips of each piece of wood, feeling for the sharpest one, then plucked it out. "Anything could happen. We have to be prepared."

"Yeah, but there should only be one or two guards waiting in the woods, right?" asked one of Quinn's women. She shot a glance at another young woman beside her, presumably her best friend, and turned back to me. "That's what everyone's been saying."

"There should be," I said. "If all goes well, we'll take them down and be miles away before the others realize what's going on. You guys have to get out of here, though," I said, waving a hand in the air. "You're drawing attention to us. Just stick to the plan, and like Quinn said, don't stop running."

The crowd around me had tripled in size, surrounding me with people I'd never seen before. As the women scattered, I turned to Quinn and my women—Coin, Hammer, Arenas, and Johnson. "If anything happens to me, I need you guys to promise me that you'll do whatever it takes to get to the Cove."

"Man, don't talk like that," Coin said. "Ain't nothin' gonna happen to you—"

"Coin, think about it for a second. You really think the Northers are gonna let us run free? Sure, we'll make it far before they come after us... But they will come after us."

"We outnumber them," Johnson said. "Even if they do—"

"We might outnumber them," Hammer cut in, "but we're not in a position to fight. They'll be shooting arrows at our backs in no time."

"Hammer's right," Quinn said.

"Maybe," Coin added, "but ain't like they're gonna send their entire army after us."

I looked up at Coin and parted my lips.

"What?" she said. "What am I missing? There ain't that many of them, Brone. At least not compared to us."

I'd never sat down and told any of them about what I'd seen behind the wooden gates. I'd never told them about the women being trained for battle—women who assumedly had been taken from the city or captured from other tribes to be used as weapons.

And what about the women I saw sitting in cages beside the mountain? The cages—thick bamboo structures—had formed a half-moon around Murk, who'd been strung up by her wrists and left to hang on her knees in the grass.

I hadn't told them any of this because I hadn't wanted to frighten them.

"They have more women," I said, "a lot of them."

Coin's eyes nearly popped out of her skull. She got up and took a step back, slapped two hands on her waist, and looked at me like she wanted to either punch me in the face or like I'd punched her in the face.

"More wom—" she said. "How? What're you talkin' about?"

"You saw Franklin, right?" I said.

"Yeah, but what—"

"They have an army," I said. "There were at least forty women back there training to fight. You know the battle sounds you hear over the fence every day? Well—"

Coin stuck out a hand to stop me. "Yeah, I get it, Brone. I assumed those were the Northers."

Quinn took a step forward, glanced around, then cleared her throat. "When they took us from our camp," she said solemnly, "half my women disappeared. I never imagined—" Her gaze fell on me, but she looked down at the dirt. "It makes sense. Why would they need so many of us to sustain them if there were only a few dozen Beasts back there? Sometimes, Zsasz asks for an entire boar or a basket of fish for supper. They *are* feeding an army."

Johnson threw her freckled hands in the air and let out a loud sigh. "So we *are* outnumbered!" She shuffled closer to me, crouched down, and stared me square in the face. "We can't do this. Not now. Not tonight. If what you're saying is true... They'll catch up to us within a few hours and slaughter all of us."

"Not if we all split ways," Hammer said.

Johnson laughed, though it came out as more of a scoff. She narrowed her eyes on Hammer and flared her nostrils. "So, what? We're all gonna run out there like a bunch of bingo balls? Take our chances and see who gets taken out?"

Quinn cocked an eyebrow and tightened the grip around her crossed arms. She wasn't a big fan of Johnson, and the lack of respect seemed to have started when Johnson asked her if her name had any relation to Batman. "You got a better idea, Batman?"

Johnson stood up, pulled her shoulders back, and met her face-to-face. She wasn't much smaller than Quinn, but she certainly wasn't bigger. "Any idea's better than asking women to run for their lives and hope they don't get shot in the back."

Quinn, who didn't appear threatened whatsoever, looked up and down at Johnson and said, "These women want to run."

"These women don't know there's a goddamn army of trained Fighters back there!"

"If they took Brone back there," Hammer said, "I'm sure she wasn't the only one to know about—"

Johnson, never breaking eye contact with Quinn, flung her hand out as if to say *Stop*. "Shut up, Hammer!"

I'd never seen this side of Johnson before. Sure, she'd always been on the grumpier side, but she'd never been outright vocal toward anyone other than Brainiac Proxy, who seemed to get under her skin. Maybe she was scared and with good reason. We were about to run straight into the unknown, which could ultimately lead to death for some.

"Johnson," I said calmly, and my tone alone seemed to soothe her. She turned slowly, finally breaking eye contact with Quinn, and stared at me.

"You don't have to come with us," I said. "We're planning on coming back once we're strong enough." She mulled over the idea, her eyes shifting from side to side. "We can come back for you."

Then, in one quick movement, she shook her head hard and let out a loud, "No, I'm coming with you guys... I just don't like... I don't like all of this uncertainty."

"Well, think of it this way," Hammer said. "If we stay here, our people are going to be killed. It's only a matter of time before Franklin leads them in the right direction."

Coin glared at everyone through the sun's bright rays. They were getting lower and lower, almost reaching the gate's highest point. "She don't even know where the Cove is," she said.

"She knows it exists, though," Hammer cut in. "That's enough to keep Zsasz hunting for days until she finds them."

I couldn't bear the thought of my friends, the Hunters, being attacked. I especially couldn't bear the thought of anyone laying a hand on Ellie. I agreed with Johnson that there was way too much uncertainty about this plan, but that was exactly it—we didn't have the time to *plan*. Zsasz, along with a small army of women and the brainwashed version of Franklin, were on their way to find the Cove. We didn't have any time to waste.

"Shit," Quinn said, averting her eyes toward the city.

And all at once, it was as if a blanket had been laid over the city, muffling the noise until it was too calm—too quiet. Countless women stopped moving, their eyes aimed in my direction. I looked behind them, toward the Northers' massive wooden gate, and that's when I saw it.

The highest point.

The setting sun's dark orange glow illuminated a sharp pike on the left-hand side of the gates, and the entire city lit up with a blinding light.

And these women, their eyes... It was as if they were waiting for my command.

It was now or never.

CHAPTER 14

I felt like a dance orchestrator.

I took a step forward, and everyone else followed suit. The frightening part of it all was how silent everyone was. There was no dramatic fleeing or flailing of the arms—instead, women walked as if on their way to the sleeping station, only, in the opposite direction.

Other women stood clueless, pointing fingers and asking questions.

It was when we drew closer to the city's perimeter that the vocals began.

At first, I'd thought it to be our women crying out as if in battle—a cry of freedom. But it wasn't us. The other women, obviously confused by what was going on, began questioning our movements aloud.

"What're you doing?" one shouted.

"Where... where are they going?"

"What's going on?"

A few of them followed like sheep glued to their shepherd, but others stared at us, eyes wide open, brows furrowed close together, and mouths hanging loose.

"Hey!" came someone else's voice, and it was as if she'd shot a gun in the air—the kind that's shot to get a race started.

All at once, everyone started running.

Crates were kicked out of the way, sheets of cotton swept through the wind as women rushed by, and dirt spat up in every direction as feet stomped through the city grounds. It was the loudest, yet most silent sound I'd ever heard coming from so many women at once.

Bodies quickly began disappearing into the forest, one after the other.

"Hey!" an old woman shouted from beside one of the market shacks. She pointed her old, wrinkly finger in our direction and shifted her weight from one foot to another so quickly it looked like she was either dancing or had to pee. "The—they're runnin'! Stop them! Someone! They're—they're getting' away!"

If I'd had my bow, I'd have probably shot an arrow through her leg to shut her up. What was she doing? Why was she turning on her own people? Was she that old and miserable she didn't want anything happening to her pathetic excuse of a life?

But she wasn't alone. Some women even went as far as to physically grab some of the runners, stopping them in their escape.

I lunged over a fallen tree trunk and landed in a bed of gooey, rotten leaves. My women followed close behind, shivs gripped tightly in their hands.

I quickly glanced at Quinn, thinking, *We're doing it—we're actually doing it*, but didn't say anything. She gave me a brief nod and we sprinted straight ahead, our bare feet splattering through the jungle's moist earth.

I missed my crocodile boots more than anything, especially right then as the idea of stepping on a venomous snake or oversized insect crept through my mind. But I didn't have time to focus on what I was wearing. There was only one thing that mattered, and that was getting out alive.

Then, the voices around us began growing louder. It was as if the women had only then realized they'd crossed the city's perimeter—as if they'd realized they were no longer prisoners of the Northers, of the Beasts. Their voices brought chills up my arms and down my back, and although I wanted to join in on the shouting, I knew it was too early to celebrate.

"Keep moving!" I shouted, and bodies stormed through the jungle's vegetation, slapping leaves and crunching down on the jungle floor.

The sun was beginning to set, lighting the trees around us with a bright orange glow, and women ran and ran and ran. Although no one was chasing us—at least not yet—it felt like we were prey. It was only a matter of time now before arrows came whistling through the trees.

I tightened my grip around the small wooden stake Hammer had carved for us and scanned our surroundings as we moved. Any minute now, one of the Northers would come into view. They would be patrolling this area, guarding the city against exterior and internal threats alike.

But no one was there.

Why wasn't there a Norther—a Beast—waiting for us? I tried to find Sumi in the crowd, but there were too many women.

And then the screaming started.

At first, it was one woman who let out a high-pitched screech. Not long after that, a few other women began shouting in agony until the sound of feet stomping on the jungle floor disappeared entirely, only to be replaced by laments, shouts, and cries.

My heart thumped hard against my chest and I wiped paste from my mouth. What the hell was going on? And why were—

My head shook violently and I took a step back, dazed. A crowd of women had stopped running and gathered around tree trunks. I rubbed my forehead and blinked several times. One of them was lying flat on the ground and no one bothered to help her up. I must have run into her. Then, women started walking backward, sweat dripping down their necks and shoulders slouched forward in submission.

They pleaded, begged, even, for mercy.

"Please," someone said.

"It was a mistake."

Who were they pleading to? I'd told them not to stop running. I grabbed a woman's shoulder and ripped her out of the way to get a look at what was going on.

I wished I hadn't.

I couldn't count how many there were exactly—twenty, maybe thirty. They all stood stiffly with blood splattered on their leather armor and furry shoulders. Some of them wore wooden masks that looked like poorly carved skulls, and others, actual skulls over their faces. It made it difficult to see their eyes, but I could sense their hatred, or at least, their brainwashed hatred.

These weren't Beasts—they were Peasants who'd been trained to fight. None of them had the Russian tattoos on their arms, and for the most part, they looked young, which meant they weren't Originals, either. It was like they'd been programmed to breathe, eat, sleep, and kill.

At their feet, bodies lay motionless—some with blood covering their faces and others with missing limbs.

Half of the Peasants held bows in the air, arrows resting on their index fingers, aimed right at us.

Then, from behind them, a Beast came out. She wore thick fur over her padded shoulders and a chest plate that looked to be made of metal. Around her wrists were metallic cuffs, and the sound of heavy weapons chafing filled the air as she walked forward.

I took a step back, but there wasn't time.

The Beast raised her chin, her black eyes scanning us from over stripes of red war paint on her face. Then, with a frighteningly deep and authoritative voice, she shouted, "Fire!" and more bodies began collapsing on the jungle floor.

PART TWO

PART TWO

PROLOGUE

Droplets of warm blood sprinkled across my face, neck, and shoulders.

For a moment, I was back in our burning Village, running among hundreds of women, surrounded by thickening smoke. Northers came stomping in with their weapons held high and their rotten mouths wide open. Screams spread around me and I watched in horror as women collapsed through the smoke, falling on their knees, their backs, and even their faces.

It was a massacre, and there was nothing I could do.

I blinked once, then again, until I came to and realized I wasn't standing amid hot flames—I hadn't gone back in time to relive my nightmare, but I hadn't left this one either.

Now, I was in another nightmare, all because I'd tried to run. I'd attempted to escape Norther imprisonment.

Northers formed a barricading wall in front of us, swinging their clubs, blades, and even swords at women who attempted to run past them. A shrill cry spread through the forest trees like a gust of wind, and a body collapsed over giant roots.

"Get back!" one of the Northers shouted in a deep, resonating snarl.

Quickly, women ran in the opposite direction and back toward the city.

What were they doing? This wasn't the plan. I'd instructed everyone to press on, no matter what happened. If we ran back to the city, there was no telling what would happen to us. Maybe they'd slaughter us all the moment they had us cornered.

"No, no!" I shouted, punching a fist in the air. But even as my own words came out, I knew they were unrealistic. I couldn't expect these women to sacrifice their lives so that I could brush past these Beasts and save my friends—to warn them about Zsasz and her army of women who'd left the city in search of the Cove.

Another scream came blasting out of a woman's lungs beside me, and when I turned, I saw a bloody sword pierce through her abdomen, pulling pieces of intestines along with it. She looked mortified, almost confused, and blood pooled over her tongue and through the cracks of her teeth. The Norther behind her tore the blade out and it made a ripping sound; she immediately fell to her knees, thick blood gurgling in the back of her throat.

The sound of rapid footsteps crunching down on jungle vegetation filled the air, and I was pushed from back and forth as women stampeded their way back to the city, their cries masking the stomping sound that shook the ground under my feet.

This couldn't be happening.

This wasn't what we had planned.

We were supposed to escape.

Everything spun around me, so much so that I had to remind myself I wasn't dreaming. I wouldn't wake up beside Coin or Quinn, prepared for another day of slavery. This would change everything. We were either going to die here, or we were going to pay afterward for trying to escape.

How the hell had the Northers known about our escape? Barely any planning had gone into this whole thing because I'd reacted on my emotions— I'd wanted nothing more than to reach the Cove to warn my friends before Zsasz and her army, along with Franklin, reached it themselves.

How could anyone have had the time to warn the Northers?

Was this Snow Face's doing? The woman who'd threatened to take me down if I attempted anything else? I thought back to that day when she stood behind me with something sharp jabbed into my throat, and a blinding rage filled me.

I'd kill her.

The sound of heavy metal breaking skull matter

resonated beside me, and I was immediately pulled back into my gruesome reality.

It didn't matter how any of this had happened. In the end, this was all my fault. As women brushed past me, I quickened my pace and joined them on their way back to the city.

I didn't want to run, but I didn't have a choice. I couldn't fight the Northers by myself.

But then, I heard a loud grunt, and though I didn't want to stop running, I couldn't help myself—I recognized the voice. I stopped in my tracks and turned around, causing several women to trip over me, but I didn't care; I couldn't move.

Only a few feet away, Hammer stood still, eyes sealed shut and teeth clenched tight. Her head appeared over a few shoulders, but everyone was running so fast I could barely see her. A Norther behind her raised what looked like a stone ax fastened around a wooden stick and came swinging down hard. Blood spat out into the air and women panicked, the skin on their faces pulled back so tight in fear they resembled a herd of terrified gazelles surrounded by hungry lions.

"Hammer!" I shouted, but my voice barely carried beyond the tip of my nose.

A firm hand suddenly grabbed me around the arm and pulled me into the moving crowd.

CHAPTER 1

The silence that had filled the city with a heavy hopelessness was eventually replaced by the city's usual chaos—women shouting over one another, elephants stomping through the city grounds, and Smith—the city's blacksmith—still pounding away on metals to forge weapons and tools. I didn't understand that woman. She'd often keep working even after the day was over, sometimes up until the sun set, and when it did, she'd be released from her cuffs and brought through the Northers' gate.

It was almost as if she was too brainwashed, too dangerous, to be allowed anywhere near the rest of us Peasants.

The voices around me, though, weren't the same as usual. They weren't lively and loud or passionately argumentative. Instead, they were angry and resentful. Several eyes kept darting my way, but I couldn't tell if the women were apologetic for running in the opposite direction or resentful of me and my plan. Did they want me to come up with a better plan, or to step forward and allow myself to be slaughtered by them?

"What the fuck just happened?" Arenas asked, her face partially shadowed by the trees around us.

I glared at the ground, my good fist balled so tightly my fingernails dug hard into my palms. My other hand, however, was slowly getting better. It was still completely discolored, and I wasn't able to make a solid fist yet, but within a few months, I'd probably be back to normal.

I looked up at Arenas and the others and shrugged, though what I wanted to do was kill someone. Who the hell had given us up? Those Northers had been waiting for us—prepared to slaughter anyone who tried to run.

And they'd done exactly that.

I glared into the distance in search of someone—anyone—who gave me the slightest indication they were responsible for this. Where was Snow Face? I stood up, shoulders drawn.

All of a sudden, I stopped breathing, teeth clenched tight.

Holland. It had to have been her. She was in on the whole thing.

I'd kill her.

I'd kill the Beasts.

All of them.

They'd slaughtered countless women, and for what? To prove to the others that we don't stand a chance against them? To discourage us from ever taking a stand? Well, it was working. All of the women who'd stood by my side surely wouldn't want to take part in some rebellion... Not after this.

I ground my teeth until my jaw popped. "Someone gave us up."

I'd said *someone* casually, though the only person I could imagine who would have given us up was Snow Face.

Quinn, who was sitting on the hammock across from me, punched the air, her septum ring bouncing up and down on her face. The sun had now entirely disappeared behind the mountain, and the only light around us was cast by small firepits dug throughout the sleeping area.

Any minute now, a few Northers would come and tell us to put out the fires and get to sleep.

Or, they'd come and slaughter us all for what we'd done.

"Fuckin' bitch is gonna pay for this," Quinn said.

She'd made it sound like she knew who the culprit was. I glanced up at her. "Who?"

"Whoever did this!" she snapped.

Several heads turned our way, including those of injured women who lay on beds of leaves, moaning in pain. By sunrise, several of them would be dead. But it didn't stop their friends from comforting them and trying to help them the best they could.

"I'll kill them with my bare fuckin' hands," she added.

I understood Quinn's rage. Not only had we not escaped, but she'd lost two of her women—her friends—in the massacre. I didn't know their names, but they were often with Quinn, and it was obvious they'd been close.

I turned my attention to everyone around me—Arenas, Coin, Johnson, and Hammer. My eyes lingered on Hammer a little longer than I'd planned, but I couldn't help myself. A few hours ago, I'd thought I'd lost her.

My voice was still hoarse from screaming, and if it hadn't been for Quinn pulling me out of the crowd, I would probably have stood there shouting for Hammer until the Northers reached me.

God, it was good to see her face.

"Don't make no sense," Coin said, staring at the ground with big eyes and nostrils wider than her lips. The only thing I could see in the darkening forest was the whites of her eyes—they looked like balls colored with highlighter marker in comparison to her dark skin. "When would anyone have had time to rat us out? Everythin' was so last minute. The whole point was to reach the Cove—"

"It was Holland," I said, my voice low and rough.

"Holland?" Arenas said.

Coin scoffed and brushed her hands through her woolly hair. It was weird to see her without her mohawk, but everyone had changed since we'd been captured, and Coin was no exception. She'd

120

slowly begun to regain her muscle, though, by eating fruits and nuts whenever possible, doing push-ups during our work hours, and doing chin-ups from tree branches before bed.

She wasn't alone in this either. Countless women were often seen exercising, though not everyone was able to due to our caloric deficit. "The bitch responsible for killin' our women," she said, and though she was talking to Arenas, her eyes were on me. It was like she was still pissed off that I hadn't killed Holland when I'd had the chance inside the fighting ring. "Apparently, she's good now," she added, but it came out as a sneer.

Johnson, being the mediator, cleared her throat and said, "The Northers didn't leave her much choice. Wouldn't you have done about anything if your sibling's life was at risk?"

Coin slapped the air in front of her. "Man, I don't got no siblings, and if I did, I'm sorry, but naw... I wouldn't kill hundreds of women to save one life."

Having someone threaten you to massacre hundreds of women in exchange for your sister's life seemed like an easy outcome—it only seemed rational to choose to save hundreds of lives over one, but in the real world, the decision wasn't all that simple.

The truth was, anyone would pick their loved one over strangers, and Holland had been no exception, even though they'd slaughtered her sister afterward anyways.

How could she have done this? How could she have possibly helped the Northers after what they'd done to her sister and her?

Quinn, who now resembled nothing more than a dark, poorly postured silhouette, said, "Yes, you would."

I didn't bother asking why she'd said that, but I could only assume it was because she'd lost someone close to her—maybe even a sibling. I instantly thought of Fisher and how she'd told me she'd found her dead sister on the island with numerous stab wounds. Though I was an only child, it hurt me to imagine the pain Fisher must have felt.

Coin didn't seem too keen on interrogating Quinn either. She sat quietly, which wasn't something she did very often.

Out of the shadows came Hammer's voice. "It wasn't Holland."

I leaned forward in my hammock, the vines holding it in place making a squeaking noise. "How do you know?"

"She gave her life for mine," Hammer said.

CHAPTER 2

Falling asleep that night was harder than any other night although every night was a challenge. I was often tossing and turning or outright kicking my legs in the air as vivid memories flashed in my mind; they were always violent memories, too, and sometimes even more violent than what had actually happened.

I'd grown accustomed to seeing dead bodies behind closed eyes. What I hated the most was when I was on the verge of falling asleep and I'd see blood splatter in my face. It made me jump every single time, and more often than not, I'd manage to wake someone up.

"You okay?" one of my women would ask me, and I'd mumble something along the lines of yes.

But tonight, everything was silent—too silent, almost.

Why hadn't the Northers done anything? Why hadn't Rainer come out? Their lack of action was more frightening than punishment. Were they content knowing they'd massacred dozens of us? Was that our punishment?

I stared overhead, trying to count stars through the dense vegetation. Then, I turned my head and gazed at the moonlit city, noting how calm it was. Aside from a few stray leaves that rolled through the sand, nothing moved.

I swallowed hard and closed my eyes. Why had Holland given her life? I hadn't seen her standing behind Hammer when the Norther's ax came down, but as Hammer had told us, she'd jumped behind her and caught the blow.

Why would someone do such a thing? Was it grief? Regret? Was she so disgusted with what she'd done—with being the reason hundreds of women had died in our Village—that she'd wanted to die herself?

Holland had lost everything. Not only had she done something atrocious, but she'd lost her sister despite having been promised by the Northers that they wouldn't harm her so long as Holland did as she was told.

Obviously, the Northers couldn't be trusted with their promises.

I thought of the pain she must have experienced when they took her life. Had the ax killed her in one blow? Or had it landed on her spine, immobilizing her instantly? Was she even dead? Or was she lying in a pool of blood, paralyzed? Did the Northers check their victims for breathing, or did they let them sit there to die?

Where was Tegan in all of this? And Sumi? Were they okay? I hadn't seen them. What about the Hunters, my friends? What was I supposed to do now? They needed to be warned.

God, why couldn't I stop thinking?

Horrible nausea sank to the bottom of my stomach. I knew there was nothing I could do about Zsasz and the Cove, and I also knew what was in store for us tomorrow. The Northers, the Beasts, would force us to clean up the bodies—to drag them away from the city's perimeter.

Maybe that alone was our punishment.

Because tomorrow, women would start finding their friends.

Would they all turn on me?

Or would they bow their heads and continue with their lives of slavery? No way were any of them going to try to stand up to the Northers—not anymore.

I sucked in moist air and let it out slowly.

Fall asleep.

Fall asleep.

Fall asleep.

It was no use. I'd probably wake up entirely unrested with aching muscles and a migraine.

A few feet away, a pained moan suddenly filled the sleeping area. The sound was immediately followed by someone snapping, "Shut up!"

Jordan, I thought. I didn't know the woman on a

personal level, but over the last few hours, I'd heard her name passed from mouth to mouth. When I finally caught a glimpse of her, I knew who it was because her ankle had swelled up to three times its size, which is how everyone was describing her. Only one woman stood by her side to help her hop on her one good leg, and undoubtedly, this same woman now was sitting at her side, wiping the sweat away from her forehead.

It wouldn't be long, I knew, before she took her last breath. She must have been bitten by a snake during our attempt to run. Was this woman going to die because of me? Because I'd foolishly inspired her—along with dozens of women who were no longer alive—to run?

I clenched my teeth and stared straight up into the blackness of the night.

I wished I could talk to my mom, even if only for a minute. Maybe she'd snap me out of this and make me realize that I was in way over my head. Yet even if given the opportunity, I'd never be able to face my mom again—not after everything I'd done.

I was a murderer, a cold-blooded killer. And for what? For survival?

Another sound caught my attention. It wasn't Jordan's moan or her friend telling her everything was going to be okay. It was the sound of something lurking nearby, a soft crunching in the jungle leaves outside our sleeping area.

It wasn't one of the guards either. Their footsteps were far brisker, almost carelessly so, like their brains weren't advanced enough to understand that even though we were their slaves, we were also human beings who required sleep.

Either that or they didn't give a rat's ass about how we felt, which was more likely.

With eyes wide open, I turned my head toward the sound and sat up in my hammock. Though it was dark, my eyes had adjusted enough for me to see the lightness of the hammocks, some skin tones, and the silhouettes of bodies lying about.

I looked past all of that and into the dense trees that formed a wall at the edge of our sleeping area.

Maybe the Hunters had come back as they'd said they would. My heart picked up in pace, and I started picturing Rocket bolting out from the forest and finding me without much effort.

But Rocket never came out.

Instead, a loud scream cracked through the air and the dreamlike image of the Hunters dashing forward heroically disappeared in an instant.

I jumped to my feet with clenched fists, feeling someone's arm crush under my heel. It was too dark—I couldn't see who I'd stepped on. Another scream filled the air around us, and this time, it was followed by a deep rumble, by the growl of what I could only assume was a large wildcat.

What I noticed first, however, were the women sitting up, the silhouettes of their arms reaching their cocked heads, as they slowly stood. No one in our sleeping area appeared to be in immediate danger.

If they were confused, where was the sound coming from?

"Attoola!" someone on the outside shouted. I knew by the incomprehensible word and by the hoarseness of their voice that they weren't one of us—they were one of the Northers—and they were under attack.

Women started shuffling in every direction as if waiting to be guided by a shepherd. Some rushed closer to the forest's perimeter to observe what was going on, and others backed away from it, not wanting any part in the attack.

Another growl filled the air, though it sounded more like a wall crumbling—incredibly loud and grumbly.

"What's going on?" a woman shouted.

"I don't know!"

"They're under attack!"

"Who is?" came a tired voice, and though I didn't know who'd said that, I envied her for having fallen into such a deep sleep.

"The Beasts!"

"It's a cat!"

"A wild animal!"

Both fear and excitement filled the air as warm bodies crashed into each other. Someone's sweaty skin slapped my shoulder, but when I turned around, no one was there. Everyone was moving about so quickly that a ball of anxiety formed in my stomach. If I hadn't heard the growl for myself, I'd have assumed that *we* were the ones under attack.

"Brone!"

It was Coin's voice.

"Yo, Brone," she continued. "You okay?"

"I'm okay," I said.

Hammer's shape came into view. She stood only a few feet away from me, and I was able to make out the shape of her nose, her eyes, and her mouth. Next, Quinn, Arenas, and Johnson squished their way through the jittery women to stand with us.

"What's going on?" Hammer asked.

"Sounded like an animal attack," I said, and as the words came out, arrows whistled in the distance. No doubt, other Northers were trying to stop the attack.

"You guys thinking what I'm thinking?" Quinn asked, and right as she said that, it was as if I'd been gifted with mind reading; I knew what she was thinking, and I was thinking the same thing.

In fact, everyone was—I could see it on their faces.

This was our chance. We had to try.

"If we run in that direction," I said, pointing west

of the noise, "we should miss the guard who ran to help the other one. There should be a gap there."

Brief nods were exchanged as if I'd announced our attack strategy for some playoff game. This was all happening too fast, but we didn't have time to waste.

"You guys sure you want—" I tried, but a loud trumpetlike sound blasted from behind the city's gates, and torches suddenly lit up, creating a bright orange glow over the wooden pikes. The gates were shot open, and out came a handful of Northers with spears and clubs at their sides.

"Now!" Quinn hissed, and without a second thought, we all bolted together, cutting through the crowd of clueless women.

And although it was safer for us to run, only the few of us, I couldn't leave the others behind—not after what had happened. What kind of a person would I have been to take advantage of an opportunity without sharing this opportunity with those I'd failed?

A coward and a heartless bitch.

"Run!" I shouted at the top of my lungs.

At first, silence filled the air and only our footsteps continued to smack against the forest floor. But within seconds, dozens upon dozens of women shouted back—not at me, but with me. The ground beneath us started to tremble as hundreds of bodies stormed away from the sleeping grounds and ran into the darkness of the jungle.

CHAPTER 3

It all felt like a dream.

It wasn't at all what you'd have expected from female prisoners running from their captors. After the first few minutes, the shouting stopped entirely, and all we could hear behind us were rapid footsteps and heavy breathing. It was already difficult enough trying to be quiet in the dead of night; we didn't need women shouting or talking over one another to attract the Northers.

We ran for hours, some women falling behind, some crashing into the ground unable to see, and others choosing to take a different path.

"No!" someone hissed.

Though I couldn't see who had spoken, I turned around in time to see her reach out into the forest as if trying to stop someone from leaving. This woman took a step forward, obviously contemplating chasing after her friend, but then several other women held her back.

I understood it, too. Our group, the large group, would be hunted by the Northers any moment now. It made sense for someone to want to try their own route. The Northers would follow our traces through the jungle's muddy floor, and once they reached us, they'd massacre as many women as possible.

Maybe the strays stood a better chance than we did.

Maybe splitting up wasn't such a bad idea.

Our running turned into more of a slow jog and voices filled the air.

"I... I c-can't," someone said, gasping.

"Me... neither."

Some breathing turned into whistling, and women began leaning forward with hands on their knees to either catch their breaths or prepare themselves to vomit.

How far had we gone? My legs burned, almost to the point of being numb. I wasn't used to this anymore. My stomach roiled from dehydration, hunger, and fatigue.

But none of that mattered. These women were relying on me. I wouldn't let feeling like shit get in the way of that.

"B-Brone," Coin said, and she swallowed so hard I heard her throat stick. "We can't stop, man. They'll be comin' after us."

"I know," I said, "but we can't force these women to run, either. Most of them have been living a life without any form of exercise for years. They probably feel like they're dying right now."

Coin's face was so close to mine that I saw a contemplative frown form on it. Her black skin suddenly lightened to a dark brown, and the shape of her lips came into view. I craned my neck back and stared into the overhead trees, where the starlit sky also began to lighten in color.

Morning was coming.

How long had we been running?

* * *

"Jesus Christ, Brone, hurry it up!"

I glared back at Mr. Torchman and his disgusting jog pants. His name suited him—he reminded me of someone who liked to light stuff on fire simply for the pleasure of it. He rested a hairy hand on his waist and played with the whistle wrapped around his neck. It looked like he was getting ready to grab it and whistle at me for the heck of it.

What a prick, I thought.

Sure, I wasn't the fastest kid in school, but that was no reason to treat me like crap. Fred Aspenson came jogging behind me, kicking little pieces of rocks at the back of my heels. He wasn't doing it on purpose; he was having such a hard time that his feet kept smacking into the ground with every step he took—so much so that the rolls around his belly jiggled. Fred was the chubbiest kid in class, and although everyone made fun of him for different reasons, not only for his weight, he never stopped trying to do better.

I admired him for that.

And then, as if out of a high school movie (with the music of triumph playing in the background), Fred appeared beside me, and I heard the sound of his arm skin flapping against his sides.

He didn't look at me—he stared straight ahead, his cheeks bright red, mouth wide open, and nose running.

"Come on, Brone!" Mr. Torchman shouted with his gruff, overly masculine voice.

Though the words didn't come out, I knew what he was trying to say: *You're going to let someone like Fred beat you, are you?*

He was such a prick.

I looked straight ahead at the finish line. It was an ugly white banner wrapped around the soccer net's metal frame, and everyone else in my class was standing around it. Some were watching Fred and me, the last two on the racetrack, but most were spread out on the grass, drinking water and chatting away.

I glanced at Fred one more time, and although the idea of the slowest kid in class beating me should have been enough to give me one final boost to the finish line, I didn't use this boost.

I could have sped things up a bit, at least enough to beat him, but I couldn't bring myself to do it. The poor kid was trying so hard, and he deserved to win. Well, to not come in last place.

So I kept my steady pace and watched as he stomped his way toward the finish line, letting out loud bark-like sounds every last step he took. And when he finally reached the finish line, he threw both hands into the air and let out a victory cry, even though no one seemed to care. A few teens rolled their eyes and walked farther away from him, but Fred was happier than I'd ever seen him.

At that moment, I didn't care that I'd be made fun of for being the slowest kid in class.

It was worth it.

* * *

This wasn't a gym class, and I wasn't fifteen anymore.

I watched the women as they spat out chunks of mucus and rubbed their legs, their big eyes aimed up at me, almost pleadingly. What did they want from me? For me to tell them it was okay to take a break? It wasn't. This wasn't some practice race. Wild and incredibly dangerous women were hunting us.

All I'd ever done in life was put the needs of others before mine. If I'd learned anything from Kormace Island, it was that every woman was responsible for her own well-being. In the end, you had to watch out for yourself, and I sure as hell wouldn't risk my life to stay behind with those who couldn't move forward.

Did that make me a bad leader? Maybe. But I didn't care. This was about survival and nothing more. I didn't even know these women. I didn't owe them anything. The Hunters, however, were my friends—my family—and I'd do pretty much anything to make sure they were safe.

"For those of you who can't keep going," I said, "I suggest you find someplace to hide."

I received a few hateful glares and wide-open mouths.

"Why the fuck should anyone be listenin' to you?" someone shouted. "My best friend died because of your stupid plan!"

The sun had risen even farther, and a cool mist licked our ankles. I could see everyone's faces perfectly now, and the one who'd spoken, a middle-aged woman with an acne-scarred face, stared at me like she wanted to tear my eyes out with her fingers.

Coin, acting as my protector, stepped forward with her chest puffed out, but I wrapped my fingers around her wrist and shook my head. "I got this," I said.

I took a step forward and elevated myself on a large flat rock. "I'm sorry about your friend," I said, and an uproar shook the forest trees.

"Bullshit!" the woman shouted.

"I suggest you all listen," I shouted. "I'm only apologizing once!"

The women suddenly went quiet. I wasn't sure whether it was due to my red face, my hoarse voice, or my aggressive posture, but they suddenly seemed curious to hear what I had to say.

"I really *am* sorry for the lives that were lost." And before the grumbling around me turned to another uproar, I added, "but this isn't black and white. This is fucking war. Those Beasts back there have held you prisoners for how long?" I stared wide-eyed at each one of them. "You were all being treated like shit, forced to cook for them, clean for them, and suffer for them. If you're standing here right now, *you* wanted to run. You aren't some mindless sheep. You had enough of the life you were living, and you were willing to risk it for a better one."

A heavy silence filled the air, and watery eyes remained glued to mine. I'd never seen so much suffering before. These women had been beaten, starved, and tortured in more ways than imaginable, yet here they were, fighting for a way out.

"You're here because you're stronger than you give yourself credit for," I said. "What happened back there was a tragedy..." I turned to Quinn, who refused to make eye contact. She stared at the moist soil with her fingers wrapped around each other. "I didn't plan for the Beasts to be waiting for us. They received insider information. That's the only reason they were ready."

Panicked whispering suddenly erupted around me, and women began searching from around them as if trying to pinpoint who was responsible for the massacre.

"I don't yet know who it was," I said, "but I swear to God that when I find them, they'll pay for what they've done."

One woman suddenly cheered raising a balled fist into the air, and the others followed suit.

"You can either follow me to safety," I said, "or, you can do whatever you want. You aren't prisoners anymore. You're free women. So you decide for yourself."

I turned away and hopped off the rock as chatter erupted behind me.

"Let's keep moving," I said.

CHAPTER 4

"How far is this place?" Quinn asked, her eyes darting between the hundred or so women behind us and me.

I didn't want to see anyone limping or hear complaints about how far we were going, so I didn't look back. This wasn't some leisure hike on a Saturday afternoon—we were in this all or nothing.

"Far enough," I said.

The problem was, we'd run east from the Northers' city, and the Cove was situated somewhere southwest. Now, we had to backtrack.

Quinn didn't seem to like this all that much. She looked straight ahead, her blotchy red cheeks jiggling a bit as she stomped forward.

"As soon as we change our path," I said, "we'll take a break. But we've been moving west for God knows how long. We need to—" But, something came to mind. I stuck a hand out in front of Quinn's face, even though she wasn't talking, and everyone stopped walking.

"You." I pointed at a short-haired woman with

rounded shoulders and a flat, muscular chest. All in all, it looked like she was handling this trek well and was precisely what I needed—muscle. She pointed at herself as if to say, *Me?*

"Grab a leafy branch... Any branch. I need you to start wiping our prints at the back of the line. Think you can handle that?"

She gave me a brief nod like a soldier trained to obey any order given and started jogging to the back.

"I'll help," came someone's voice, and my gaze moved to a tall dark-skinned woman with thick arms and a soft smile.

I nodded as a way of thanking her, and she disappeared into the crowd.

"If each and every one of you can start stepping out of line to make it look like you ran, do it. Let's keep this messy."

A loud whisper broke out, filling the air with an energy that we'd need over the next few hours.

"Let's throw them off their game," I added. "Then, we stop to rest."

This seemed to excite them. A few women at the front with arms wrapped around the shoulders of others straightened their stances, and an elderly woman with a round back and a sweaty forehead jabbed her walking stick into the ground, flicked her wrist into the air, and shouted, "Let's keep movin', ladies!"

And with that, we kept on marching.

By the time we reached a distance where I felt we were safe, the sun was on its way to setting, and a cool breeze ruffled the leaves overhead. I'd spent the entire day staring straight ahead, refusing to make conversation with anyone.

The only thing on my mind was to get these women as far away from the Northers as possible, and that was precisely what I'd done.

In an instant, the melodic sound of birds chirping filled the moist air, and the scent of damp earth entered my nostrils.

"Do you see that?" someone asked.

"Is that—"

"Water," I breathed, gazing through the gaps of giant banana leaves, where crystal-blue water glistened in the sun. I rushed toward the leaves and pushed them aside, revealing what could only be described as a hidden paradise.

The water looked like glass, reflecting the sunlight from every angle, and large, bright green leaves hung overhead, almost touching the water. A small, yet powerful waterfall sat at the far end, falling down hard enough to create ripples and white foam.

A young woman with sticklike legs, a protruding collarbone, and big eyes that looked like gumballs came running out from the crowd in the direction of the water.

"Stop!" I shouted, but like a starving dog hunting its prey, she didn't see or hear me.

Then, as she ran toward me, I did the easiest thing I could think of—I stuck my leg out in front of her and she flew into the air like a safety cone in the wind and landed flat on her face.

Everyone stared at me, probably thinking I was nuts for tripping someone who only wanted water.

The young woman finally unstuck her face from the dirt and pulled herself up onto her knees. She turned around and shot me a nasty glare as though getting ready to come at me, but she wiped that look off her face the second Coin's hand came swinging at the side of her head.

A loud slap sound echoed through the trees around us, and the woman's face went blank.

"Have some respect, for fuck's sake," Coin said. "You wouldn't even be here if it weren't for Brone. So if you're goin' to be followin' us, you do what she says, when she says it. And when she tells you to stop, you stop."

"She only wanted water!" someone shouted from inside the crowd of dirty faces.

Quinn then stepped forward with her arms crossed over her thick chest. She looked as mean as Coin, only, in a different way. That septum ring and those colorful tattoos, along with the way her golden brows came together when she was upset made her look like the kind of badass no one wanted to mess with.

Like a loyal pack of wolves, Johnson, Hammer, and Arenas also stepped forward with crossed arms and elevated chins.

It was as if they were saying, *You mess with Brone, you mess with us.*

And although we were greatly outnumbered, it seemed to work. The women started breaking eye contact—some nodding, while others stood silently with their heads bowed.

"The water could be contaminated," I said. "I'm trying to protect you."

The girl I'd tripped rubbed the back of her head and scurried back into the crowd.

"Brone, look," Johnson said, extending a freckled arm through the wall of hanging leaves.

I followed her finger to the water, where several antelope-looking creatures stood, their snouts dipped into the water. Thick horns sat at the tops of their head on an angle with their points aimed over their backs, and bright white vertical stripes decorated their orange coats.

I'd never seen anything like it.

"What is that?" Arenas asked, squinting.

Coin did the same, but she gave up and threw her arms in the air. "Man, we can't all see that far."

"That looks like a bongo," came someone's voice.

It was an elderly woman with thick-looking

skin, a small mouth with brown teeth, and a chin that stuck out farther than her curved nose. It made me think of Olga, the Russian woman who'd cared for the Orphans when they'd first crashed their plane on Kormace Island.

She wiggled a wrinkly finger in the direction of the creatures. "That right there's an African rainforest antelope." She stretched her crisp lips into what I could only assume was a smile and added, "Worked in a zoo in 2032."

"African?" someone said.

I glanced at Quinn, then at the others, but they all offered the same response—a clueless shrug.

Where the hell were we? I swallowed hard, afraid of what else we might find on this island, but then Arenas blurted, "So, water's good then?"

I sighed and flung a hand in the air, and everyone stormed loudly through the narrow entrance between two angled trees. Within seconds, the sound of water splashing filled the air, and women with excited voices talked over one another.

"You think we're in Africa?" Johnson asked, her big mouth hanging open so wide it made her neck disappear.

I didn't know what to think. The only thing I could think of was Mr. Milas, Attorney General of the Department of Justice, and the way he'd smiled so cockily at the camera when being interviewed about the penal islands. I remembered his bleached teeth, his crisp white suit, and his blond hair pulled back into a small bun.

He'd already admitted that the government had played a part in populating the island with wildlife. But to what extent? Had they added a single species, such as wild boar, to keep us fed? Or had they populated the whole damn thing? If so, how many species had died off due to climate? How many more were there? And what else hadn't we seen yet?

"Brone!"

I glanced up, suddenly realizing that I was standing alone at the entrance of the small bay.

Hammer stood tall with a proud grin on her face. She held something in her hand, though I couldn't tell what it was from this distance.

"What is it?" I asked.

She took a few steps forward, her index finger poking the top of whatever it was she was holding. She twirled it around in her hands a few times until it landed flat in her palm. It was a small triangular rock, no bigger than the size of a golf ball, with a natural point to it.

"Looks like we hit a goldmine," she said, her smile growing wider.

I wanted to hug her and tell her how amazing she was for always finding ways to craft us weapons. Without Hammer, we wouldn't have survived this long. But instead, I found myself unable to express anything. Had I lost my emotions? When was the last time I'd laughed? Was I depressed, or was this the new me?

"You think you can make me a new bow?" I asked.

CHAPTER 5

"As soon as the sun sets," I said, "we'll have to put out the fire."

A few eyeballs rolled my way as I spoke, and although no one said anything, I knew they'd do as they were told and put it out. The last thing we needed was something to draw the Northers to us, and what better way to do that than to have bright orange flames dancing and crackling in the middle of the night?

Hammer hadn't spoken a word all evening—it was like watching a robot at work. The only difference between the two was that Hammer mumbled to herself every few minutes. She'd spent the last several hours forcing her way through crisp vegetation and loose vines in search of quality wood, collecting dozens upon dozens of stones, and slicing apart bamboo sticks to create strings.

A year ago, Hammer would have collapsed by now. But there she was, working away like an ant from an oversized colony as if fatigue was nothing more than a myth told to children by parents wanting a few hours of peace.

Everyone else, however, lay in awkward positions with limbs overtop one another and small lines for eyes on their faces. This wasn't fatigue, it was exhaustion. Some women complained that their ankles were swollen, while others scratched at blisters on their feet.

"Hey," I heard as I sat on a cracked log. I knew who it was before I glanced up to find her shadowed, disfigured face.

Sumi stood in front of me, the melted half of her figure hidden from view.

"Sumi," I said, content to see a familiar face. "Where were you? I thought you—"

"Relax, spaz. I'm okay," she said.

It was strange to think that a few months prior, I hated Sumi, all over sheer pettiness. But I didn't look at her as the Village cook anymore; I considered her a friend.

"Thank you," she breathed, and a soft hand touched my shoulder.

"For what?"

She scoffed, her attitude still as fierce as ever. "For getting our asses out of there."

I laughed, even though nothing about the situation was funny. "It's not over yet."

"No," she said, "but we're almost there. Keep doing what you do, Brone."

Before giving me the chance to say anything

else, she turned around and made her way to a group of Asian women, assumedly friends of hers.

The log I sat on suddenly shifted, and I turned to find Johnson sitting next to me. She didn't look over. Instead, she stared straight ahead at Sumi and her friends and at the women lying around the bay of water. She slid her bare toes into the sand in front of us and let out a sigh.

"Are you sure you know where you're going?" she asked.

Although her words sounded insulting, I knew they weren't. She rubbed at the freckled skin on her face, then turned her head to the side and stared at me with her odd, orange-brown eyes. "I don't want them to stop believing in you, Brone."

I wasn't sure whether to be shocked or confused. The majority of Johnson's vocabulary consisted of insults and idiotic comments—it wasn't like her to want to have a serious one-on-one with anyone.

"I know where I'm going," I said.

She cocked an eyebrow and leaned away from me. "Where *you're* going?"

"You saw Zsasz," I said. "She left with Franklin and a bunch of other women. They're looking for the Cove."

She nodded and chewed her bottom lip, and I couldn't tell if she understood what I was getting at, or if it wasn't clicking for her.

"I can't sit here and wait—"

"You aren't *sitting* here," she interrupted. "We've been walking all day, and before then, we ran for hours. We need to rest a bit. We aren't machines. And what're you talking about, Brone? I thought we were headed to the Cove together."

I parted my lips to speak, but nothing came out. The truth was, I wasn't taking these women to the Cove. One of them, if not several of them, had given us away to the Northers the first time we'd tried to escape. Why would I bring all these women, some of them potential traitors, to my friends? It wouldn't be long after that until the Northers came destroying everything again.

And as I stared at Johnson's galaxy of a face, I realized I didn't trust her.

Why?

Why didn't I trust one of my own?

"We *are* headed to the Cove," I said quickly. "We need to keep moving fast, that's all."

She stared at me and I became uncomfortable. She was either far more intelligent than I gave her credit for and knew I was lying, or she trusted me.

Either way, I felt awful.

The truth was, I'd have to leave these women behind. I couldn't continue to drag them through the jungle while my friends were in danger. I'd guided them far away from the Northers—the rest was up to them.

"What's goin' on here?" Coin asked. She sat down on the other side of me and I wobbled back and forth. She stretched her back and let out a pained moan.

"Nothing," I mumbled.

"Ain't look like nothin' to me," she said. "I can see it all over your face."

"Jesus, Coin, back off. I said *nothing*," I blurted. I hadn't meant to be so mean, but I didn't need anyone overhearing her—I didn't need anyone else questioning me.

She playfully rested her cheek on a closed fist. "Wow, okay. Guess it's *that* time of the month." She then slapped her knees, got up, and walked away.

Why was I being so mean? It was like I was trying to push everyone away—like I was trying to handle the situation on my own. I looked at Quinn who sat quietly against a tree stump with her forehead resting in the palms of her hands.

Poor Quinn.

She'd recently lost one of her best friends, and now, she didn't want anyone talking to her. A few of her other girls came to see her, but she didn't even look up at them.

Who did I have on my side? Who could I trust? Was it wrong of me to want to take off on my own? I'd be faster without anyone slowing me down. That's what I needed in the end—speed. I needed to reach the Cove before Zsasz did.

If I brought anyone with me, they'd only slow me down.

I couldn't risk that.

My heart started pounding in my chest and the back of my neck became hot and sticky.

Fuck.

It seemed like I was losing my mind all because I had no control over anything.

The worst part of it all was that I wanted to leave at that very moment, but I knew I couldn't. If I was going to make it to the Cove alive, I needed my strength—and my bow.

I looked up in time to see Hammer walking toward me with a brand-new bow, a quiver, and a handful of arrows. The sun shone down hard over the bay of water, making it difficult to see her features. When she finally reached me, though, she had a tired smile on her sunken face.

"Here you go," she said, and dozens of eyes turned my way.

I grabbed the bow and ran my fingers along every edge. It was soft—though not incredibly soft given the amount of time she'd had to make it. It sure as hell wasn't perfect, but it would do. I wondered if I'd ever get Eagle's bow back. I'd dropped it before Zsasz and her goons grabbed me, and now, for all I knew, it was being used to decorate some sacrificial Ogre altar.

"It'll hold?" I asked, looking up at her.

She raised both eyebrows as if to say, *Are you kidding me?*

I smirked up at her and shook my head. Of course it would hold. Hammer was the best at what she did. When she made something, she made it right the first time around.

"Might take some practice with these broken things," I said, wiggling my slowly healing fingers, "but I'll manage. Thanks, Hammer."

She dropped the quiver and arrows at my feet. "Don't mention it."

At the same time, Johnson let out a loud sigh and stormed off.

"What's up her a—" Hammer started, but I waved a hand in the air.

"Don't worry about her," I said.

When Hammer didn't answer me, I looked up to catch her staring at me with two balled fists on her waist. Why was she looking at me like that? It was like she'd entered my mind and was now attempting to sort through my thoughts.

"What?" I blurted.

"You're an idiot if you think you're going alone," she said.

My eyes shot from side to side, but when I realized no one was close enough to hear us, I glared at her. "What're you talk—"

"Cut the bullshit, Brone."

She plopped herself down beside me and the log

rolled back and forth again.

"The only reason we ran in the first place was because of Franklin," she continued. "Zsasz has her as leverage, and she's hoping to use her to find the Cove. I know you. There's no way you're going to waste time leading hundreds of women to the Cove over the next few days when your friends— our friends—are sitting ducks over there."

I parted my lips, but I didn't know what to say.

"So when are you leaving?" she asked. "Tonight? Tomorrow? I'll be ready."

"Look, Hammer—" I tried, but she nudged me hard in the ribs and I let out a grunt.

"No, *you* listen," she hissed. Her thick eyebrows came together under her curly bangs. It was hard to imagine that over a year ago, Hammer had bullied me and threatened me at knifepoint. And now, even though she pointed stiffly at my face, I didn't feel threatened at all. I knew her anger was coming from a good place. "I'm really impressed with how far you've come, Brone, but stop trying to be a fucking hero. You must be insane if you think I'm letting you go after Zsasz alone."

When I didn't say anything, she let out a forced laugh. "What? Did you think it would be simple? Do you honestly think you'll show up at the Cove before Zsasz, warn everyone, and save them all? For all we know, Zsasz is already there. We have no idea what happened. Or, maybe she never found

156

the place. Either way, we need to be prepared to fight, and to do that, you need us."

I wanted to tell her to shut up, but I couldn't. She was right.

"Who's us?" I asked reluctantly.

"The gang, Brone: Me, Coin, Johnson, Arenas, Quinn, and whoever else you know for sure is on our side. Probably Sumi, too."

"That's exactly it. I don't know who—"

"We are." She jabbed the log's cracking bark with her finger. "So is Quinn. Just look at her."

I peered over at Quinn, who still refused to talk to anyone, then over at Johnson, who was now sitting alone at the edge of the water playing with river stones.

"I know it's hard to trust anyone right now," she said, "but you can't go around doubting everyone, either."

I closed my eyes and sucked in the hot air around me.

"How many more weapons did you make?" I asked.

Without breaking eye contact, she said, "I have us covered."

"Okay," I breathed. "And what are we supposed to tell everyone else?"

Hammer suddenly smacked me on the shoulder and I flinched. "Don't push your luck, Brone. You're the leader here. You figure it out."

CHAPTER 6

By the time the sun began to lift the morning fog, I was nauseous and unrested. Had I even slept? I'd spent most of the night tossing and turning over a pile of freshly plucked banana leaves, debating whether or not to take off in the middle of the night.

The truth was, thinking with my emotions was making me entirely reckless. The jungle was no place for one person to venture. There was a reason Trim used to banish women from the Village—solitude was a death sentence.

Hammer was right; I needed my team, same as Trim had needed us.

I sat upright but almost fell back into a lying position when Arenas's face appeared right beside mine.

"Mornin', chica," she said. She held a spear in her right hand, its shaft jabbed into the jungle's moist earth by her feet.

"Where'd you get that?" I groaned.

"Same place you got yours," she said, wiggling a finger at my funny-looking bow that lay in the dirt.

Then, another spear shaft stabbed the earth and I followed it up to Coin's face. She grinned from ear to ear, revealing that shiny gold tooth I hadn't seen in a while.

"What's going on?" I asked.

Then, Johnson appeared beside Coin with two arms crossed over her chest. She wore some kind of mesh belt with two stone daggers attached to it. I stared at her a bit longer than the others, wondering if she still held on to any resentment for my having lied to her.

But, a sly smirk curved the corner of her freckled lip. "Knew something was up."

Hammer stomped her way over—a habit she hadn't given up despite all the weight she had lost—with another handful of arrows and shivs, and I glowered at her.

Her eyes popped out at me and she opened her mouth as if to say, *What?*

I lunged up onto my feet. "You told everyone?"

"Not *everyone*," she said, almost sarcastically. "Like I told you last night—you aren't going alone."

"Who's not going alone?" I heard.

It was Quinn—she was standing behind me with her hands on her waist and her light eyebrows so close together they looked like a unibrow. I shot Hammer a quick glance, but all she did was shrug and look away. Why hadn't she told Quinn?

"I'm going after Zsasz," I said, matter-of-factly.

A heavy silence weighed down on us. Was Quinn upset? Would she feel betrayed? Would she ask to come with us? I trusted Quinn, but I didn't trust her girls—I didn't know them.

What came out of her mouth next was the last thing I'd have expected to hear.

She let out a loud, broken laugh and patted a hand on her chest. Everyone's attention fell on her. Even the women who sat in the near distance rubbing their aching feet and stiff muscles perked up.

"What's so funny?" I asked.

The smile on her face disappeared almost instantly. "Fuck, Brone, I thought you were joking."

When I didn't answer, she took two brisk steps toward me. "Are you out of your mind? You know how Zsasz is. If she sees you, she'll tear you to shreds."

"And if she finds the Cove," I said, "she'll kill everyone in there."

"I thought you said your friends were coming for you," she said.

I thought back to the city and to the woman inside the bamboo cell that night. She'd held her fingers through the holes of the prison's bamboo gate, her orange, fire-lit eye floating in the darkness.

"We're alive. Fisher made it. We're coming for you."

That was what the woman had told me, only more choppily. I hadn't seen her since that night. Had the Northers taken her behind the wooden gates? Had they taken her to where Murk and other prisoners sat in cages, undoubtedly being beaten or tortured?

"That's what someone told me," I said, returning to reality. "That my friends were coming back. That they were going to get us out."

"So, what if this Cove you're talking about is empty when you get there?" Quinn asked.

I slapped the air in front of me. "I don't care about the what-ifs. They didn't come back in time, and I'm happy they didn't. The Northers would have killed them. All I can do now is make my way toward the Cove and try to reach them before Zsasz does. If you want to come, Quinn—"

"I do," she said, "but I won't."

I raised an eyebrow but didn't say anything.

"I can't leave my women behind," she continued. "Not after everything that's happened."

And then, it hit me.

"How do you feel about leading more than just your women?" I asked.

"What?" she blurted.

Quinn *not* coming with us may have been what everyone needed. She was the kind of leader the women needed—all of the women, not only her own. I parted my lips to say something along those lines, but someone's boisterous voice exploded behind us, waking women from their sleep.

"Fuck off, you half-brained twit!"

"You fuck off!"

Leaves shuffled, and branches snapped as two women started pulling at each other. From where I stood, it looked like a tug-of-war competition, only with hateful scowls rather than competitive frowns. What were they fighting over?

They both appeared to be of the same age—somewhere in their early thirties with smooth skin but mature features. If I hadn't known any better, I'd have presumed them to be related. They both had golden-brown hair that looked like thousands of little wires atop their heads and they both wore the same clothing—ragged scraps made of old cotton. The only difference between them was that one was short with her hair tied in a messy bun, and the other was a few inches taller and her hair formed wings at her shoulders.

The taller one seemed to have the advantage. She tugged back so hard that the short one scurried toward her in an attempt to remain on her feet.

I took a step forward to intervene, but Quinn beat me to it.

"Hey!" she shouted, her big voice masking theirs.

She grabbed the tall one by the collar and

pushed her back, then stuck out an arm toward the short one, which was a translation for, *Stay back*.

It was obvious Quinn had done this before— broken fights apart. I wondered how many times she'd stopped her own women from killing each other.

"That's fuckin' mine!" the short one yelled.

The taller one, looking a bit smug now that she held whatever it was they were fighting over, pulled her shoulders back. "No, it isn't."

"You're not goddamn animals," Quinn snapped. "There won't be any fighting here."

The shorter one fell into a lazy stance, almost as if completely forgetting why she was even fighting in the first place. It looked like she was amused by Quinn. She cocked her head to one side and gave Quinn a nasty, yellow-toothed smile.

"You don't dictate what I can or can't do," she said.

"This isn't about dictating—" Quinn tried, but the short woman scoffed in her face and gave her the middle finger.

"Hey!" I shouted, and everyone turned toward me.

An uncomfortable silence filled the space around us as women's eyes shifted between the woman who'd flipped Quinn off and me. I walked toward her with my fists clenched. Old Brone would have remained quiet somewhere at the back of the crowd. New Brone, however, didn't give a shit about confrontation anymore. If someone was out of line, I needed to say something.

The woman must have sensed that I wasn't in a playful mood, because she immediately broke eye contact.

Although it wasn't my intention to intimidate anyone, there was something satisfying about the amount of respect I was receiving. I'd always been the new girl—little Brone—who'd been given a bow and arrow because of her perfect vision.

But now, as I walked forward, women took a few steps away from me and aimed their gazes at the ground.

It was the strangest feeling, yet I couldn't help but enjoy it.

"What Quinn says, goes," I said plainly.

I sensed Quinn's stare. She hadn't expected this, which was why she was so deserving of it. Quinn had a big heart, and although seemingly loud and obnoxious at times, she was the right choice for this group of women if they were going to survive.

"Her?" the woman sneered, waving a finger in Quinn's direction.

I stared at the woman but didn't say anything. There was something about her childish attitude that made me want to either slap her across the head or point an arrow at her face. I was so sick and tired of snide remarks from grown-ass women.

The short woman, obviously uncomfortable by the length of my stare, threw both hands into the air and said, "Okay, whatever."

It looked like she was about to turn around, when the tall one let out a short, condescending laugh and said, "Yeah, that's right."

Even if I had known what was about to happen, I wouldn't have had the time to stop it. Within seconds, the shortest of the two lunged backward with such force that Quinn was pushed out of the way, arms flailing and septum ring flopping up and down on her face. The women around us screamed and stepped back as the two enemies came crashing down onto the jungle floor.

I ran toward them, expecting to see a struggle—dirt flying up, legs kicking out, and loud grunts—but that didn't happen. In fact, the tallest one wasn't fighting back at all. She lay underneath her attacker, her limbs twitching. The short woman made jerking motions with the upper half of her body.

"Enough!" I shouted, but it was too late.

I heard the sound before I saw the body—an all too familiar gargling sound that immediately brought me back to the day we were captured by the Northers.

Trim.

* * *

I watched as she stood calm, her dark eyes almost smiling. It was as if she knew what was about to happen but was at peace with it. She glanced at me one more time, and though I may have imagined it, it almost looked like she gave me a brief nod—a wordless goodbye that told me to stay strong.

Then, in one swift motion, Zsasz's knife slid through Trim's throat like a freshly sharpened knife through a sweet, local strawberry. Dark blood came oozing out, and at first, panic spread over Trim's dirt-stained face—an instinctive reaction to the fact that she was about to die—before her eyes glazed over and she collapsed onto the river stones.

* * *

"No!" I shouted, and suddenly everyone's eyes were on me as I was drawn back into reality.

I stood at the center of the crowd as the short woman continued her struggle atop her victim. Beastly grunts escaped her lungs, and she muttered things I couldn't understand. It almost sounded like she was swearing to herself.

I aggressively reached down, grabbed her messy bun, and tugged back as hard as possible. I pulled her up into a standing position, her swinging arms and cotton-covered chest stained in blood. In her fist, she held what appeared to be a shiv made of either bone or wood.

Was this one of Hammer's weapons? One I'd

asked her to carve for protection during our first escape?

The woman on the ground lay still, her face pale and lifeless. What remained of her throat was nothing more than a wide gash flooded with dark red, almost black, blood.

Gasps erupted around us, followed by whispers and pointing fingers.

"What the fuck did you do?" Quinn snapped.

Then, as the killer's eyes turned on Quinn, I reacted without thinking and swung a closed fist to the side of the woman's head. She fell like a pillar—flat on her side, face-first in the dirt.

"Stell? Stell?" came someone's voice. "Oh my God," said the woman, who I could only assume was friends with the dead one. "Oh God, no," she whimpered. She grabbed her friend's head and kissed it hard, then with two fingers, closed the dead woman's eyelids.

"Fight, fight, fight," the crowd started to crescendo.

"Quiet!" I shouted, and the cheering stopped.

With my fist still held tight, I glared at the crowd around me, seeing nothing but shells. Though I knew they'd been programmed—trained, if you will—to behave like this, it still made it nearly impossible to imagine integrating them into a society without constant fights and violence.

I couldn't think like this. The truth was, these

women were still human beings. They needed guidance, and they needed to be taught that a life without constant fighting and suffering was entirely possible.

"We aren't prisoners anymore," I shouted, my voice carrying over their heads. "If you want to survive this shitty island, you'd better get used to being around each other. You won't survive on your own!"

I didn't mean to sound so angry, but I realized by the look on Arenas's face that I was coming across as hateful. She stood at the back of the crowd, her head bowed, almost the way a bullied child tries to evade their bully.

"Quinn here"—I pointed at Quinn, who looked more confused than anything—"is in charge until I return."

I pulled my shoulders back and the arrows in my newly constructed quiver slid to the other side. God, I missed that sound. Wood scraping wood.

"Until you get back?" someone asked, and voices erupted around me.

"Back?"

"Where's she going?"

"I thought she was guiding us somewhere."

"Some leader she is."

Stiffly, I raised a hand and everyone went quiet. It would probably take me a while to get used to that, but I'd be lying if I said I hadn't enjoyed it. It made me feel important—valued.

"The Northers—the Beasts," I corrected, "are on their way to kill my friends. I know where they're going, and I have to stop them."

I realized as the words came out of my mouth that I probably sounded like some cheesy superhero, like some too-good-to-be-true woman willing to risk her life to save the day.

"Why don't we come with you?" someone shouted. She had paint markings across both her cheeks and teeth so rotten it looked like they were missing entirely upon first glance. She punched a solid fist in the air and added, "'Cause I'd like to fuckin' hit 'em where it hurts!"

"Same here!"

"Let us at 'em!"

I fought the urge to smile. They weren't Battlewomen, but I was willing to bet the anger they carried was enough to take on Zsasz and her crew.

"I can't be held back—" I started.

"I won't hold you back!" the woman shouted, a dirty smile stretching her blotchy face.

"Me neither!" someone else said.

"Me n-n-n-either!" came a familiar voice.

I caught sight of Tegan's messy hair, and then her big eyes appeared over a woman's shoulder. She was smiling—something I hadn't seen her do since the Village. It wasn't a shy smile either. It revealed sheer excitement and anticipation.

"Tegan!" I said, but my voice barely carried over the shouts of enthusiastic women. They started stomping their feet and punching invisible targets, and as they did, Tegan was shoved backward and forward until she disappeared, blending in with the crowd.

"I'm in!"

"Me too!"

"Let's fuckin' kill them!"

I turned my attention to Coin, then Hammer, who both shrugged at the same time. What was going on? This wasn't the plan. It was only supposed to be me and my women. And what about trust? How was I supposed to trust a bunch of strangers? I'd already explained to Hammer that I couldn't risk a traitor entering the Cove, our safe haven.

But, maybe this wasn't about protecting the Cove.

The Northers would never stop hunting us until they killed our people, all of our people. And they'd try time and time again until they succeeded.

Rainer's hatred couldn't be eliminated.

Instead, we had to eliminate Rainer.

What we needed wasn't a safe haven—we needed an army.

CHAPTER 7

"What're you gonna do with 'er?" asked the rotten-toothed woman. "Name's Jack, by the way." She stuck out a brown-nailed hand, but I couldn't bring myself to grab it. Not on this island. Not in a place without hand sanitizer. Her short hair appeared as dirty as her grimy face—an ash brown that looked oil black. Hundreds of dandruff specs sat on her head, and every time she talked, I worried one of them might come flying into my mouth.

"Brone," I said simply.

"Oh, I know who you are," she spat. "Everyone's been sayin' yer name all damn day. If ya ask me, all I'm startin' ta hear is *bone*." She humped the air with a nasty smile on her face, and I grimaced. "If ya know what I mean." And she burst out into a barking laugh.

I peered down at the woman, the murderer, who was still unconscious. She lay with her mouth wide open, almost lazily so, as if her jaw were too heavy for her lips to stay closed. It wasn't only Jack who'd asked me about her—everyone was asking me what the woman's punishment would be.

What was I supposed to do? Banish her? What if she followed us for revenge? It wasn't like we had a village surrounded by a barrier or guards to keep her away from us. And even if she didn't follow us, how long would it take before she died a violent or painful death?

I hated myself for feeling any form of empathy for this woman. She didn't deserve it. As I kept toying back and forth between my survival instincts and morals, I realized something: in the Village, this woman would have been banished without question, and if I wanted any hope for our future, I had to follow the path of the only capable leader I'd ever known—Murk.

Had she witnessed this, she'd have banished the woman with the click of her fingers.

I pointed at Coin and then at the unconscious woman. "Tie her up and leave her behind."

Coin didn't make a face at me or attempt to argue. She pulled her shoulders back, almost as if proud to have been the one asked to help, then made her way toward the killer. I was happy to see that Coin's body was back to being the way she'd always intended it to be—thick and well-defined. It was evident that her physique was her main source of confidence. Ever since she'd regained her muscles, her steps thundered with strength and she walked with purpose. Her chin, too, was elevated at all times.

Coin cut overhanging vines down and grabbed the woman's wrists. As I watched her tie them tight around her arms, her ankles, and even her waist, I couldn't help but wonder: was I making the right decision? Was I cruel for tying her up, rendering her helpless against enemies?

If I gave it too much thought, I'd back out of my decision. I needed to remain strong and consistent if I wanted these women to view me as someone fit to lead. How would I ever forgive myself if this woman followed us from a distance and killed someone else? It was one life to potentially save another, if not several.

Instead of focusing on my feelings, I told myself that I didn't have any—that I couldn't afford to have any—if I wanted to save my friends.

"Let's move," I said, and as I turned away, Arenas's dark-skinned face almost crashed into mine.

"Hey, chica," she said, her abnormally long eyelashes far apart. "You okay?"

What was that even supposed to mean? How was I supposed to be okay? I was indirectly murdering someone else. Another life, on my hands. Was it obvious that I felt like I wanted to shed my skin? That I wanted to vomit until only air came out? I was doing everything in my power to look composed—to look like the leader everyone wanted me to be—but inside, I felt like I was breaking apart into thousands of decomposing pieces.

I swatted the air beside my face when a huge, long-legged, winged bug tickled my cheek. Although I'd gotten used to critters on Kormace Island, I still didn't like them.

Arenas stared at me.

"I'm fine," I said coldly.

The truth was, I wanted everything to be over. But at the same time, I felt responsible for seeing this through to the end. If I didn't keep moving, everything might fall apart. I worried the women would turn on each other or part ways, which would inevitably lead to their deaths.

They needed me, and deep down, I needed to serve a purpose.

"You did good," came Johnson's voice.

I looked at her in my peripheral but didn't turn my head. Were these supposed to be words of encouragement? Was this supposed to erase the fact that I'd basically left a woman to die? Not only to die, but undoubtedly tortured by either some sharp-toothed carnivore or worse, Ogres.

"She's a killer anyway," Johnson continued.

I swung my head sideways to look at her. I was getting sick of the word *killer*, or *murderer*. "Aren't we all?" I snapped.

She seemed taken aback. Her eyebrows came together, forming freckled lumps on her forehead.

"Yeah, but—"

"We're all here because we killed someone," I said.

"You can't look at it that way," Hammer said. With the back of her forearm, she wiped a line of sweat from underneath her lip. "Everything's circumstantial. Sure, we're all murderers, but I'd be willing to bet that most of us have a story behind it. Betrayal, heartbreak, self-defense—you name it. To kill someone over a fucking bracelet? Letting her be a part of our society would be a mistake."

"It was a bracelet?" Arenas asked, now walking backward at the front of the crowd to look at us.

Coin suddenly appeared beside Hammer with a look of utter disgust on her face. "Crazy bitch." She wiggled what appeared to be a bracelet made of string and rock. The string had turned a deep pink, and some of the rocks still had dark blood splattered on them. "Had it clutched in her bloody hand."

"Wonder if it belonged to someone they knew," Hammer said.

"That don't excuse it," Coin grumbled.

"Either way," Johnson cut in, "I agree with Hammer. You did what you had to do to protect the rest of us."

I nodded, even though all I wanted to say was, *Shut up.*

What was wrong with me? Why was I so bitter?

Was it resentment? Was I resentful that I'd been put in this role? Forced into an impossible leadership position when all I wanted was freedom? Or, was I angry with myself? Maybe I didn't want to be consoled because deep down, I knew I'd killed someone else.

Deep down, I wasn't Lydia anymore—the girl who'd *accidentally* killed her mom's abusive boyfriend. I was Brone, an island woman who'd violently taken several lives.

And this time, it hadn't been a Norther's life. All this time, I'd told myself that those I'd killed had been monsters—soulless women who deserved to be removed from this planet.

But then again, this woman was no different from a Norther. She'd killed someone in cold blood over a goddamn bracelet.

Maybe she deserved to die like the Northers.

I clenched my teeth, disgusted with myself for having such thoughts, and quickened my pace. "We need to hurry."

I hadn't counted them all—the women who argued they wanted to fight by my side—but if I had to guess, I would have estimated approximately twenty to thirty women. They all held weapons of sorts—rocks, sticks, and shivs—and they all looked the same to me: barbaric clones with dirt-covered faces, thick-browed scowls, and postures so poor they resembled cavewomen.

I caught sight of Quinn in the distance, over the heads of all the women. She waved a tattooed arm and gave me a firm nod, almost as if to say, *It'll be okay.*

Would it be? After this was over—after I'd ensured that my people were safe at the Cove—the plan was to find Quinn and the rest of the survivors. She'd given me one of her women, Aisha, and said that so long as her friend remained alive, she'd be able to lead us back to Quinn—back to her old society of women hidden near the southeast shore.

I had no idea how Quinn planned on integrating over a hundred women into her old society, but if anyone could do it, she could.

My shoulders jerked forward when Jack, the greasy, short-haired woman with rotten teeth, jabbed a stick into the air and shouted, "Death to the Beasts! Death to the Beasts!"

Several women started joining in, fists pumping in the air and looks of fearlessness on their faces.

"Guys!" I hissed, and they all went quiet.

Jack's head sank into her shoulders like a turtle caught in a crowd. Poor woman. It looked like all she'd wanted to do was get her fellow warriors pumped up for the big fight, but now wasn't the time, and shouting "Death to the Beasts" when the Beasts were hunting us wasn't exactly a brilliant idea either.

It was obvious she'd never fought or hunted before.

"We have to be quiet," I said. "Let's focus on stealth right now, and when the time's right, you'll have your chance to rip those Beasts apart."

This seemed to satisfy their hunger for blood. The crowd broke out into rapid nods, and Jack waved at everyone, urging them to move faster.

"You got it, boss," Jack said, a glob of slime dripping down her chin.

She reminded me of an overly eager office assistant. It was as if she wanted to enforce everything I said, almost to the point of taking charge herself. I wondered how long she'd been here, on Kormace Island. More specifically, how long she'd been held prisoner by the Northers.

Then, from within the crowd of women came Tegan, her frail figure swaying from side to side. She stealthily slipped past shoulders, arms, and chests. The woman was so skinny she'd have probably been able to hide behind the narrow trunk of a palm tree.

"Tegan!" I said, surprised to find her here.

I was certain she'd stayed behind with Quinn and Sumi. Why would she want to join the fight? She wasn't fit for battle.

"I-I want to help," she said, her stutter far less prominent than it had been the last few times she'd spoken.

"Help?" I said.

I hadn't meant to sound unappreciative, but the truth was, I wasn't sure how Tegan would be of any assistance in her condition.

"Heal," she said. She scratched at her throat—so much so that her skin turned pink. It was as if she was trying to drown out her horrid memories with physical pain. "I can help, Brone," she said.

For the first time since the Village, I felt like I was looking at Tegan—like I was standing before our potions expert in admiration. Tegan had a lot of knowledge, but ever since finding her in the city, I figured she'd been broken beyond repair.

She looked away and stared at her feet, her ratty hair falling over her face.

"All right, Tegan," I said. "You can be our Medic."

Her head jolted up and her bangs fell away from her sunken face. She looked like a friendly dinosaur from a kid's television program: big joints, awkwardly shaped, and with an oversized grin. It was obvious that being given a title, a purpose, meant the world to her.

I knew no one could take Navi's place as Medic, but Tegan was the next best thing. If anyone could fill her shoes, it was Tegan.

We continued through dense forestry, swatting giant leaves and hanging vines from our path as we moved. That was one thing I missed most from the real world: paved asphalt. I missed the feeling of thick, memory foam sneakers against solid ground.

The thought made me want to look down at my feet, but I resisted the urge. I knew how bad they looked. The last time I'd taken a moment to inspect them, my thick yellow toenails had grown three times their usual length, and curly black hairs sat on my big toes. The pads of my feet had become entirely calloused, which in a sense served its purpose because I didn't feel anything when I walked.

Everyone around me was barefoot, and although I cringed at the very thought of it, there was nothing I could do. We weren't in a position to start building wooden slabs or leaf boots. We had to keep moving, and if that meant putting our lives at risk, so be it. The idea of being bitten by a highly venomous snake was less disturbing than the thought of being slaughtered by a Norther.

I slid to my right when I suddenly stepped in something slimy.

Two solid arms caught me midfall, and in my peripheral, I caught sight of Coin's golden tooth.

"Yo, what the f—" she said, and as soon as I landed back on my feet, the smell hit me.

I jumped backward, away from the carcass at my feet, and pressed my forearm up against my nostrils. The women behind me started flocking like seagulls at a beach party, their necks craned and their heads moving this way and that.

"What's going on?"

"What is it?"

The reason I hadn't seen her body was that it lay in a bed of rotten leaves, her dark skin blending effortlessly with the combination of brown, black, and red around her. The skin of her chest was missing entirely, revealing torn pectoral muscles, and I could see her broken bones protruding from her arms.

What the fuck was this?

I slowly glanced up and wished I hadn't. It was almost as if I'd stepped into a time machine and found myself standing in front of Sunny's lifeless, upside-down body. The only reason I'd recognized her that day was because of her dandelion eyes—her face had been swollen like a balloon, so much so it became unrecognizable.

"Brone," came Rocket's voice.

Rocket.

Was she here?

"Brone," the voice repeated, but this time, it was Hammer's voice.

Was I losing my mind?

I squeezed my eyes shut and opened them again, bringing into focus the dozens of mutilated carcasses hanging overhead hidden amid thousands of vivid green leaves. Limbs were amputated and throats slit wide open, so much so that some vocal chords could be seen.

On the ground, throughout the bloody leaves, was a white powder that formed some sort of symbolic design. I couldn't make out what it was, but I'd seen symbols like this before.

"Brone," Hammer hissed again.

A woman behind me whimpered, and the sound of skin being slapped echoed up into the trees.

"Shut up," someone else hissed.

"Dear God..."

"Oh my God... What the fuck is this?"

I knew exactly what this was.

I slowly drew an arrow from my quiver, my glare fixated on the dense greenery around us.

CHAPTER 8

"An Ogre?"

"The fuck is an Ogre?"

"Keep your voice down!"

I swung my body around so fast that the arrows in my quiver shifted to one side, and everyone went quiet.

Had they never been told the stories of Ogres? It didn't make sense to me, seeing as Death Sprinters—women who attempted to flee the city—were beaten and strung up alive for Ogres to find.

"Oh God have mercy," one woman started, and for a moment, I thought it was Georgia, only, this woman didn't have a Southern accent. When I finally caught sight of her, I realized she looked nothing like Georgia. Her skin was as black as fresh earth, and curly white hairs topped her head. From a distance, she looked frail, which made me wonder why she'd followed us to fight, but upon closer observation, it was obvious she had some muscle on her. She quickly drew crosses over her forehead and lips with the back of her thumb, then stared at the sky and pressed a clenched fist over her chest. "Remove these demons," she went on.

One Latina-looking woman beside her rolled her eyes. "Jesus ain't gonna save you here, sister."

The religious one, obviously ignoring the nonbeliever's opinion, bowed her head and started searching the ground. Had she dropped something of value? This wasn't the time to hunt for a lost item.

We needed to get the hell out of here.

The only problem was, I couldn't move.

Why couldn't I move?

The black-skinned woman suddenly bent over, dug up a sharp-edged rocked from beside her big toe, and pulled it up. "In the name of the Lord, I fight."

"Deemas," everyone else started muttering.

It sounded like *demons*, but with a thick accent. What the hell were they saying?

Another woman made the cross symbol over her chest and kissed something that was held tightly between her thumb and index finger.

Jack must have sensed my irritation because her big, crusty eyes rolled my way and she took a gentle step forward. "All they sayin' is *Demon*, but in Russian. Ya know, 'cause of da Beasts bein' Russian and all. Told us there're demons out here. Now, I ain't religious mahself, so I don't believe all that bullshit. But these women do. Don't know what kinda monster could do somethin' like this. I can see why they're called *demons*. Man, if—"

"Okay," I hissed, and she stopped talking.

I jerked my head sideways, signaling everyone to follow me.

Dry vegetation cracked under our feet as we moved beneath the bodies, and every time we walked underneath a carcass, I cringed. The death appeared to be fairly recent—a few days, maybe. I'd seen enough dead bodies to know that it took, on average, three to five days before the bloating started. These bodies weren't bloated at all. The foul smell, however, was noticeable, which meant their organs had started decaying. The smell wasn't as bad as some bodies I'd smelled—those that I'd found without teeth and nails, which meant they'd been sitting for over a week. But it was enough to make my stomach churn; it was a smell I'd never gotten used to, nor would I ever.

I glanced at Johnson, Arenas, Hammer, and Coin, and made the international signal for *keep your eyes open*—two fingers pointed at my eyes and then directed into the thickness of the jungle.

Although I'd never wish this sight on anyone, part of me wished that Franklin were still around to see it. She'd been the most skeptical of the gang, constantly belittling anyone who spoke of the Ogres. I wondered if she'd encountered some along her path with Zsasz.

Hopefully.

Maybe Ogres had attacked Zsasz and her crew and resolved this entire problem for me. Maybe they'd killed Franklin, and now Zsasz had no way of reaching the Cove.

Or, maybe I wouldn't even reach the Cove myself, so I'd never know.

I swallowed hard and took another step forward when the sound of something snapping echoed from above. A dozen women screamed and scurried sporadically in a panic.

"What happened?" I asked, but the swaying carcass overhead immediately grabbed my attention. Its face was soaked in blood, masking its features entirely, and its legs had been messily hacked off, leaving only half a naked body hung by the neck. It hovered several feet lower than the other bodies, presumably because the rope had come loose, which I assumed had also been the cause of the loud snap.

I looked away; the sight made me sick to my stomach.

"Keep moving," I growled.

We rushed through the sacrificial opening, hands and forearms covering our mouths. There was no worse feeling than wanting to run but knowing it might draw unnecessary attention. It reminded me of those awful nightmares—the ones in which you're being chased, but you can't run.

The harder you try, the slower you become as your killer moves closer. It's as if you stand jogging in one spot, or as if your limbs suddenly weigh a thousand pounds.

This was precisely what it felt like and it was worse than being hunted by the Northers because the Ogres were absolute savages.

They truly were demons.

We moved past what appeared to be an altar, atop which sat a decomposing severed head, its brown eyes wide open and its colorless lips parted only enough to reveal bloody gums. In front of it, several teeth lay in a perfectly straight row. I couldn't tell whether they'd fallen out or if they'd been torn out.

I regripped my arrow and held the elastic back tight enough to release a quick shot if necessary.

What kind of sick piece of shit would ever do something like this?

What was the purpose of this? Was it religion? Fanatics? Pure barbarism? How on Earth had I ever convinced myself that Ogres deserved the same treatment as any other human being? They deserved to be killed—all of them.

You're a killer, Brone.

I shook these thoughts away. I wasn't a killer. I was a survivor. And I was also a protector. I clenched my teeth at the thought of women screaming while being tortured. I couldn't even imagine the pain they'd endured—the fear they'd experienced—before being brutally murdered.

Had they even been murdered, or had they been cut up and strung to die a slow, painful death, their minds still intact?

My jaw clicked and I released my clench.

The more I thought about these victims, the more I hoped an Ogre would come out.

Come out and face me.

I'll shoot an arrow right through your fucking eye.

Goddamn piece of fucking shit.

I inhaled a deep breath and rushed passed the altar. On the ground, several dozen seashells formed a hollow circle, which most probably meant something to the Ogres. It was positioned right underneath the severed head, allowing the victim's blood to spill off the altar and directly at the center of it.

Without thinking, I kicked my foot right through the shells and they flew straight into the air. Two of them made a clanking noise against the wooden altar, and the others landed softly on the jungle floor.

I felt Coin's stare, but I didn't look at her.

Then, I did something stupid.

I angrily forced the weight of my body against the altar, knocking it down to the ground. The severed head rolled, causing some of the women to scream and hop away from it.

"The fuck are you doin'?" Coin asked.

"What's it look like?" I said, my voice pure gravel.

"Sick pieces of shit," Arenas said, obviously taking my side.

"Yeah!" a woman rasped from behind us.

I continued through a narrow opening, beneath a thick sheet of hanging leaves, and led the women away from the site as quickly as possible. It felt darker here than it had only minutes ago, probably because of the density of the trees overhead.

Carvings were dug into every other trunk, almost as if forming a welcoming path to the Ogre's territory. Was this their exit, or their entrance?

I ground my teeth and stared straight ahead, praying for one to lunge out in front of me.

Was I being reckless? Maybe. But I didn't care. I was so angry, all I wanted was blood. And I knew this feeling—I knew that if I wasn't careful, I'd lose control, but I couldn't even bring myself to care about that either.

I wanted to lose control.

I wanted to slaughter the person responsible for this.

I tore a giant spider web from my path and stomped over a protruding, green moss tree root.

"Brone!" someone hissed so sharply that I couldn't tell who it had come from.

I turned around to find Coin's menacing scowl aimed right at me.

"What?" I said through gritted teeth.

Though the others wouldn't admit it—Johnson, Arenas, and Hammer—I could tell by the look of horror on their faces that they also thought I needed to calm down.

Seeing the look on Hammer's face had the most impact of all. Over the last few months, I'd come to learn that Hammer was probably the most levelheaded of us all. It was almost as if a switch had been flipped ever since the day I'd beaten her face in.

I had nearly killed her, after all. Had she had a near-death experience?

This new Hammer wasn't the Hammer I'd met in the Village.

She wasn't scowling at me like the others were. Her face was much softer, and if I'd had to guess what she was thinking, it would have been, *Are you okay in there, Brone?*

No, I wasn't okay, but it also wasn't okay for me to risk the lives of these women by attracting danger. I had no idea how many Ogres there truly were.

I inhaled a long breath through my nostrils and let it out through my mouth, an unfamiliar calm immediately washing over me.

"Yo, man," Arenas said, "she looked like the Hulk there for a second, no?" She wiggled a finger in my direction with a cheesy grin stretching the bottom half of her face. Her wiggling finger made its way in the direction of the leaves overhead, and her smile grew even bigger. "'Specially with all them leaves up there. Givin' off a green tint and shit."

It almost looked like she was about to burst out laughing when Coin jabbed an elbow in her ribs.

"Aye! Chica! The fuck was that—"

Johnson, suddenly looking like a tired mother of two disobedient twins, smacked her hands on her waist, and gave them both the stink eye—the look that said, *Shut up, or else*—and Arenas went quiet.

I rolled my eyes and kept moving until we reached a tree with what appeared to be human hair attached to its decaying trunk. It sat so still, almost as if it had been placed there over a hundred years ago.

Beyond it, the narrow path continued as far as I could see, its trail disappearing at a bend up ahead. The last thing I wanted to do, despite my wanting to encounter an Ogre only minutes ago, was lead these women directly toward danger.

I couldn't be selfish about this.

Where did this path go? Was there some sort

of Ogre nest up ahead? Had we passed through their sacrificial land, only to be venturing toward their home? This was the longest stretch of Ogre territory I'd ever seen.

Though I much preferred to walk through a predefined path, I knew it was a stupid idea to keep using it. It had obviously been made by someone, just as our path from the Village to the Working Grounds had been created through years and years of usage.

So instead of moving past the tree with the hair, I turned right and ducked beneath a fallen tree branch. Its cracked tip was black, making me wonder if it had been struck by lightning.

"Great," I heard Arenas in the background, ducking. "We got a clear path, but we're goin' where it's dark."

"Shut up," Johnson hissed.

"You both shut up," Coin joined in, and she moved beneath the branch behind me.

"Oh, ow, aye," I heard.

I turned around to spot Jack attempting to crawl underneath the branch to follow me. It was too high up to climb over, but not high enough to walk under—only crawl. Around it were large boulders and tree trunks so close together that there was no other option but to get on one's hands and knees.

She bent over low to the ground and took a

step, then yelped out again and restraightened her posture.

"Go!" someone behind her snarled.

"What's going on?" Coin said, moving toward the condensed crowd forming on the other side of the branch.

"It's mah back," Jack said, wincing. "Isn't what it used to be, ya know?"

Jack didn't look all that old. If I'd had to guess, I would have placed her in her midforties. It wasn't like she was a senior. What had she done? Injured herself? If so, why the hell had she asked to come along? I'd specifically told them all that I didn't need anyone slowing us down.

I must have been glaring at her because the grimace on her face disappeared. She quickly dropped to her knees, careful not to curve her back, then let herself fall flat on her face like a sausage wiener. It was the strangest thing I'd ever seen, and if I hadn't been so preoccupied with wanting to reach the Cove, I'd have probably laughed.

Then, she rolled.

Arenas snorted behind me and slapped a hand over her mouth.

The moment Jack reached my side of the branch, Coin grabbed her by the arms and helped her up. Several gooey leaves stuck to her knees, but she flicked them away.

She gave me a rotten smile, threw both arms in the air, and said, "I'm okay!" but tucked her chin into her neck when she realized she was yelling again.

I turned away from her and stepped through a wall of leaves, fearfully hoping that I was leading these women in the right direction.

CHAPTER 9

"So it's true?" Arenas finally asked.

It was like she'd been holding the question in ever since we'd found the dead bodies. She'd probably kept her mouth shut to keep the vomit from coming out. That hadn't worked for everyone, though.

I was glad we were out from underneath that bloody scene. I'd learned to cope with dead bodies, but mutilated ones, that was a different story. And by the amount of bile that had come out of the women, they weren't all that used to it either.

"The whole 'Ogre' thing," Arenas pressed, forming air quotes beside her dark-skinned face.

"Ogre?" came Jack's voice. With her fingers, she formed a hollow zero and placed it over her eyes, obviously trying to portray a one-eyed creature. She then let out a stupid laugh and stomped the weight of her body from one leg to the other.

What was she doing? She looked like a complete idiot.

"That's actually a misconception," Hammer said, matter-of-factly. The playful smile on Jack's face vanished, and she dropped the whole one-eyed look and stared at Hammer. "It's folklore," Hammer continued, "and all it means is a man-eating giant."

Jack, who seemed unimpressed with Hammer's amount of knowledge, made her eyelids go flat.

"Gotta admit," Coin chimed in, "Hammer's right. Plenty of two-eyed ogres out there. Sounds to me like you're generalizin', girl."

Jack rolled her eyes like a kid who'd been told to stop making funny faces because they weren't funny.

I glared at all of them, but Johnson must have been the first to notice. In a sharp whisper, she said, "We aren't safe yet, so shut up, all of you."

The markings on the trees became inconsistent until finally, I couldn't see any more. I slid my arrow back into my quiver and fastened my bow around my back.

"We may be off Ogre territory," I said, turning to the women behind me, "but we're still on Kormace Island. Stay focused."

The jungle's wildlife seemed to amplify as the women became quiet. Leaves rustled overhead, and I glanced up in time to see a capuchin monkey hopping from one branch to another. The air was hot and sticky as it usually was toward early afternoon. Fortunately, the greenery around us was far too dense for the sun to sink its rays into our skin.

Why hadn't we seen an Ogre, anyway?

Were they hiding?

Did they only massacre women who were defenseless?

Cowards.

And who were those women we'd seen hanging from above? Our own? I couldn't imagine they were, being that we were still pretty far from the Village. Murk wasn't the type to let women venture far away from the Village.

Murk, I thought, remembering how her defeated body leaned forward, her arms strapped by the wrists. If only I'd had the courage to fight Zsasz—to kill her where she stood—I could have rescued Murk. But then, rationality kicked in, and I realized that even if I'd miraculously won a fight against Zsasz, there had been countless Northers outside, in front of the mountain.

How was Murk doing, anyway? Had she been punished for our escape? I hadn't been able to save her, but I'd get her out, one way or another.

"Hold up," someone suddenly said, pulling me out of my daze.

She didn't look very old—late thirties, if that. But the way she walked made me believe she was in her late sixties. Her clothes fit loosely over her undefined body, and it looked like at any minute, she would collapse. She clutched a sun-damaged hand over her heart and winced.

"What's up?" asked one of the women beside her, looking both concerned and agitated at the fact that we'd stopped walking.

But the woman didn't answer. Instead, she inhaled a deep breath through reddening nostrils and let it out through her mouth.

"I—" she tried. "I need a break."

I wanted to sympathize, I honestly did. But I didn't have an ounce of empathy in me—not when my friends' lives were at risk, and we were on a time-sensitive mission to reach them.

Several eyes turned my way; the women were waiting for me to say something. And judging by everyone's sweaty skin and heavy breathing, they weren't opposed to the idea of a break.

"I'm not stopping anyone from taking a break," I said, "but I'm not stopping."

The air around us went even quieter, and for a moment, it sounded like even the insects had stopped humming.

Without another word, I turned around and continued forcing my way through giant leaves and intertwined vines. Women muttered behind me, and I was certain they thought I was a bitch, but I didn't care—I couldn't care.

This wasn't about them, nor was it about me. What if sitting for ten minutes prevented me from saving my friends? What if Zsasz reached the Cove ten minutes before us, only to massacre not only my friends, by countless innocent women?

We would rest when we finally reached safety.

"Girl, it wouldn't change anything to let the women rest for five minutes," came Coin's voice. "They're exhausted."

"So am I," I said sharply. I let out another long breath before turning to Coin, a little calmer this time. "I was supposed to be doing this on my own, Coin. I appreciate that everyone wants to help—I do. And I couldn't be more thankful to have you and the gang here with me. But I already told everyone that if they're coming, they can't slow me down."

She gave me a gentle nod, her way of saying, *Yeah, you're right, but you're also wrong.*

Maybe I was.

Had I been alone right then, an Ogre or a predator might have killed me. Or, I could have reached the Cove, only to then be attacked by Zsasz and her crew. The truth was, I didn't stand a chance alone, just as Trim wouldn't have survived the jungle had she gone hunting without us, her Hunters. Kormace Island was about working together, and I'd been so caught up with wanting to save my friends that I'd begun to view everyone else as either an obstacle or a means to getting what I wanted.

These women weren't objects, and the last

thing I wanted was to end up becoming a bitter leader like Rainer—someone who abused her people for her own gain.

I stopped walking so abruptly that Arenas's face hit me flat in the shoulder blades.

"Watch it!" she shouted, but her eyes went big when I swung around. She let out a nervous laugh and raised two hands on either side of her face. "My fault, chica, my fault."

Was she scared of me? My gaze shifted toward the women. Some of them were quite a way back, no doubt trying to decide whether taking a break was worth having to run to catch up. Some of them looked back at me wrinkling their brows, others biting their lips while most avoided eye contact altogether.

Were they all scared of me? I felt like a complete asshole. This wasn't what I'd wanted.

"Sorry, guys," I said, and this seemed to catch their interest. "I'm stressed out about getting to my friends before anyone gets hurt. Let's rest for a bit, okay? I know some of you are really hurting, and it's completely understandable."

At first, no one responded. It was almost as if they thought that any second, I would let out a maniacal laugh and say, "Just kidding! Keep moving, bitches."

So instead of waiting for the women to rest, I pulled my bow off my back and rested the weight of my body against a slanted tree trunk. Something tickled the top of my head, and I swatted hard at it, only to feel a bunch of leaves dance through my fingers.

The women slowly followed suit, finding something to either lean on or sit on.

How far were we, anyway? A few hours away? All I knew, based on the sun's location, was that I was headed in the right direction. Whether we'd find the Cove or not was an entirely different story.

But I had to hope.

I had to hold on to the possibility of seeing Ellie again—of holding her in my arms and feeling her soft face against mine. Then, I thought of Fisher, Biggie, Rocket, and Flander.

God, I missed them so much. It felt like I'd been torn away from my family.

I couldn't sit here anymore. We'd rested enough.

With a swing of my upper body, I threw myself up onto my feet.

"All right, time to keep moving."

"What?" someone blurted. "But we only just—"

"You heard the boss," came Jack's voice. She marched ahead of me with her chin held high, arms swinging on either side of her body. "Let's keep moving, ladies."

A few sighs and groans spread through the jungle around us, but it was something else that caught my attention—another sound. It was subtle, almost undetectable, but it was a sound so distinct that I couldn't ignore it.

Jack, now at the front of the line, had stopped moving. She held her open palms up in the air, almost as if to say, I *didn't do it*.

What was *it*, anyways?

Suddenly, everything felt like it was moving in slow motion.

I turned toward Coin, who I knew had the best ears out of all of us, and caught the look of horror on her face before it happened.

Leaves instantly bunched together, and the sound of fast-moving rope filled the air. It sounded like a zip line coming loose, or like someone descending quickly with a rappel—high pitched and rapidly approaching.

It may have lasted all of one second, but it felt like ten.

All at once, arms and legs swung through the air like those of fifty-year-old rag dolls. Women screamed as they were scooped up into what appeared to be a giant mesh trap. One woman, having only been caught by the leg, hung upside down, her red hair reaching as far as her dangling arms, and her face entirely contorted with every fearful shout.

"Shut up!" I hissed, and the dozen women on top of one another inside the trap went quiet.

The women who hadn't been caught hesitated, taking one step backward, but then stopping in fear of activating another trap. I whipped an arrow from my quiver, my gaze fixated not on the trap that hung twenty feet overhead, but at the greenery around us.

And then I saw them.

At first glance, there only appeared to be one, but as she moved in on us and as the leaves beside her began to separate, it was clear she wasn't alone. Shadowed faces slowly stepped out from behind the jungle's lush vegetation, red and white markings across their cheeks and eyes as dark as coal.

The only clothing they wore were underwear-like leather around their groin area, while some wore long fur over their shoulders. Their chests were bare, revealing sagging breasts. Some of them had large wooden pikes hanging from oversized holes on their earlobes, while others wore long necklaces made of what appeared to be human teeth.

"Agra amoolar!" one shouted, and the others jerked their spears in the air, their breasts swaying with their motions.

If I'd had to guess, I would have pinned this one as their leader. Her black hair was long and scraggly, and it split down the middle of her head and hung on both shoulders. Across her high cheeks were big black markings that looked like oil had been splattered on her face. She was the palest of the group, reminding me of an ancient vampire who'd recently awoken from its tomb. She had muscle definition, though no more than any of us. It wasn't her size I was frightened by; it was the look in her eyes. It was the emptiness—the void that made me wonder if she even had a soul.

Her gaze fell on me and then on my bow.

The string of my bow felt hot against my skin, and although all I wanted to do was fire a shot, it would be suicide. I didn't know how many of them were hiding behind trees or how dangerous they were. All I knew was that they wanted blood.

And although my women had stated they'd wanted to fight, the way they'd frozen told me they weren't ready for battle.

"Agra umaro!" the same one shouted, and this time, the others shouted the same thing, dark lips flapping over rotten teeth.

My heart pounded so hard I could hear it in my left ear. This couldn't be happening. Any moment now, cameras would descend from the sky, and music would fill the air. Some man's obnoxious voice would carry through the jungle—something along the lines of, *Ladies and gentlemen, thank you for coming to the show*, and everything would end.

Everyone would drop their weapons and shake hands, commending one another for their outstanding acting skills.

Because this streak of bad luck couldn't be real.

We couldn't have possibly escaped the Northers only to be caught by Ogres.

PART THREE

PROLOGUE

"You are my sunshine, my lovely sunshine. You make me happy, ev-er-y-day," my mom sang, the tip of her nose nearly touching mine. Obviously, she wasn't the best at remembering lyrics, but she still sang them as if she'd been the one to write them, grinning from ear to ear with little wrinkles forming at the corners of her eyes.

Behind her, the hallway light created a yellow glow. She always left the hallway light on for me even though she hated leaving lights on as it was *a complete waste of electricity*.

"Money doesn't grow on trees, Lydia," she'd say, flicking a light switch off. I'd usually make some smartass remark like, "Well, Mrs. Appleton says paper is made from trees..."

Mrs. Appleton was my fourth-grade teacher, and Mom didn't seem too impressed when I quoted her. She'd give me the *look*, so I'd shut my mouth.

She reached for Beakly, my favorite table lamp from my favorite TV show. It was a big yellow bird head, and it went dark the moment she tugged on the string hanging underneath its beak. She then brushed the back of her index finger along my cheek and whispered, "Good night, sweetheart."

Although she was smiling, I could tell she was hurting.

She tried to hide it, but I could always tell when she didn't feel well. I didn't understand it at the time, but looking back, I realized it was because of all the work hours she was putting in to put food on our table.

"Good night, Mom," I said, and I closed my eyes as she walked away, picturing hundreds of dollars sitting on our dining room table.

I did this every night. Maybe if I thought about it enough, I'd make it happen, like magic. And if I could make money appear somehow, I could take care of my mom as she took care of me.

I went to bed that night, visualizing a life in which my mother wasn't suffering. Instead, she was sitting by a huge inground pool in the middle of a sizzling summer day, sipping on a fancy, overly colorful cocktail.

When she caught me staring, she turned her head sideways and glanced at me over her oversized sunglasses, and a smile stretched across her entire face.

For the first in a long time, she looked happy.

Wasn't that what she deserved?

Happiness.

A life without suffering.

The only problem with this world is, people don't always get what they deserve.

CHAPTER 1

You are my sunshine, my lovely sunshine.

My mom's interpretation of that song played in my head as if being emitted from old wired speakers attached to a television, crackling every few seconds.

Perhaps that's all this was—a TV show, a reality program designed to amuse the most shameless and heartless of people as violent gladiator battles had once been a form of entertainment.

But the sweat inside my palms reminded me that I was very much alive—I wasn't playing a part, nor was I under the protection of television directors. My heart pounded against my rib cage, and I breathed in the jungle's moist, earthy air. It smelled of earthworms, tree moss, and fungus.

Although my legs should have been shaking, they weren't. Could be I was getting used to controlling my adrenaline.

You make me happy, ever-y-day.

As I stared at their paint-smeared faces, one word came to mind: monsters. If I hadn't known any better, I'd have assumed them to be native to

Kormace Island. They didn't look like prisoners or convicts. They looked like savages who had spent their entire lives on this island.

And since when did Ogres stick together in such large groups? I'd always been under the impression that they were either lone wolves or tiny clans. But from what I could tell, there was at least a dozen of them pointing their sharp-tipped spears at us while chanting along with the leader. Saliva spat out from their mouths as they chanted, and the paint markings on their skin resembled a giant maze—red and green lines that ran in unusual directions, seemingly nowhere, and appeared connected from one Ogre to the next as their arms touched.

Their spears, weapons constructed of finely carved wood and sharp bone, seemed to dance with their words. Every time they spoke out, their spears jabbed out at the same time, threatening us.

They spoke words that weren't English, but I couldn't determine what it was. It was the strangest thing I'd ever heard, sounding like complete gibberish, but they appeared to understand each other.

"*Lupa arkama!*" the leader shouted again, her ugly, soulless eyes rolling toward me.

What the hell was she saying?

You have to know dear, how much I love you.

I inhaled a slow, deep breath as my mom's song

continued to play in my head. I eyed every Ogre in sight, wondering how they'd turned out to be this way. They stood with their backs hunched and their heads bowed forward, creating shadows beneath their already sunken eyes. Their eyebrows sat close together on their dirt-stained foreheads, above eyes that rolled from side to side like those of an animal.

And then, as the leader jabbed her spear into the air and shouted something else, I heard my mother's voice one last time.

You can't take my sunlight away.

In one quick motion, I raised my bow and fired a shot straight for the leader's face. Everything happened in slow motion—eyes widened as the arrow flew toward her, but no one moved, or at least, didn't have the time to move. The leader's head shot backward as the arrow penetrated her left eye, blood gushing out and soaking the arrow's stem. Her head faced forward one last time, almost as if she wanted to look her killer in the face, and she fell backward.

Before her body hit the leaves on the ground, I plucked three more arrows from my quiver and began firing faster than I'd ever fired before. They whistled through the air, over the heads of my women, and landed on the necks, shoulders, and chests of the Ogres.

Several of them fell to the ground, clasping at

the arrows lodged in their bodies and grunting in pain. By the time they realized what was going on, four of them lay on the jungle floor, either dead or severely injured.

"Lupa arkama!" shouted one of the Ogres standing on the far right.

Their faces suddenly warped. I understood why Northers referred to them as demons. Their mouths stretched open so much so that they no longer looked human, and their eyes seemed to double in size.

Before I had the time to reach for another arrow, they charged into the crowd with their spears pointed forward.

And then, everything happened so fast.

I managed to fire two more arrows into the throats of our enemies before the shouting began—it carried over the sound of wood clanking against wood, and colors blended together. As I stood there, my arrow drawn back, its tip swaying from side to side as I tried to find a target, I couldn't make out who was who.

Having never received combat training, I felt useless.

What was I supposed to do? Charge mindlessly?

A loud scream came blasting out of Coin's lungs beside me, and with a shiv held over her head, she made a run for it, her dark skin disappearing into the group of women.

I side-glanced Hammer and Arenas and Johnson.

We couldn't stand around while our women fought for their lives.

Plucking an arrow from my quiver, I dropped my bow. If I couldn't fire it from a distance, it would serve as a melee weapon.

I let out a shout so loud I didn't recognize myself. I was like an animal or a wild huntress raised on the island—but it felt good. In a sense, it was a release; all of my anger, my fear, and my hatred had been set free.

My voice carried over everyone as I charged straight into the crowd, prepared to jab my arrowhead into someone's throat. There was no hesitation, no thought process. I was in survival mode, and although I'd never killed in cold blood at close range before—I'd always convinced myself that shooting someone was less barbaric than stabbing them—I wasn't afraid to do it.

I wasn't afraid to take the life of someone who, moments ago, was prepared to capture us and torture us until we wished for death.

Bodies moved out of the way as I came charging full force toward what appeared to be the last Ogre standing. It was almost as if I'd been given the honor to finish this fight. Her lips curled over her disgusting, slime-covered teeth, and she stared into me looking like the soulless monster she was.

Had she slaughtered some of our people? Had she been the one to hang women upside down and slit their throats open? This Ogre was no woman—she *was* a demon. She slouched forward and stabbed her spear toward me, but I wasn't dumb. Of course she'd try that. I dodged sideways, grabbed her spear with both hands, and with my elbow, knocked her flat in the nose. There was a loud crack and she threw her head back, blood spewing over her lips and onto her neck.

And then, I did something I'd never done before... something I knew would change me.

Tightening my grip around my arrow, I stabbed the arrowhead straight into the side of her neck, up toward her jaw, and pushed as hard as I could. A growl slipped past her lips, but nothing more, and blood came squirting out onto my cheeks. I turned away but didn't let go of my arrow until we fell to the ground together.

The warmth of her blood was the first sensation I felt, followed by the pounding of my heart against her motionless body. She let out a long rotten breath that smelled like milk left in a container for a week, and her grip around my forearm loosened.

I yanked the arrow from her neck and wiped the head's stone tip in the dirt by my feet before slipping it back into my quiver.

Everyone slowly stepped back, gazes fixated on the countless bodies around me. Most were Ogres, but a few were our own. I waited for the lamenting to begin—for grief to set in once the adrenaline had died down, but not a sound other than rapid breathing escaped the lungs around me.

No one cried for the dead, which led me to believe no one knew them.

Slowly I stood and with the back of my forearm wiped a thick line of blood from my face.

"You aren't prisoners anymore," I said, shifting my gaze from one woman to another.

My breaths came hard, and I could only imagine what I looked like: a complete savage with blood on her face, a wide-legged stance, and broad shoulders bouncing with every breath.

It was clear their nerves were shot. Most, if not all of them, had no combat training. They'd reacted instinctively. Were they in shock, or frightened by me? Some trembled so much their legs shook, and their eyes were so large that they resembled owls.

I didn't miss that feeling, the shaking.

"These Ogres, these *demons*," I corrected, "would have slaughtered us like pigs."

No one said anything, though I knew they agreed with me.

"Come on." I broke the silence and wiggled a finger toward the trees overhead, where many of our women sat quietly in the large net that had captured them moments ago. Bare feet dangled, fingers clasped the rope, and dirty faces stuck out from open spaces. "Let's get these women down."

CHAPTER 2

"One more," Coin shouted.

The woman who'd climbed the tree—Jordan, I believe her name was—hung upside down from a thick branch, slicing one piece of mesh at a time. Branches snapped every time she did this, causing the net to abruptly fall a few inches, and the captured women screamed.

The closer Jordan could get them to the ground before the entire thing snapped, the better.

If I hadn't seen her climb that tree, I'd probably have mistaken her for a monkey: long, lanky limbs, short hair, and smooth skin that looked black beneath the shadow of hundreds of leaves overhead. She moved about so effortlessly it seemed like she'd done this a thousand times before.

She slipped the knife in between her teeth, and with two bony hands, tugged at the rope she'd cut. It made a small tearing noise, which caused its prisoners to release gentle gasps.

But something ripped, and the small noises escaping their mouths evolved to screaming.

"Careful!" Coin twirled around the trap from below like a shark in water.

"I'm trying," Jordan growled through teeth clenched around her knife.

Dozens of women gathered underneath, prepared to catch those in the giant net. There was a final snap, and the ball of dangling limbs came crashing toward the ground. Grunts and screeches filled the sticky air around us, but the fall didn't appear to have injured anyone.

Those who were free joined together to pull the net apart, and one by one, the captured women came out stretching and rubbing their backs, shoulders, and necks.

"Is everyone okay?" someone asked.

Several eyes shifted toward the bodies lying on the ground and then to me. At first, I was afraid everyone would accuse me of causing our women's deaths, but a soft whisper broke out from the bickering crowd. "She saved us."

"Did you see that?"

"They would've cut us into little pieces."

"She's brave."

A sense of pride washed over me. I wasn't proud for having killed so many women, but I was proud for having protected mine. I made my way toward the front of the line, where my circle met me, and I plucked my bow out of the dirt.

"Hey, chica," came Arenas's voice. "That was

some badass shit."

Although a part of me wanted to smile, the other part suddenly became conscious of the bloodstains on my hands, arms, and shirt. It felt hot and foreign against my skin.

I saved them. I saved us all.

I wasn't even sure where the bravery had come from. Maybe it was my mom. Maybe thinking about her again had made me realize that I wasn't ready to die, at least, not at the hands of Ogres. And if I did die, I wanted it to be in battle, not by being cut into pieces, limb by limb, while still alive.

"Hey, you hear that?" Coin asked.

I stopped walking. "Hear what?"

I closed my eyes and listened. My mom used to do something like this when we drove into downtown's core. If the radio was on, she'd turn it down, and I remember laughing and asking, "Does sound affect your ability to see?"

She'd chuckle and brush me off every time.

As I'd learned on Kormace Island, removing one sense always heightened another, if not all. That might explain why Coin's hearing was so strong— her sight was horrible.

I was about to say, "I don't hear it," when I opened my eyes. Her cracked lips began to stretch wide until they formed a huge, out-of-place grin on her face. It made me think of a kid who'd farted, waiting for the smell to enter their best friend's nose.

What did she have to smile about?

But then, I heard it. At first, it sounded like a distant trickle, like water dripping from a leaky faucet. Then the sounds began to blend until the trickling transformed to a staticky flow.

"Is that—" I tried.

Coin's smile didn't fade. "A river."

"The *river*?" Hammer cut in.

"What're you talkin' about?" Arenas said. "What river?"

"I think it is," Johnson said, showing more excitement than I'd ever seen from her. She extended her neck and took a few rapid steps ahead of me.

"I think it—" Hammer started, but she winced so hard that little lines formed on her face.

Something was wrong.

"Hammer?" I rushed toward her and grabbed her by the shoulder, then inspected every inch of her body for blood. "What's wrong? Were you hit?"

She shook her head and reached for the side of her face.

"What's goin' on?" came Jack's unevenly toned voice that mimicked an annoying chihuahua left in someone's backyard—a noise that did nothing but irritate.

I fought the urge to glare at her. Had she not stumbled her way toward us earlier, none of this would have happened and she wouldn't have set off that Ogre trap that nearly got us killed.

I shook these thoughts away. Had she not set off the trap, it would have been someone else.

"My toof," Hammer mumbled.

"I thought you had your tooth pulled," I said.

"I did," she growled, then sucked in a big breath.

"Open up," I said.

She gave me a one-shouldered shrug that said, No, *really*, I'm fine.

I wasn't buying it. I eyed her closely. "Open up."

She let her lungful of air out through her nose and dropped her jaw open. Arenas's and Johnson's faces came up beside me, their cheeks nearly touching mine, and we all looked inside. It didn't take a dentist to see that it was infected.

The hole where her tooth used to be was oozing with slimy yellow puss, and the gum around it was red and severely swollen.

"Fuck," Arenas blurted. She made a *that's disgusting* face and pulled away.

Hammer closed her mouth and forced a smile. "It looks worse than it is. Really. It's not that bad."

"There's puss," Johnson said, matter-of-factly. "Anything with puss on this island is a bad thing, Hammer."

Hammer didn't say anything.

"What? What?" Jack said. She popped up beside

Coin, who was surprisingly taller than her, and craned her neck from side to side as if trying to catch radio waves with her head. "What is it? An infection? A tooth infection? Oh God. Did she go to Ripper? Did she let her work on her teeth? 'Cause that woman ain't got no background in dentissing."

"Dentissing?" Johnson scoffed. "You mean dentistry?"

Jack stopped making her over-the-top hand gestures and dropped both arms at her sides. She stared at Johnson a bit longer than necessary until blurting, "Does it look like I gotta dictionary?"

Someone cleared her throat and I turned around to find Jordan—the woman who'd helped bring the net down—standing behind me. She looked even more slender up close, but it suited her even though she may have been considered unhealthily skinny by some standards. Her tiny frame made her hazelnut-colored eyes look almost cartoonish, the way anime characters often have oversized features.

"What's up?" Jack asked, but all Jordan did was give her an up-and-down look before returning her attention to me. "I'm not trying to rush you in any way, but I thought it worth pointing out that we're still on demon territory. We should probably get out of here in case there are more coming."

With a firm nod, I looked at Coin. "Take us to the river."

CHAPTER 3

The soothing sound of the water's flow and the thousands of stones decorating the river's borders made it evident we were following the same river Coin and I had found before meeting with the Hunters.

Had we passed Redwood?

While we'd thought Redwood to be the ideal spot for resting, it had turned out to be Ogre territory. And we'd been attacked on Ogre territory. It was possible we'd been close to Redwood and hadn't noticed. I'd come to learn that the jungle's thick walls of vegetation made it easy to pass by someone, or something, without realizing it.

"Ahhh, that's nice," said Jack, opening her mouth to catch some mist like a kid trying to catch snowflakes on Christmas Eve.

She scurried toward the river, dancing this way and that as stones wobbled underneath her bare feet. Her flabby arms—a result of aging skin—jiggled on either side of her body as she fought to maintain balance.

"I wouldn't do that," I shouted.

She spun as fast as a wooden spinning toy, her arms still outstretched on each side.

"Do what?"

"Go near the water, dipshit," Johnson said.

I shot Johnson a warning glare, but all she did was smirk sideways at me like being rude to Jack was fun for her. She acted as though Jack was the dumb kid in the gang, which made it okay to be condescending toward her. I wasn't Jack's biggest fan, but she didn't deserve to be bullied, either.

The last thing I wanted was for Johnson to provoke someone again and a cause a fight. She tended to get under one's skin.

With eyelids flat and mouth in a straight line, Jack stared at her. "It's fresh water. I'm thirsty. I'd be willing to bet we're all thirsty."

The women behind me muttered, but no one stepped forward. Instead, their eyes shot my way every few seconds as if wired to a metronome.

Had I done this to them? Had I caused them to fear me? Or, were they so accustomed to fearing a leader that this was all they knew? While I didn't enjoy feeling like an abuser, I appreciated that no one acted without my consent.

I wasn't trying to be controlling, either. But the truth was, as a Hunter, I'd learned a lot about the dangers of the jungle, and it was my responsibility to ensure the safety of these women. How could I protect them if they didn't listen?

I stopped searching the crowd when my eyes met those of the woman I'd tripped earlier that day. Although I didn't know her name, I remembered how confused she was when I stuck my leg out to prevent her from running to the water. She averted her gaze the moment she caught me looking and locked her fingers together. She didn't look all that old, either—probably as old as me. How had she ended up here? Had it been accidental, the way it was with me? Or was she a cold-blooded killer? Would she try to slit my throat in my sleep?

When she shifted her weight uncomfortably, her right foot squishing the dirt underneath her, I realized I was glaring at her.

"You," I said, and she looked at me again. "Can you explain to Jack why we don't go running toward water?"

She glanced around, obviously not understanding why I was singling her out. But no one spoke, so she cleared her throat. "Could be contaminated."

Before I had the time to say anything, Jack scoffed. "It's not contaminated. It's flowing water. Not like we're in the city."

She was probably right, but she wasn't getting the point. She'd decided to follow *me*, not the other way around.

"'Cause Brone didn't say you could run up ahead of her!" Arenas shouted, but she rounded her shoulders when her voice carried all the way down the river.

In an instant, Jack pulled her head low to her shoulders She likely wasn't trying to be disobedient or rebellious. Jack, as far as I knew, was being *Jack*—thoughtless and rash.

"It's the open space, too," Hammer said. Her stare fell to the river stones at her feet, and I could only imagine what she was thinking. Was she reliving that dreadful day? The day we were ambushed by Zsasz and her goons? The day I'd pushed Ellie, along with Rocket, Fisher, and Proxy into the river? The day Trim was slaughtered right in front of us?

And then, almost as if Mother Nature were in tune with our thoughts, color slowly faded from our surroundings. Overhead, hundreds of lumpy gray clouds slid across the sky and in front of the sun, darkening the trees around us.

Jack opened her mouth to say something, but thunder clapped so loudly that she hopped where she stood and rushed back to us.

"Holy mother of—" she said, but a tremendous amount of water suddenly fell from the sky, causing the river to spit in every direction imaginable. The water, which had appeared blue seconds ago, now looked like spilled oil.

"Stay in the forest!" I shouted.

The women huddled close together, some dry and some drenched, depending on where they'd been standing.

The sound became static-like, a loud hum that seemed to fuse with the jungle's preexisting orchestra of insect and mammal cries. If I weren't trying to save my friends, I'd probably have asked the women to find a comfortable, dry area for us to lay low.

But there wasn't time to rest.

Not now. Not while Zsasz and her army were making their way toward the Cove to slaughter people I loved.

Rain, shine, storm, tornado—I didn't care. We'd make it to the Cove. I quickened my pace a bit, but I slipped in the mud and caught myself before I fell.

"You okay?" Coin asked.

"I'm good." I turned my head sideways, but only enough for my voice to carry over my shoulder. "Try to stay dry. The last thing we need is someone getting sick."

Hammer cleared her throat but didn't say anything.

"What?" I asked.

She hesitated, which meant she had something to say but was making every effort possible not to embarrass me

"That's not true," she said in a soft voice.

"What's not?"

"This stuff drippin' out of my nose," Jack blurted out. "That's snot."

I let out a soft sigh and returned my focus to Hammer.

"The whole getting sick because of rain thing," she said. "It isn't true."

"Oh, well," I said, "my mom always—" But I stopped myself, feeling like I'd reverted to my ten-year-old self.

My mom...

I squeezed my eyes shut and rainwater dripped off my eyelashes. I couldn't think about that right now.

"Who cares?" came Johnson's voice. "I'm sure it isn't good for anyone. I got drenched a long time ago in the Working Grounds... You know, when Murk came out waving her hands, telling everyone to go back to the Village. Anyways, I was working on something special, and I didn't want to go back."

"Get to the point, chica!" said Arenas.

Johnson winced at her. "I didn't dry off all day and I ended up getting this nasty rash on my back. Took weeks to clear it up. So yeah, there're dangers to being wet."

Jack smirked, her head bowed forward. "Not in my book..."

Hammer glowered at her, evidently not a fan of sexual jokes. "Anyways, it's not a good thing, but rain itself doesn't make you sick—"

"Made me sick when I was a kid," Coin cut in. "Got bronchitis and shit."

"It wasn't the rain that did that," Hammer said.

"All right," I said, waving two hands in front of me like giant scissor blades. "Just stop."

I felt a bit stupid for having passed along information I'd learned from my mom. It made me seem like I wasn't fit to be a leader, like I had no place guiding so many women when I believed something as trivial as rain gave people colds.

What else was I wrong about? It wasn't like I had the internet to confirm my beliefs.

We continued our walk as I pondered whether I was too young to be in charge.

It's only rain, I told myself.

It was impossible for one person to have every answer out there. In truth, I was the reason these women had escaped the Northers' grasp in the first place and the reason they were still alive despite having been found by Ogres.

That had to count for something.

Had Ellie been by my side, she would have wrapped her warm arms around my shoulders and told me everything was going to be fine.

"Ellie."

I hadn't realized I'd breathed her name aloud until Coin shot me a side glance and said, "What?"

I shook my head and she let it go—probably

because something else immediately caught her attention.

"Yo, Brone, check it out!" She rushed toward a thin-trunked tree and brushed her fingers along the bark's grooves.

I didn't bother asking her what she was trying to show me. I already knew—it was one of the markings she'd left behind when she and I had traveled this same path.

Instead of wasting my energy on speech, I offered a weak smile.

"What's that?" Hammer asked, but before either one of us had the time to answer, Tegan's matted head popped in front of us all. She forced her way through fallen leaves and pressed her cheek against the bark.

What the hell was she doing?

Her long, bony fingers slid along the tree's trunk and she looked back at us, eyes so large she resembled a pug.

"What?" Johnson said, though it came out as more of a sneer. She was still as impatient as always especially when it came to eccentricity or intelligence. It was almost as if she thought herself better than others, but it wasn't hard to figure out that her anger was probably the result of low esteem and insecurity.

"La-la-lapacho," Tegan said. She tilted her head back with a childish grin on her face, and my gaze followed hers.

High above, hidden among the thick green leaves surrounding the tree, were leaves so bright and pink that for a moment, everything around me disappeared. The contrast made me think of a ball of cotton candy surrounded by dirt. It was the most beautiful thing I'd ever seen before. How had Coin and I not seen its colors? Had we been so preoccupied that our surroundings had become one giant blur of green?

At the trunk's base, tree roots hid neatly beneath the earth, and around it, hundreds of vividly pink leaves lay still, droplets of rainwater making them look even shinier than they were. Had I walked right over these, thinking they were flowers? I'd grown so accustomed to seeing colorful flowers around trees that I never took the time to observe anything anymore.

"What... is... that?" Jack asked. She was so mesmerized that she sounded high.

"She just told you!" said Arenas. "Lapucho!"

"Lapacho," Hammer cut in.

"Never heard of it." Jack continued staring up into the leaves. Her bottom jaw hung loose, making her neck disappear entirely, and her rotten teeth looked like pieces of old toffee.

"Me neither," someone said.

"Me neither."

"What's that?"

"Did you see that?"

"Move, let me see."

"L-l-apach-ch-cho," Tegan repeated. With her nails, she began pulling at pieces of bark and slipping them into what appeared to be a bag or a saddle made of suede. Then, she dropped onto her hands and knees and started scavenging through the dirt, throwing mushrooms and branches out of her way as she searched for what I assumed were healthy fallen leaves.

"Ah," she groaned, and she wrapped her fingers around a handful of bright leaves. She slipped them into her bag and continued searching.

Arenas tilted her body toward me and crossed her arms over her stomach. "What's she doin'?"

I shrugged. "Supplies, I'm guessing."

"Chica, what you doin'?" Arenas shouted.

Tegan didn't look back. Her arms kept swinging around in every direction as she searched for her previous leaves. "H-heal," she said.

"Heal what?" Jack asked. She'd stopped staring at the overhead leaves, and now, she stood with both hands on her waist as if surveilling Tegan were some important job she'd been assigned.

"T-tumors," Tegan said, never once looking back. "Every... Everything." She shoved another handful of colorful leaves into her bag. "Cancer."

Perhaps if I'd had ten eyes around my head, they'd have met everyone else's at the same time. I sensed their attention on me, but my gaze landed on Coin, who looked as dumbfounded as I probably did.

"Franklin," she whispered.

CHAPTER 4

"I'm not trying to be a downer," Hammer said, "but what you're thinking is completely insane and would never work."

"You heard Tegan babblin' under that tree," Coin said. "That shit treats cancer."

"She has pancreatic cancer," Johnson said. "I'm sorry, but leaves aren't going to cure that."

"Why you guys arguin' about curing?" Arenas said. "Man, the girl's with Zsasz now. Not like you'd be able to help her anyway. She ain't on our side anymore."

"Arenas is right," Hammer said.

Coin scoffed and flicked her wrist in the air. "You women ain't got no faith."

Though I admired Coin's positive attitude, I was beginning to side with everyone else. It was delusional to think that some leaves and tree bark could eliminate a disease so far progressed, wasn't it?

"All's I'm sayin' is—" Coin started, but she stopped talking and turned her head toward the river. "You hear that?"

"Hear what?" Arenas's big eyes shot from side to side. "Fuckin' spit it out! What is it?"

Coin sucked on her golden tooth and assessed Arenas up and down. "Calm your ass down. It's the waterfall."

"The waterfall?" Arenas asked.

"We're getting closer," I said. "Come on."

Coin looked at me, and I knew what she was thinking: *Yeah, the waterfall, where Brone kicked that Norther's ass (literally) and sent her flying to her death.*

But she must have known I didn't want it brought up because she kept her lips sealed tight.

We continued along the riverbed, careful not to step out into the rain.

At the same time, Tegan kept digging through her leaves, counting them with a whisper. It was like watching a kid count their candy on Halloween night. Every time she dug deeper inside her pouch, several pink leaves flew out and twirled around her ankles. Then, she'd stop walking and crouch down, nearly tripping the person walking behind her every time.

"Would you stop doing that?" Johnson said.

Tegan didn't look up. Instead, she picked up one of the fallen leaves with both hands and brushed its ridges along her bottom lip, before delicately placing it back into her pouch.

Johnson arched an eyebrow and leaned into

242

the rest of us. "What's she doing?"

"Being Tegan," Hammer said.

I turned my attention to Hammer, wondering if she'd known Tegan during our time in the Village. After all, she'd owned a shop near hers. They could have once been friends.

I hadn't known Tegan long enough to determine whether her unusual behavior was the result of the abuse she'd endured or her eccentricity. All I cared about was that she was still in there—that she was still capable of mixing plants and herbs to cure diseases or fight infection.

"What do those do?" Arenas asked. It came out as if she were speaking to a child—soft and curious—which was surprising coming out of her mouth. "Can they fight cancer?"

Maybe Arenas had left a child, or several, in the real world.

Tegan lit up and nodded excitedly. "Lapacho. P-p-powerful enough to k-kill fetuses in pregnant r-r-rats."

"Jesus," Arenas said, her motherly tone instantly gone. "Why the fuck would you wanna do that?"

Tegan shrugged. "I don't. Studies."

"Girl, how do you know all of this?" Coin asked. "You some kind of pharmacist?"

Tegan shook her head, her matted hair resembling an oversized hat. "W-worked at the B-

Blue Crystal. A gift shop." She then smirked, almost mischievously, and added, "It was a P-pagan shop, but with the n-n-new laws..."

"No religion anywhere," Hammer cut in. "Yeah, I remember."

"What'd you care?" Coin said.

Hammer glowered at her but didn't say anything. No doubt she had her own reasons for being affected by the abolishment of religion that took effect January 17, 2059. I remember the date because it was all over TV.

* * *

"Lydia, would you turn that off?" came my mom's voice.

"Don't you want to know what's going on?" I asked, phone glued to my nose. Contradictory headlines appeared all over its built-in search engine:

Goodbye God, Hello Hell

Praying Won't Save You Now

Finally, We've Adapted

Toss your Bible or Pay the Price

I couldn't believe it had happened—they'd successfully illegalized public practice of religion. Why? Because of all the wars and hatred it was causing. The government, which had managed to piss off millions of people, thought it fair to shove its nose into people's beliefs.

While I agreed that religion was responsible for

a lot of problems in this world, I didn't understand how anyone had the right to tell you what to, or what not to, believe.

"There are protests everywhere, Mom. You think this will last?"

My mom sighed and flopped herself down on the couch. She rubbed at her aching legs and leaned her head back. "I don't know, Lydia. I'm sure they'll realize it isn't doing any good, and they'll reverse everything."

I ran my finger along the latest headline: "Dozens of Churches Burned to the Ground."

"Holy shit," I said.

"Language," my mom said.

"I'm thirteen, Mom, not eight."

My mom didn't look at me. Instead, she winced and stretched her neck. "You're under my roof. Now get ready for school. Your bus'll be here in half an hour."

* * *

"You think they reversed the law by now?" Coin asked.

I shook my head. "Doubt it. It was still around when I was sentenced, which was in 2064.

"What law?" came Jack's voice.

I didn't understand how she always managed to butt her nose into everything. She reminded me of this guy we had in high school—Peter Puttmore. No one liked him all that much, yet he thought he was loved by everyone. Each time he joined a group of people, he shoved his hands in his pockets and sported a grin. And, although they went quiet every time, he'd stand there, simply smiling.

That's who Jack was to me—Peter Puttmore.

"The abolishment of religion," Hammer told her.

Jack let out a laugh so loud I instinctively smacked her on the shoulder. I hadn't meant to, but she didn't seem offended by it.

Instead, she laughed nervously. "Sorry, Brone. Won't happen again." She gave Hammer a disbelieving look. "This some kind of joke?"

"How long have you been here?" Hammer asked. "On this island, I mean."

Jack glanced up at the sky and breathed out numbers as she counted them on her fingers. It almost looked like she'd recently been taught to count.

"Ya know... I don't know," she said at last. "Ten, fifteen, twenty years. I lost count a long time ago."

I clenched my teeth and closed a tight fist. I still couldn't get over the fact that the government had been hiding this place for so long. I remembered reading holographic advertisements all over the underground subway stations—they were actually called LR stations, short for lightning rail stations, but Mom always referred to them as *subway* stations. I supposed it was from her time. The trains hovered on the tracks, something Mom never understood nor wanted to try, and traveled at speeds of 200 miles per hour—something Mom was especially freaked out about. The advertisements always flickered on with dramatic music and talked about how the government was in the process of selecting the islands. I supposed it was an attempt to reduce crime rates, though it didn't seem to make much of a difference.

How were they getting away with this? Was Ellie right? Was there a chance the general public would find out about the government's corruption and come to our aid? Or was the public happy to have criminals off their land?

"Well," Johnson said, "they got rid of it."

Jack scoffed. "Ain't nobody going to tell me who I can or can't pray to."

"Amen, sister!" came someone's voice.

Then, someone laughed, and Jordan stepped out from the crowd and to the front of the line. She gawked at Jack, flared her nostrils, and cocked one eyebrow high up on her forehead. "You didn't know?"

"Weren't you listening?" Jack asked. "Been here too damn long. How am I supposed to keep up with American politics? And frankly, why would I give a shit? They don't apply to us."

She puffed her chest out and tightened her dry lips so much they almost disappeared from her face. I'd never seen Jack get angry before, fortunately, because that ugly look on her face made her look like a goblin.

"You think I wanted to be sent here? Away from goddamn civilization? You think I fuckin' asked for this?" she continued.

Her face was beet red now, and she took a step toward Jordan, her eyes nearly triple the size they were two seconds ago. Squiggly blue veins appeared on her temples, and she breathed out so hard that a cracking noise—the sound of dried snot being pushed out—released from her nostrils.

Her shoulders bounced, and it looked like any moment, she'd lunge straight at Jordan.

"I'll cut you like a fuckin' pig, little girl," she said. "Just like I did my husband!"

"Whoa," Coin said. "Easy."

Everyone stared in silence as Jack's eyes remained glued to Jordan. It was as if she'd been possessed. What was going on? Who was this woman? I didn't recognize her, not that I'd known her well to begin with. But on the outside, she looked like someone other than Jack. Jordan didn't say anything. Instead, she stood tall, never once backing down, and stared back at Jack with a relaxed smirk on her face.

I wasn't sure who was more frightening—Jack, the Hulk-looking one, or Jordan, the young, arrogant girl with nothing to lose.

"Enough!" I snapped, tightening my grip around my bow.

Within a split second, the veins on Jack's forehead disappeared and her face lightened in color. She looked over at me with that same rotten smile. Then, without looking back at Jordan, she let out a loud laugh—a cackle, almost—and said, "I oughta stop bottlin' up all that rage."

She walked past me with a hop in her step as if nothing had happened.

I arched an eyebrow at Jordan, who gave me a lazy shrug as if to say, *I have no idea what just happened, but it's cool.*

How had she stayed so calm?

Jack walked ahead of us, shoulders drawn back, a soft whistle escaping her mouth. The short hairs on her head barely moved as she stepped over a huge, moss-covered tree root, and she kept going.

"The fuck is she doing?" Johnson said.

I sighed.

Now I understood what Fisher had meant about not wanting to be a leader—about not wanting to babysit anyone.

"Jack," I shouted, and she turned around so fast she looked like a cartoon on fast-forward.

She stared at me stupidly as though not understanding why I was calling out her name. I jerked my head sideways to say, *Get back in line.*

"Oh, right," she said and came back running

with her knees bouncing up high as if charging through an obstacle course.

I didn't bother asking if she was okay after her outburst—it was apparent she suffered from either rage or mental problems. Asking her to talk about her mental state wasn't going to fix anything.

Murk and Trim came to mind, and a lump swelled in my throat. I remembered learning that people with severe mental illnesses weren't accepted inside the Village. Though I thought it cruel and absurd at the time, I now understood it from a safety standpoint.

It wasn't about discriminating against those with mental illness—it was about trying to protect everyone else. But what if there was a way to help? What if, rather than banishing, we were able to find coping mechanisms or herbal remedies to alleviate certain symptoms?

What was I supposed to do? Banish Jack for snapping? For being unstable? She was still a human being, and I couldn't let her rot in the jungle or be torn alive by predators simply because her state of mind was fragile. For all we knew, the island had made her this way.

It would have been like reverting to ancient times when people with mental illnesses were diagnosed as *insane*, kept in an asylum, and tortured day in and day out. I'd learned about that in class and found it barbaric.

I glanced sideways at her, observing her goofy smile. Had she meant what she'd said about cutting her husband to pieces? If this was true, then she also posed a risk to every other woman here, and banishment was our one option.

I ground my teeth and kept walking.

How was anyone supposed to make a decision like this? How was anyone supposed to play God?

A firm hand suddenly grabbed me by the shoulder. I swung around with a tight fist held by my face, prepared to knock out my attacker's teeth, assumedly Jack's, but it was Coin's big eyes that greeted me, and she slapped a finger over her lips.

She then pointed up ahead and tapped her ear.

I dropped into a crouched position, and everyone behind me did the same.

CHAPTER 5

I squinted and pressed my face against the coarse bark of the tree beside me. I couldn't see what it was, but I could hear it. Soft footsteps crackled through the jungle's wet vegetation.

It didn't sound like human footsteps, though.

And now that the rain had stopped, I could hear every movement—every step. They weren't heavy but rather short and soft and familiar to my ears.

A wild boar?

I inched a bit closer, trying to catch a glimpse of it when I finally saw it. It was light brown, though it looked much darker with its wet fur, and its eyes looked like small black buttons sewn on its face.

I'd seen boars much bigger than this before. Either it was young or a female. It was slender, and its shoulders looked weak in comparison to some of the monster boars I'd seen before. The tusk, no longer than adolescent thumbs, sat at the bottom of its jaw and became only visible from certain angles.

I drew an arrow from my quiver, my focus

never leaving the animal. Though I didn't want to drag a dead carcass along with us, there was no telling when we'd find another one.

"You got this," Jack whispered, rubbing her hands together so fast it looked like she was trying to start a fire.

I gave her a look, one that said, *Not another word*, and it was enough for her to retreat. She gave me an apologetic nod and sealed her lips with an invisible zipper.

I glanced back at the others, who stared at me expectantly, and placed a finger over my lips. Everyone nodded, and to my surprise, despite there being many of us, not a single sound escaped into the air.

Everyone was so still they looked like wax manikins—the kind you'd find in a horror movie.

Slowly, I made my way toward the animal, matching its movements to mask my sounds.

I raised my bow, pressed my face against my shoulder, and stared at the creature over the tip of my arrowhead. Its jaw moved up and down, chewing on something, entirely oblivious that it was about to die.

A soft snap resonated the moment I released my arrow, and the boar let out a loud squeal. It ran in circles, leaves kicking through the air, before taking off in the opposite direction.

"Damn it," I muttered.

I pulled my knife from my belt—another one of Hammer's constructions—and charged straight into the bushes, slapping away leaves, branches, and vines as I plowed through. Damp vegetation rustled behind me as my women followed, and for a moment, it sounded like a wave was crashing through the jungle—a loud staticky hum that moved with impressive force.

A hind leg kicked into the air and disappeared behind a bright, orange-and-yellow-flowered bush. Where had I hit it? Why wasn't it dead yet? Perhaps I'd only caused injury.

I stepped around the bush, but before even spotting the animal, it let out another loud squeal, followed by a disturbing silence.

What had happened?

But I didn't have the time to react because right in front of me stood a masked woman. Her mouth shot wide open as a horrendous scream blasted out of her lungs.

CHAPTER 6

Her hair resembled a setting sun—bright orange and rich in color. Her eyes, two light green circles above what appeared to be a tiger mask, shot from me to my women. In her right hand hung a bloody, bone-constructed knife, the weapon she'd obviously used to kill the wild boar.

She looked petite, but it was hard to tell how small she was because she wore a mass of seaweed and dried plants over her shoulders. It had made her nearly impossible to see—a giant mess of greenery that fused effortlessly with the jungle around us.

She stabbed her knife into the air and let out another broken scream.

One arrow, I thought.

That's all it would take to shut her up. Otherwise, she was going to attract predators our way. What if Zsasz was nearby? She'd hear us a mile away.

"Shhh," I said softly. "We're not here to hurt anyone."

She hesitated, her eyes searching me. What

was she trying to find?

Then, without warning, she let out another scream.

I whipped an arrow from my quiver and pulled it against the elastic of my bow.

The intention had been to shut her up, but it had done far more than that. She lowered her head, glowering at me. Quite possibly, she was preparing to charge. What kind of an idiot charged straight at an archer?

When she lunged forward, I pulled back on the arrow, prepared to defend myself. But then, a loud, birdlike cry resonated around us, and the woman stopped in her tracks. She searched the sky, then looked behind her, and started walking backward toward wherever the cry had come from.

And that's when I saw them—eyes.

Several of them, too. They sat in the darkness of the trees, watching us.

Were they with this woman? If so, why hadn't they come out to fight? Because we outnumbered them? I scanned their faces, though it was nearly impossible to see any kind of detail.

That was... until I saw a set of emerald green eyes.

There was something familiar about them— something homey. I couldn't see the woman's face, only her eyes, but that was enough to pique my curiosity.

I watched the seaweed-entangled woman run back toward the trees, her rat's nest hair bouncing as she moved.

That hair, I thought. It looked familiar, too.

I took a step forward and squinted. Something was going on. I could feel it. The redhead punched a closed fist in the air, communicating something to the others, but it wasn't her gesture I was preoccupied with; I couldn't stop staring at her bony little arm.

Was she even a *woman*?

Then, without thinking, I shouted, "Elektra!" and the woman turned around. She slid her mask off and looked back with a hand over her eyebrows to block the late afternoon sun. At first, her face resembled that of a teenager being asked to do some chores—contorted to the point of being unrecognizable.

But then, something must have clicked, and when it did, her features softened and I saw her.

"Elektra!" I shouted.

Instead of shouting my name, she turned sideways and searched the forest. Clearly, she wasn't the one in charge. Then, out of the darkness came several bodies covered in sheets of green leaves. Their faces were painted like that of soldiers—black and green—and two of them held bows, while the others held on to hunting spears.

The shortest of the bunch bolted out ahead of

everyone.

I knew those eyes. They were the ones I'd seen earlier; they were the ones I'd recognized. I knew who she was before she pulled off her headpiece— a hat made of intertwined twigs, seaweed, and big leaves.

"Brone!" Rocket shouted.

Without thinking, I dropped my bow and ran straight for her. I didn't even have the time to open my arms in preparation of the embrace because she lunged straight at me. My head rocked forward, and together, we were propelled into the air.

I landed flat on my back and let out a grunt when something sharp jabbed me in the shoulder. Rocket, on the one hand, didn't seem all that concerned with the fall. She'd landed flat on top of me as if having intentionally used me as a landing pillow.

"Brone!" she said again, this time, her face inches from mine.

She smiled from ear to ear, and I couldn't help but observe every feature on her face—her cute button nose, her bright eyes that almost looked like green highlighter in contrast to the forest green and black paint on her face, and finally, the unsightly scar she'd had since the first day I'd met her. It was crooked, squiggly almost, and ran down from her left eyebrow and to her cheek. Her hair, too, still looked the same—caramel-brown dreadlocks pulled away from her face. She'd always worn them in a tight knot at the base of her skull, but now, they were pulled back into a thick ponytail. It looked great on her.

Then, that beautiful smile of hers disappeared, and she gave me a solemn look—one that made me want to vomit. Out of nowhere, our reunion went from magical to unpleasant. What news did she have? Had someone else died? Was it Ellie? Oh God.

I sat upright.

"What?" I blurted.

"How'd you get out of there, Brone? How'd you survive?"

Was that all it was? Was it sinking in for her that I'd spent months captured by the Northers? Why wouldn't we have ignored my disturbing reality? I didn't want to be reminded of it. I looked away. Thinking about my time, however long it was, being abused by the Northers and treated like a slave in the Middle Ages brought out such despair that if I focused on it for too long, it would evolve into an unconquerable depression.

I couldn't dwell on the past.

Suddenly, a sharp pain radiated from my healing hand, up my arm, and into my spine and I was immediately pulled into a nightmare of a daze. In front of me, Beasts stood side by side, their figures hunched, and the bottom halves of their faces covered with dirty skull masks. Their soulless eyes hovered over their masks' lines, staring into me with such ferocity that the one thing I could think about was the afterlife.

Then, Zsasz's face emerged from the row of monsters, and she grinned demonically from ear to ear like a sociopath relishing in its victim's screams.

She looked at me, then pointed a pink-scarred hand in my direction. It was a hand gesture that said, *I'm coming for you.*

No, this wasn't happening.

We weren't on their territory anymore.

We made it out.

We made it out.

"Brone?"

I looked up at Rocket, and although I should have felt peace, all I felt was panic.

"Where's Biggie?" I blurted, my gaze shifting toward the women around her. They'd slid off their camouflage helmets same as Rocket had, but I didn't recognize any of them. "And Flander? And Fisher? Rocket, where are they? Where's Ellie? Is she okay?"

She looked at my women, then back at me, the way a concerned parent does to another when what they want to say is, "Do you honestly want to blow up like this in front of the kids?" I had to maintain my levelheadedness and couldn't afford to lose my cool.

Clearing my throat, I grabbed Rocket by the arm, hoping to pull her aside for a moment. But the second I touched her, hunting spearheads came so close to my face, they created a small gust of wind through my hair.

Behind me, my women withdrew their weapons and started shouting.

We outnumbered Rocket's women tenfold, but that didn't matter. If Rocket was leading them, they weren't our enemy—we were all on the same side.

"Whoa, whoa," Rocket said. "Stand down. Brone here's a good friend."

Her women lowered their spears, and when I raised a hand behind me, mine did the same. The two crowds stared hatefully at each other as we walked away and slipped underneath a low-hanging tree. Its sharp-edged leaves formed a thick canopy overhead, masking everyone from sight.

"What's going on?" I hissed.

"Brone, relax," Rocket said.

I'd forgotten how short she was. She craned her neck back to look up at me, and I wasn't a giant by any means.

"Everyone's fine," she continued, and I took in a choppy breath. "But things have changed, Brone."

"What do you mean, *changed*?"

"We're surviving at the Cove, but barely. Ever since Murk's been gone, shit's hit the fan."

"What do you mean?" I asked. "Are people fighting?"

She glanced at the leaves over our heads, almost as if trying to see through them to monitor our women.

"They're fine," I said, waving a hand.

She frowned at me. "It's not my girls I'm worried about. Who are these women, Brone? I don't recognize any of them. And to be honest, they look a little rough around the—"

"They're survivors," I said. "Look, you have no idea what happened to us, okay? The Northers... It isn't what you think. They're enslaving people."

The muscles in her face relaxed, and she stared into me—not at me, but into me as if the insides of my eyes were television screens capable of replaying every moment of what had happened to me.

I turned away. "Look, we can talk about this later. How's Ellie doing?"

"She's fine," Rocket said. "But like I said, shit's changed."

What was she trying to say? I paced from side to side and let out a sharp breath. "You're gonna have to be more specific than that, Rocket. What's *changed*? It can't be any fuckin' worse than what I... What we... went through with those monsters." I pointed toward the North.

When she pulled her face back and looked me up and down, I realized how angry I sounded. "Looks like you've changed, too."

"Where were you?" I snapped. "Someone gave us a message. They told us you guys were coming to get us out. But you didn't. You never showed, and we had to do it alone."

"We tried," Rocket said, but she cast shameful eyes toward the ground. "I managed to gather over a dozen women willing to stand up to the Northers. The moment we left the Cove, though, a band of Northers attacked us." She pointed at a scab on her shoulder. It looked like it had once been deep—a puncture wound. "Lucky I even got out. The others weren't so fortunate. It doesn't take a genius to figure out what happened after that, Brone. No one wanted to risk their lives by leaving the Cove again."

I suddenly remembered Zsasz bragging about the little brunette she'd killed—the one I'd initially thought to be Rocket. I wondered if it had been one of Rocket's women. It must have been.

In any other circumstance, I'd have nodded and told Rocket I completely understood—that it wasn't up to women who didn't even know us to sacrifice their lives to save ours.

But all I could think about was the torture I'd endured, and even though it wasn't Rocket's fault, at that moment, I hated her for having given me false hope.

"They starved us, Rocket," I hissed. "Beat us. Every day, they'd beat on someone. Forced us to fight to the death. You have no fucking idea—" My eyes watered.

"Oh my God, Brone." She reached a gentle hand toward my shoulder, but I slapped it away.

If I allowed anyone to comfort me, especially by Rocket, I might collapse for hours, days, or weeks. I had to remain strong... to be the leader my women needed even though it seemed like I was decaying inside.

"Can we get to the Cove?" I said.

She nodded without a word, but she didn't have to speak for me to see myself through her eyes—it was as if she didn't recognize me anymore.

CHAPTER 7

"This is Tay, and that's Ginger." Rocket pointed toward her women. "That right there's Alice—"

"Are you fuckin' kidding me?" came Johnson's obnoxious voice. She let out an exaggerated scoff. "Alice Number Three."

Rocket cocked an eyebrow, but I shook my head to say, *Ignore her.*

"That's Mackenzie," she continued, "and this right here's Kira."

Stop talking, I wished I could tell her, but I didn't. Beyond my anger and resentment, I loved Rocket and was ecstatic to see her again. For some reason, though, it was difficult to express it. So much anger remained inside me that I was unsure what to do with myself, and on a rational level, I knew it wasn't her fault.

I gave a brief nod to each woman as she introduced them but didn't pay much attention to them. What were the chances I'd remember their names anyway?

"You know Elektra," she added.

Elektra grinned up at me, her freckled face

slightly more mature than it had been the last time I'd seen her. She'd grown at least a few inches, which brought her up to Rocket's height. I wondered why the Hunters had brought her along. Was she no longer having her outbursts?

"Listen, Rocket," I said, and it suddenly seemed like I was standing on a stage, preparing to perform a solo act. Everyone around me went quiet, fixated on my every movement. Rocket's followers were no doubt waiting to see if I'd disrespect her in any way—if I'd say something warranting an attack or an offensive comment—while mine waited for us to make a decision. "Can we save the introductions for the Cove?"

She seemed taken aback, and I couldn't tell if she was offended or concerned.

"What's going on, Brone?"

I glanced sideways at my people—at Coin, Hammer, Johnson, Arenas, and it was apparent by the way they stood with their arms crossed over their chests that they were prepared to defend anything I said.

"The Cove's in danger and we need to get back."

Her eyes popped out at me, her back as stiff as a piece of plywood. Then, her followers became uneasy, repositioning their stances and shifting their weapons.

Rocket bowed her head toward me, eyebrows so low on her face that her eyes looked brown.

"What're you talking about?"

"It's a long story," I said, and a warm hand grasped me around the back of my neck—it was a gentle touch, something I wasn't used to.

"They got Franklin," Coin said, appearing beside me.

Rocket pulled back, looking even more confused than before. "Who's Franklin?"

"Tall girl, tattoos," Johnson cut in. She gestured a measuring hand over her head. "She was with us when Trim"—she cleared her throat—"when the Northers got us."

"You mean when Brone saved us," Rocket said, and a hiss-like whisper broke out among her women.

"That's her?"

"That's the one who saved them?"

For the first time since I'd met them, they weren't glaring at me with animosity. Instead, they almost looked starstruck. It was as if in my absence, Rocket had fabricated fantasy-like tales about me, and everyone knew my name.

"Yeah!" Rocket raised her voice, silencing her women. "She's the one. So if she says the Cove's in danger, we need to move now."

I turned toward the circle of women that had gathered behind us. "Can you guys drag the boar? That's our supper."

Someone within the crowd scoffed. "If we're

even alive long enough to eat supper."

I took a step forward, fists clenched, but Rocket's hand landed across my chest. "What are we walking into here, exactly?"

I let out a long breath through my nostrils. "Franklin knows about the Cove. She doesn't know where it is, but she knows about it, which makes her dangerous. They turned her—"

"Turned her?" Rocket sneered. "How fucking easy was it? How do you take a side like that? They're murderers!"

Jack, who'd been quiet up until now, let out a smug laugh. "Girl, we're all murderers."

Rocket's hateful gaze turned to Jack, but she didn't say anything.

"Rocket, you don't understand," Hammer said. "They were beating on her every day. I have no doubt they were using brainwashing techniques of some sort."

"You should have seen her," I said. "It wasn't *her*." I squinted to emphasize the word *her*, and Rocket seemed to understand.

"So, what?" Rocket said. "She's bringing the Northers to the Cove? Trying to find it so they can slaughter us? Those women aren't prepared to fight, Brone. I told you things have changed. There's no order."

"No order?" Johnson asked.

Rocket ignored her and kept talking. "How

many of them are there? What kinds of weapons do they have?"

"Kinds that'll cut you to pieces," Jack said, head bowed and a grin on her face. She looked demonic enough to make me uncomfortable. Had she been medicated in the real world?

"The fuck's that supposed to mean?" said one of Rocket's women. She was the tallest of the bunch and easily the most muscular. It was like she'd been waiting for any excuse to punch someone in the nose.

"It means they have metal," Johnson said apathetically, and then an explosion of voices broke out.

"What?"

"How the fuck's that even possible?"

"Rocket, we need to do something."

"Metal?" Rocket asked, and everyone went quiet.

I nodded. "Like I said, it's a long story. We need to move."

"You didn't answer me." The muscles in her face hardened. "Is she bringing an army of Northers with her?"

"Worse," Coin said.

Rocket arched an eyebrow as if to say, *What could possibly be worse than an army of barbaric, self-serving monsters?*

Coin sucked on her gold tooth. "She's bringing

Zsasz."

CHAPTER 8

"Who's Zsasz?" Rocket asked.

A mixture of confusion and disgust clouded her face. It was almost as if the sound of Zsasz's name alone was enough to make her queasy.

"A crazy bitch," Coin said. "That's who."

The women behind me went even quieter than before. It was like Zsasz's name had triggered something. And who could blame them? Her name always made me sick to my stomach. Every time I thought of her—every time I pictured her scaly zebra-striped lips and pink-scarred body—all I wanted to do was crawl out of my skin. I'd never felt that way about anyone, but Zsasz, although I'd never admit it, scared me.

She was also twice my size and easily mistakable for a man from a distance. Not only did she have incredible strength, but she was also a complete psychopath.

"She's a killer." I didn't know how else to describe her. And before Jack could open her big mouth again and point out that we were all killers, I added, "She keeps track of how many people she's killed, and it's easily over a hundred."

Rocket grimaced.

"She's also huge," Jack said, swinging her arms out over her head. "Could crush ya like a bug."

Rocket didn't seem all that impressed with Jack. She tended to lack patience when it came to immaturity, and that *was* how Jack presented herself—like a big kid in a woman's body. It was as if she'd never grown up. Either that, or she was downright crazy.

"Back off, puta!"

"Let go!"

I swung around like a mother dragging her kids along on a shopping trip—tired and testy.

Two middle-aged women, either Mexican or Latina, held onto each other's wrists, pulling back and forth as if playing a game of tug-o-war. It was like watching a wildlife documentary—the ones with commentary that often repeated the same thing: "*In their natural habitat...*"

Because that was precisely what they looked like—animals.

"Hey!" I shouted.

They stopped at the same time but didn't let go of each other's hair.

"We're on the verge of standing up to the people who imprisoned you, and you're fighting like a bunch of high school kids." I slapped a hand against my thigh. "For fuck's sake, you're both old enough to be my moms, and you're acting younger than me."

I sensed Rocket staring at me. No doubt she was trying to determine where the old Brone had disappeared to, and she had every reason. Who had I become? Not the same Brone I was a few months ago and sure as hell not the same person I was when I first landed on Kormace Island.

I'd become hard—cold, even.

At times, I didn't recognize myself, and when words came pouring out of my mouth, it was like I was a third-party observer rather than the one in control. The filter I'd once possessed—the brain functionality that held back certain words for fear of offending or upsetting someone—was gone.

The two women I'd scolded slowly let go of each other's hair, their hateful, low-browed gazes remaining in place. They looked like preschoolers forced to share one cookie. It was embarrassing.

These were the women who were going to fight back against Zsasz? They couldn't keep their hands off each other.

Rocket continued walking, feet kicking through the jungle's fallen vegetation.

"Who are these women?" she asked, leaning in close to my ear.

I rolled my eyes, but the words that came out next made me realize I needed to be more understanding. "They were prisoners, too. Slaves, really."

"Oh shit," Rocket said.

"I think it'll take awhile for them to realize that there doesn't always have to be a fight," I said. "It's like they're programmed to hate, and that's probably from being abused day in, day out. They're bitter."

Rocket scoffed at me, and if looks could harm, I'd have melted the skin right off her face.

"Like you?" she said.

"I'm not bitter," I growled.

She gave me a sarcastic smile, the kind that said, *Okay, whatever you say.*

"It obviously fucked you up." She stepped over a rotten coconut.

"Yeah, well, I have no excuse," I said. "Some of these women have been there for years."

"So?" Rocket said.

I stared at her. Was she seriously trying to undermine their suffering?

"Their pain has nothing to do with yours, Brone. That's like breaking an arm, then turning around and telling me your neighbor's kid broke an arm *and* a leg, so now you have nothing to complain about. Your arm's still gonna hurt."

Rocket was right, but I didn't know how to respond, so I kept walking.

"Hey." She turned to me. "Thanks."

"For what?"

She playfully punched me in the shoulder. "For throwing me into that goddamn river." She pointed out through the jungle's trees, where the river's flow filled the air with tranquility. The rain had stopped, and the sun reflected on top of the water. "You could have jumped in, Brone, but you didn't. You threw us in and sacrificed yourself. These women are lucky to have you."

CHAPTER 9

The waterfall's powerful chute filled the air with a loud hum, almost as if in song. The moisture around us thickened, and it smelled like wet earth and fish—so much so that I became hungry.

I glanced back at my women. Two of them dragged the dead boar's body with sliced vines wrapped around its ankles. I'd never much liked looking at any dead animal, let alone one that was going to end up in my stomach, but as I stared at its wiry hairs, its open mouth, and its glazed eyes, I became even hungrier.

Had there not been urgency in reaching the Cove, I'd have probably cut the creature open myself and staked it over a fire.

I glanced down at my fingers and the few freckles on my knuckles, then at my sun-kissed forearm, my elbow, my feet—everything looked the same, so why did I feel different?

It was as if I'd evolved into a woman capable of surviving this island, which was all I could have done. Had I not changed, I wouldn't have survived.

But would Ellie be happy to see me, or would she sense the change and lose the feelings she'd once had for me?

I shook these thoughts away when I remembered something—Trim.

I reached for Rocket's hand, and though she didn't stop walking, she glanced back at me.

"Rocket, I have to tell you something."

Remarkably, she didn't seem all that surprised by my words. It was as if she'd been waiting for me to speak them. She wasn't taken aback or fearful of what I might say next.

"Is this about Trim?"

I stared at her. How did she know about Trim? I'd pushed her into the river before any of that happened.

"You don't have to tell me, Brone. I already know."

She looked defeated, heartbroken, even. But it was apparent she'd already prepared herself for news like this. It was as if she hadn't expected to see any of us again and had already mourned us. Now, she was simply grateful for the ones who remained.

"How do you know?" I asked.

She offered a weak shrug. "I know Trim. She wouldn't have stayed behind. She's too..." But she stopped herself and cleared her tight throat. "She was too hardheaded for that."

She turned away, her eyes watery and her head bowed forward. It looked like she was fighting every urge to cry—as if showing emotion in front of her women would somehow weaken her as a leader.

I understood that.

"Let's save the head count for the Cove," she added. "And Brone"—she looked back at me, eyebrows slanted and mouth forming an upside-down smile—"be delicate about it when you tell Fisher. I don't know how she's gonna handle it."

"Fisher," I said. "How is sh—"

But I cut myself short when she shot me another look, one that said, Do I *need to repeat myself?*

I kept my mouth shut and followed her toward the waterfall, bow in hand and eyes sharp. There was no telling what lurked nearby, and no matter how close we were to the Cove, danger still existed. To assume we were safe was equivalent to trying to convince an aircraft passenger with a flying phobia that there was nothing to be afraid of now that the plane was landing, when in reality, landing accidents happened all the time.

Rocket led us down the same path Coin and I traveled before finding Navi's body in the open field. Every day since that day, I'd asked myself the same question: what if I'd done one thing differently? What if, instead of leaving Redwood, we'd stayed there? Perhaps then, the Northers would have never found us.

But thinking this way was useless. I couldn't change what had happened—all I could do was focus on the future—on what I *could* do, not what I could have done.

Bickering erupted behind me every now and then, but all it took was a side glance to stop it. Being capable of changing someone's behavior with a mere look was the strangest of feelings. I wondered if it was like that for Trim when she was leader of the Hunters, or if this was how Rainer felt on her territory.

One thing set us apart: Rainer was a monster hungry for power. I didn't want power. All I wanted was peace and for things to be the way they were when Murk was in control. As I listened to the petty arguments behind me, I realized why it was so important to have one person in charge of a society. Not having any form of leadership on the island would have been like having a sports team play in a championship without a coach.

And what had Rocket meant when she'd said everything had changed? Was she not in charge? Was Fisher in charge? Someone had to be, right?

To my surprise, Coin, Hammer, Johnson, and Arenas remained silent during the trek. They walked behind me, two on either side, and scanned the area for danger.

Fortunately, danger didn't make an appearance. It was almost too calm, which kicked my anxiety into overdrive. My palms became clammy and my mouth so dry I didn't want to breathe because every bit of air that came through my nose felt like sandpaper going down into my lungs.

When the feeling became too unpleasant, I lowered my bow and slipped the arrow back into its quiver.

"Water break," I croaked, rushing to the base of the waterfall.

I stepped over flat rocks, careful not to catch a wet or slimy spot. The women did the same, though they looked more like a pack of dogs given the order to hunt. At the river, I hadn't let them fill their water bladders—for those who had some—for fear of being spotted out in the open. Now, they rushed as quickly as they could toward the water.

It looked dark green down at the base, in part thanks to the slowly setting sun. The sky had turned an iris purple on the horizon, which meant it was going to be a hot, sticky night. While I didn't enjoy cool jungle evenings, especially without adequate clothing, I much preferred them over high humidity.

Unclipping my water bladder from my belt, I knelt by the water. A mist swept through the air and landed on my face, my neck, and my chest, cooling me instantly. I filled my bladder, thankful that the Northers hadn't taken this away from me, and swallowed the cold liquid in one gulp.

As I bent forward to refill it, Hammer appeared beside me.

"Hey," she said simply.

"Hey," I said.

She sat down on the flattest rock she could find, let out a long breath, and tilted her head back, allowing the waterfall's chilly mist to encompass her.

"You okay?" she asked.

Why did everyone keep asking me if I was okay? Did I not look okay?

"I'm fine," I said.

She rested her face on her shoulder and gave me a warm smile. I wasn't sure what she wanted, so I shifted my eyes to the side before looking at her again.

Then, she punched me gently on the arm. "Just wanted to say I'm proud of you."

When I didn't say anything, her smile grew into a grin. "A lot's changed since the day I first met you."

I glared at her, though not hatefully. I knew what she was referring to—pathetic, weak little Brone who'd allowed herself to be bullied and manipulated into paying out a portion of her weekly earnings by none other than Hammer herself.

"Too soon to joke about that?" she asked.

I smiled, and it felt foreign to me. I couldn't remember the last time I'd genuinely smiled. For a second, even if only briefly, it seemed like everything would be okay—like we weren't all destined to live a horrible life surrounded by violence and chaos.

Then, Coin plopped herself down and rested the weight of her body on her hands behind her. She opened her mouth at the mist like a kid trying to catch a snowflake on their tongue, and I let out a soft chuckle.

"Holy shit," came Arenas's voice. "The girl ain't a robot. I was beginnin' to think you had no feelings, Brone." She dropped to her hands and knees and dunked her entire head into the river. When she pulled her head out, she swung back so fast that her wet hair whipped her in the back.

I shook my head, still smiling until I saw Rocket standing at the edge of the river, away from everyone. She stood stiffly with two hands on her waist and stared out into the open grass.

And then, as if being propelled back into reality by some unseen force, I thought about the Cove. I thought of Ellie, of Fisher, of everyone else I cared about, and I lunged away from the rocks.

"That's enough," I said. "Let's keep moving."

Women rose to their feet, and those who had jumped into the water came splashing out. The moment Rocket saw us approach, she kept moving.

"How much farther?" I asked, catching up.

"We're almost there," she said.

She led us out of the open field, away from the river, and toward greenery so thick I wondered if she was out of her mind.

"You expect us to walk through there?" I asked.

She looked back at me, an arrogant smirk on her lips. "There's a reason we've survived this long at the Cove, Brone. Can you ask your women to go inside? To keep walking until they reach the water? I need to stay out here and make sure no one's following."

"Watch out!" someone suddenly shouted.

I turned around to spot a handful of women hopping away from something, arms flailing over their heads.

I moved toward them, whipping tall grass out of my way. "What's going on?"

No one answered. Instead, they pointed at the ground, and two of them covered their mouths. I inched closer, a bit nervous by what I might find when I saw her.

She lay there like a child's abandoned doll—pale and lifeless. The tattoos on her arm looked even darker than usual in comparison to her translucent skin. Women gathered around me, and though I couldn't see them, I could hear them.

Franklin's body lay still in a bed of grass.

CHAPTER 10

"Brone, slow down," Rocket said.

I shouldered my way through a wall of vined flowers, and petals flew into the air.

Slow down? If Franklin's body was this close to the Cove, it meant Zsasz wasn't far. And odds were, she'd already found the Cove.

"We don't have time to waste." I angrily tore through hanging vines, then nearly fell when dozens of tree roots appeared in front of me. I say appeared because that's precisely what it felt like— as though they'd manifested to spite me.

Planting a firm hand on my shoulder, Rocket forced me to stop marching forward.

"Relax," she said, her voice low. "Unless they were brought to the Cove by one of our own, there's a good chance they didn't make it all the way. Look." She pointed straight ahead into the darkness. "The trees, the bushes, the branches... Everything's still intact."

I arched an eyebrow, and she continued. "They must have followed prints or seen someone from a distance enter the forest. Doesn't look like they came through here, though. Come on."

She hopped her way to the front of the line and I followed at arm's length.

The vegetation became so thick that some of my women began snapping branches off the trees.

"Don't do that," Rocket warned, pointing a menacing finger toward them. "Push your way through, but don't break the one thing that's keeping us hidden." Almost as if only now realizing these women were complete strangers, she turned to me. "You sure we can trust these women?"

I wasn't sure. In fact, I had my suspicions that at least one, if not several, were loyal to the Northers. But that was all it was—suspicion. I couldn't rely on my anxiety, especially seeing as I'd gone as far as to suspect my own women of treason. This gnawing doubt constantly made me sick to my stomach. I didn't know who to trust, and at times, I didn't even trust myself.

How could I point a finger at someone and accuse them of not being true? I had no proof, and for all I knew, these women all wanted the same thing—revenge. Why wouldn't they? They'd been held captive for weeks, months, years, by the Northers. Surely they wanted revenge for that. Why else would they have escaped while others stayed behind?

I gave Rocket a look, one that said, *I hope so.* That's all I had to offer. I truly did hope these women were as eager to fight back as I was.

My reaction was sufficient for Rocket. She gave me a quick nod and plowed her way through the remainder of the vegetation, elbows swinging from side to side.

Though it felt like an eternity, we may have been inside the forest for a few minutes at most. As if the sun had risen from a long night, a burst of light came blasting through the cracks of greenery up ahead.

At first, the light was yellow, but then, a bright blue came into sight.

I recognized that color.

That smell, too.

It was the smell of salt water, sand, and fish. I listened carefully, and a sound I'd once found annoying as a child entered my ears as pleasantly as one of Mozart's symphonies. It was the sound of seagulls flying overheard—they cried and cried and cried, undoubtedly circling their prey or hunting for fish.

"Water," someone behind me said.

"Is that—"

With both hands, Rocket slid aside a final wall of leaves—something that looked like it had been constructed by hand—and the entire ocean came into view. A small piece of land covered in sand decorated the border of the jungle, and on either side of us were large stone walls—giant cliffs—that made it impossible to see anything other than the ocean.

Women gathered one by one, squishing their bodies into one another as they stepped out onto the sand. Some of them, including Jack, fell to their hands and knees, running their fingers through the sand. Others walked right into the ocean and began splashing water around with childish grins on their faces.

Though I knew it wasn't time to celebrate, I couldn't help but smile.

This was the most beautiful thing I'd seen in a long time.

The ocean water felt warm against the tips of my toes, and its color was unlike anything I'd seen before—it was so clear, so transparent that I could see multicolored fish swimming below the surface. In the distance, white foam sat at the top of the water, breaking apart as gentle waves came through.

Everything was so calm—so peaceful—that for a moment, I forgot where I was; I forgot that the Northers existed and that our lives were dependent on our ability to survive on this island. None of that mattered. All that mattered was this moment right now.

I inhaled the warm scent of salt water and felt at home. It reminded me of the Working Grounds' waterfall, where I'd spent countless evenings relaxing in the sun after a long day of work or showering beneath trickling water at the far side of the waterfall.

"Watch out," Rocket said, nudging her way through my women.

She grabbed the leaf wall—something that looked like it was built of bamboo, seaweed, and vine leaves—and pulled sideways until it hid the opening we'd come through. Though I knew it was a door, it was nearly impossible to tell by looking at it.

Rocket fought her way back to the front of the crowd and followed the base of the cliff, one footstep at a time through the shallow water until she found something and let out, "Aha."

She tugged on a rope and a poorly constructed wooden floating device came into view. "Water must have pushed it away."

"Check it out!" Coin said, though it sounded more like she was talking to herself.

She crouched and began examining every detail of the platform—the size of its planks, the rope holding it together, and the quality of the wood.

"Not bad..." she said.

Not bad was Coin's way of saying that points would be received for effort, but that was it. She was incredibly meticulous when it came to building anything with wood, and if I'd had to guess

293

what she was thinking, it would have been: *I could have done a way better job.*

"What's that?" someone asked.

One of Rocket's women swung around, looking unimpressed with the one who'd asked the question, and said, "What's it look like? A fucking kitchen counter?"

"Easy," Rocket said, and her Hunter backed down.

"A secret floater!" Elektra shouted, hopping up and down from within the crowd, but she stopped hopping and slapped a hand over her mouth when Rocket's eyes narrowed on her.

"Mackenzie," Rocket said, wiggling an instructive finger toward the floating device. "You grab the second raft and start bringing women over. I'll take Brone and her crew to meet old friends."

Mackenzie, a young-looking woman with dark brown hair pulled into a high ponytail, a purple heart tattoo on her shoulder, and a shiny black eye gave Rocket a firm nod and started splashing through the water. She came back with a rope in her hands, and behind it, a large raft floated atop the crystal clear water. It was like watching butter melt on top of a hot ear of corn—it moved so smoothly that it made the water look like silk.

Rocket climbed on and jerked her head sideways at me. "Come on, get on."

I led the way, followed by Coin, Hammer, Johnson, and Arenas, who huddled so close the heat of their bodies spread across my back.

"You should have fastened those two pieces together," Coin said, pointing at the corner of the raft.

Rocket, not knowing anything about Coin, gave her a dull look and ignored her comment.

"Come on," I said, slowly climbing onto the raft.

Warm water pooled through the cracks as the weight of my body pushed it down, but it remained surprisingly sturdy. Coin followed, crawling forward with her butt in the air, and Johnson and Arenas jumped on, their momentum causing the raft to drift away from the cliff wall and out toward the ocean.

"Whoa," Rocket said, her leg muscles bulging to maintain balance.

Still standing, she reached down and picked up what looked like a giant paddle, while the rest of us sat still, knees pressed against our chests. I watched as the other women stayed behind, eyeing us like a bunch of curious monkeys—necks craned, eyes wide, and mouths partially open.

Rocket soaked her paddle in the water and swept sideways. She did this over and over again, at times switching sides. Every few seconds, she'd rush over to the other side as if trying to see fish, when in reality, she was trying to keep us from going off course.

"Watch out," she said when Johnson's leg got in the way, and Johnson, without so much as a peep, pulled her leg back and kept on looking forward. She must have had a lot on her mind. Any other time, she'd have probably let out a snarky remark like, "You have legs, use them."

Slowly, we disappeared around the cliff and all the other women disappeared from sight.

"They'll catch up soon," Rocket said. "We're a bit limited on the rafts right now. Some women decided to take them to the other side of the Cove, and they refuse to bring them back."

"Refuse?" Johnson said. "Who's in charge?"

But instead of answering, Rocket threw her chin out, her jaw muscles tense, and we followed her stare.

Up ahead, hundreds of women gathered across the shore, tending to different tasks as they'd done in the Village—some tore apart carcasses and fish while others worked at building platforms or houses out of old wood. It didn't look like they were getting far with it, but they were trying. The Cove, or the open shore, was surrounded by giant cliffs that hid everyone from the remainder of the island. It was like a secret enclosure accessible by water—and only accessible from the ocean.

The late afternoon sun came down hard on the sand, making it look almost like cream. A handful of palm trees decorated the shoreline. Aside from that, there wasn't much greenery.

But the lack of greenery was easily made up by the shore's striking beauty. It reminded me of the Working Grounds' waterfall though brighter and cleaner. The water, a transparent pool, was filled with minimal algae and instead, multicolored fish created an underwater rainbow.

The sand beneath the water looked like butter—like something I'd step into simply to relieve the pain in my feet and legs.

Arching my neck backward, I spotted an abundance of greenery overhead, which almost made the cliffs look like they'd sprouted hair.

The walls at the far back of the Cove and along its sides were steep—a flat wall, even—that looked like thousands of long yellow-brown stones flattened over top one another. The lower part of the walls was dull gray, and large stain lines ran horizontally across the stone, making me wonder if this was the result of high tide.

Was this truly the safest place to be?

"Welcome to the Cove," Rocket said, and although I should have been happy at the prospect of a new home, I couldn't help but notice that Rocket wasn't smiling.

CHAPTER 11

At first, it seemed she thought she was high. She turned sideways to grimace at Proxy, who stood like a statue as she'd always done—completely emotionless.

She grabbed Proxy's stick-for-an-arm and pulled herself up, limped on one leg, then grabbed something handed to her by Proxy—a staff of some kind—that she used to support the weight of her body.

I couldn't sit on the raft and wait for it to reach shore.

She raised a hand over her brows, probably thinking that the sun was causing her to hallucinate. But she wasn't hallucinating, and neither was I.

I was staring right at her, and although I'd heard she'd survived, it was hard to believe what I was seeing.

"Fisher!" I shouted, and without thinking, I dived headfirst into the ocean water.

It was smooth against my skin—neither warm nor cold—and the taste of salt entered my mouth.

When I resurfaced, I caught a glimpse of her limping faster and faster toward the shoreline.

Countless heads turned to look at us, but I didn't care. They could stare all they wanted. I was reuniting with a friend, with Fisher, who I thought for sure wouldn't survive.

The moment I reached shallow water, I pressed my feet into the ocean sand and started running, my knees nearly touching my chest as I hopped over the water.

"Fisher!" I repeated.

She came splashing in, and as soon as I was at arm's length, I threw both arms around her neck. She patted me hard on the back and squeezed me tight, but within seconds, her grip loosened as if she'd realized things had gotten too emotional, and she needed to take a step back.

That was Fisher being Fisher.

She cleared her throat and slapped water off her arms. "Man, you're all wet."

"Nice to see you too," I said.

She smirked, and I was about to force her into another hug when a few voices started shouting. I followed the noise and nearly collapsed to my knees.

Biggie and Flander ran through the sand, arms flailing in the air, and behind them came the most beautiful sight I'd seen in a long time—Ellie. She wore a white cotton dress, and her long dark hair was tied, hanging gently over her shoulder. In her arms, she held what appeared to be a basket constructed of bamboo, resting on her hip. She pulled a thick strand of hair out of her face and winced like someone does when they aren't wearing their glasses.

I wasn't sure what her eyesight was like, but it was apparent she didn't know it was me.

Biggie's feet came down so hard in the sand that the rolls on her body jiggled. She clapped hard over her head, a wide white smile on her face and big bright eyes to match it.

"Brooooooooooone," she shouted, and Ellie perked up, dropping the basket at her feet.

Colorful fruit rolled out into the sand, but she didn't seem to care. With both hands, she raised her dress and started running behind Biggie and Flander.

"Holy mother of Joseph!" Flander said, getting closer. "It's really you, kiddo!"

Her hair had grown quite a bit, now reaching the sides of her face. It was wavy and split right down the middle of her overly tanned head. Although her short hair had suited her well before, this doo gave her a softer, more bohemian look. It was the same gray it had been before but rougher looking, assumedly because of the salt water and sand around here.

I grinned from ear to ear when they got closer,

but I didn't even have the time to say anything. In one swift motion, Biggie scooped me up into her arms and squeezed me so tight, my spine cracked. I almost told her off, but I'd missed her too much, and the crack felt surprisingly good.

"Oh, Brone!" she shouted, her mouth so close to my ear that I flinched. She shook me from back and forth, and I felt like a helpless cat in a five-year-old's arms.

"Okay," I mumbled. "Let me go, Big—"

I fell flat on my side, into the water. When I reemerged, Ellie was almost with us. I looked at Flander, who was smiling at me like she was my long-lost grandmother.

She jerked her head sideways as if to say, Go get 'er, tiger.

I lunged straight toward Ellie and threw my arms around her, pulling her tight against me. She wrapped her hand around the back of my head and pulled me into her neck. Although I had so much to say, nothing came out. I wanted to tell her how much I'd missed her and how stupid I'd been for pulling away emotionally before all of this happened, but I couldn't. I wanted to apologize for pushing her into the river, but at the same time, I didn't feel like that mattered anymore. All I cared about was that she was alive.

She kissed my neck, and it was the warmest sensation I'd had in as long as I could remember.

Pressing my cheek against hers, it felt like I'd taken Ecstasy even though I'd never experienced that particular type of rebelliousness in the real world. I wanted to touch her everywhere, confirm that she was actually standing there. I pulled away enough to stare her square in the face.

I looked at her perfectly arched eyebrows; the two freckles on her right cheek; her chocolate brown eyes that made me feel like my insides were melting; her plush lips that always looked like they were coated in lipstick; and then, without thinking, I pressed mine against hers.

Warm air blew from her nostrils and onto my face, smelling like perfume, and I held her tight, refusing to let go. I kissed her again and again until my lips parted, and the warm tip of her tongue tickled mine. I was about to kiss her hard again when I lost my footing and we both fell into the sand with her underneath me.

She let out a cute laugh, and I couldn't help but join in.

"Yo, chicas," came Arenas's voice. "Get a damn room."

"Oh, shut up," Hammer said. "Can't you see they're having a cheesy beach moment?"

Biggie let out a laugh so loud I flinched again.

"Hey," Fisher said, now standing beside me. I stretched my neck to look at her, and as soon as we made eye contact, my fleeting moment of happiness was stripped away and replaced with reality. She leaned the weight of her body on her good leg, while the other leg reminded me of Sumi's face—pink and bubbly. "When you're done making out, come see me over there." She pointed to where she'd been sitting before, right beside Proxy. "We have a lot to talk about."

CHAPTER 12

My fairy-tale moment didn't last long. It crumbled almost instantly.

Across the shore, curious eyes turned my way—some women looked intrigued, others bitter, and some even downright vicious. For a moment, it seemed as though I was back on Norther territory. What caught my attention most of all were the segregated groups dispersed around the Cove. In the middle of the Cove, sprawled unevenly in the sand, were women with dark skin. A bit farther down, a group of Asian women had gathered beneath a palm tree, carving away at either weapons or fishing gear. Then, there were the Latinas, the Native Americans, the Caucasians, and the Middle Eastern women all separated from each other.

Fisher sat in the sand where I was headed, her back pressed against the cliff wall and her face shadowed beneath a rock overhang. It was apparent that her group, or clique, continued to honor Murk's interracial approach.

What was going on? Was this what Rocket had

meant when she said there was no order? This was never an issue under Murk's reign. We were all equal regardless of ethnicity or belief. Aside from a few rogue groups like Snow Face's women, this wasn't even an issue when enslaved by the Northers.

"Hey, stranger," Fisher said, smirking up at me. She was sitting in the sand, one leg crossed in front of her and her damaged leg lying straight out.

"Fisher, I have to tell you something," I said, unable to stop thinking about Trim. Then, all I kept hearing in my head were Rocket's words: "Be delicate about it when you tell Fisher. I don't know how she's gonna handle it."

I had no idea how to tell her—all I knew was that I needed to get it out into the open as soon as possible. As I parted my lips to continue talking, she waved a hand in the air.

"If this is about Trim, I don't want to hear it."

A lump formed in my throat. Did she already know what had happened? Or, like Rocket, had she already concluded that Trim was dead considering she wasn't with us? Maybe all she was asking was for me to spare her the gory details.

But I needed to be sure—I needed her to know and not learn it from someone else.

"You know?" I asked.

She swallowed hard, looked away, then drew an odd shape in the sand by her thigh. "Trim would be here if she were still alive."

Her dark eyes rolled up at me, almost pleadingly—almost as if she were waiting for me to argue and to say something along the lines of, "Trim's still alive, but she didn't make it out. We have to go back to her."

I wished I could say that. I wanted nothing more than to have Trim with us by our sides during all of this. She was a far better leader than I'd ever be, and she deserved to be the one standing here, breathing in the crisp ocean air.

Fisher patted the sand beside her, breaking the awkward silence. "Have a seat."

I was already covered in wet sand from having fallen over with Ellie and didn't mind her invitation. I carefully slid against the cliff wall, grimacing as my leg muscles tightened to lower me. I was so sore I didn't know what to do with myself. At long last, I could breathe again and relax without worrying about Alice Number Two threatening us or Zsasz beating me to a pulp.

Zsasz, I suddenly remembered.

Where was she? Had she returned to Rainer? Was she coming back? Was it truly possible that Zsasz and her army had missed the Cove, even though they'd walked right by it? Then, I thought of Franklin, and how she lay there in the tall grass, looking like nothing more than a porcelain doll.

How much had they tortured her to break her?

I didn't want to think about it.

"Hey," Fisher said, and I was pulled back into reality. "Whatever happened there... It's over."

I couldn't even look at her. She had no idea what had happened to me, to us, because if she did, she wouldn't be telling me that it was *over*.

It would never be over.

Not until the Northers were dead and Murk was safely returned.

"Watch out!" someone shouted.

I glared out toward shore. Mackenzie, the woman with the purple heart tattoo and the shiner, was now bringing her fourth round of women. She jabbed her paddle in the sand and pulled the raft closer to the shore—so close that it got stuck.

"Come on," someone shouted, and then the boar came into view.

Three women struggled to pull it off the raft, and when it landed in the sand, the three of them tripped backward but caught their footing.

"You brought food?" Fisher asked.

This time, I glanced sideways at her. She'd lost so much weight since I'd last seen her. Her cheekbones looked even higher than usual, though, in reality, her sunken-in cheeks had more to do with it. Dark bags sat below her eyes, and her lips were pale and flaky. She still wore that same tight ponytail on her head, but it had grown quite a bit longer, sitting on top of her right shoulder.

I turned my attention toward the boar. "Yeah, I did. Well, I can't take all the credit. Elektra took a shot at it, too." I smirked, realizing how coincidental it was that we'd found each other—it was all because of this boar. "She's good."

Fisher smiled, though her lips barely moved. She stared out toward the horizon, and I followed her gaze, the setting sun making it easier to see the entire shore now. The water behind the raft darkened, and above it, the sky turned a fire orange with streaks of purple overtop. The palm trees nearest to the shoreline began to lose color, slowly transforming into nothing more than a dark silhouette.

Women gathered around the boar, but with the setting sun, it was impossible to see their features.

"Those survivors from the Village?" I asked.

From what I could tell, they wore the same suede clothing I'd seen through the Village and the Working Grounds.

Fisher shrugged. "Most of them."

"Most?" I asked.

Without looking at me, she stretched her neck and scratched at her scarred leg. "We found some new drops here and there. Couldn't let them die."

"So you brought them here?"

She nodded slowly. "Yeah, but I'm starting to think it was a mistake."

"What do you mean?" I asked.

At last, she looked at me, her eyes resembling black gumballs. "Rocket didn't tell you?"

"She said there's no order," I said. "I assumed that meant things aren't going well, but I still have no idea what's going on here."

Fisher scoffed. "No order," she repeated. "It's more than that, Brone. These women are acting like they would in prison. It's like they've reverted back to being their criminal selves. I don't know how Murk did it, but she made us forget we were convicts. She made us feel like a big family. Sure, there were fights every now and then, but nothing like it is now. It's like everyone's fighting to be top dog. I'm so fucking sick of it." She dropped her head against the rocky surface behind her. "It's exhausting, you know?"

"Hey!" someone shouted.

"Fuck off, that's ours!"

I followed the shouts to find Elektra's silhouette pulling at the vines wrapped around the boar's leg. Then, a woman—much taller than Elektra—shoved her into the sand and with the aid of a few others, started pulling the boar to the other side of the beach.

I couldn't tell who they were, but it was apparent by the sharp objects they held in their hands that they were willing to fight to steal what we'd caught.

I picked up my bow and lunged forward, but Fisher grabbed me by the back of my shirt, pulling me down.

"Don't bother," she said.

"Did you see that?" I growled. "They shoved Elektra. She's a kid!"

Fisher's eyelids went flat, making her look sleep deprived. "Yeah, I know. But that's Hawkins. Most women here call her Hawk. She was dropped on the island last month."

"So? Who is she?" I asked.

She let out a defeated breath through her nostrils. "Someone trying to be the leader. She has a lot of followers, and she's not scared to fight anyone. She's already killed two women here."

I clenched my teeth. "How're you letting her get away with that?"

Fisher turned to me, giving me that feisty look I'd forgotten—the one that said, *Are you an idiot?* "Look around, Brone. We're safe here. At least from the Northers. If we leave, we're as good as dead. You know how bad Rainer wants us dead."

I scoffed—not because I found any of this funny, but because I was infuriated. I'd run away from imprisonment only to end up alongside someone else who was hungry for power—so much so that they were willing to shed blood for it.

"So what?" I said. "We catch food and they take it from us?"

Fisher shrugged again. "Yeah, if they feel like it."

"How many followers are we talking about, here?" I asked.

"I don't know, Brone—" But then, Elektra came storming toward us, punching invisible enemies in the air.

"Stupid, stupid, stupid," she growled. "Stupid bitch."

"Hey!" Fisher said, her tone deep and stern.

I'd never pegged Fisher as the parental type, but it was clear she was doing her best to contribute to Elektra's development.

"Sorry," Elektra mumbled. Then, she dropped her hunting bow into the sand and plopped herself down. "Why can't we kill her?"

Fisher glowered at her. "You don't just kill people, Elektra."

"But you do," she said, and Fisher gave me an awkward glance.

"Just because we've all done bad things in the past, it doesn't mean we have to continue to do them."

As Fisher tried to convince Elektra that we didn't have the right to take someone's life even though there were criminals on the island, I wondered... Would she look at me differently if she knew about the lives I'd taken? If she knew about the Northers I'd killed, the women I'd nearly killed in a blackout, and the countless Ogres I'd slaughtered?

Would she think I was a ticking time bomb?

The whole gang joined us at the back of the Cove—Coin, Hammer, Biggie, Flander, Arenas, Rocket, Ellie, Johnson, and Proxy.

Although I felt at home, it also seemed like I was again sitting on enemy territory.

"Where we sleepin'?" Arenas asked.

She sounded like an entitled teenager. I almost said, "In the sand," but Rocket pointed toward what appeared to be an opening in the cliff wall—a cavern that led into the cliff. I couldn't tell how deep it was, but it looked deep enough for someone to walk into and disappear from one's sight.

"What's that?" I asked.

"Where we sleep," Fisher said. "Feels safer than sleeping out on the beach, right in Hawkins's view. I'm surprised she hasn't come to take this from us, too."

I clenched my fists. I didn't even know the woman, but the sound of her name made me want to punch her in the face.

"Flander told us all about it," Coin said. "Man, that's bullshit. Why can't you all enjoy the Cove together? Ain't no reason to still be fighting. Haven't we all suffered enough already?"

"Human beings are dumb," Hammer said

pensively.

"Look, stay out of her way, and she'll stay out of ours," Fisher said. "There's no use trying to get revenge. We're outnumbered."

I was so sick of hearing that—outnumbered.

It wasn't fair. Why was evil always winning over good? Coin was right. We'd suffered enough already. We'd had our Village burned to the ground, yet our own women, survivors of the massacre, had allowed some newcomer to ruin our society.

Was it because they were weak? Devasted from the attack? Were they too afraid to fight? Or, could it be they wanted someone to follow, and they'd allow anyone strong enough to lead them?

None of that mattered because I realized something.

Before I could say anything, Jack came jogging toward us. "Hey, guys!" she said, waving her hand high over her head. "You must be Brone's friends. Holy moly, has she ever talked about you guys."

What was she talking about? I hadn't talked about any of them.

"Can't believe I'm meeting you finally!" The sun-damaged skin on her face stretched, revealing her rotten teeth. "So, is this our new camp? Our freedom land? Our safe haven?" she rambled. "What a gorgeous place." She sucked hard through her nostrils, and the clicking sound of mucus being pulled into her throat filled the air. Then, she hacked and spat a glob in the sand.

"Ew!" Elektra shouted.

Jack pointed at the cave in the wall, completely ignoring Elektra. "That where we're sleeping? Smart place. Especially if it's raining!"

She continued to ramble, but her voice slowly faded from my ears. It became a distant hum—a radio host talking in the background. The one thing I could focus on was the group of women— my women—walking toward us.

They looked exhausted, their feet dragging in the sand, but they were all looking at the same thing—me.

They were still following me, even though we'd made it to our destination.

Was I their leader now?

Then, I remembered Quinn and the countless women she'd been instructed to guide to safety. How many were there? Eighty? One hundred? All survivors who'd escaped imprisonment. While I didn't know where they'd gone, one of her women, Aisha, had come with me to guide the way.

I turned to Fisher, the loud bickering around me suddenly returning. I must have gasped with excitement because everyone went quiet and looked at me.

"We aren't outnumbered," I said.

"What're you talking about?" Fisher asked.

But I didn't have to answer.

The women who'd followed me—the ones I'd saved—formed a half circle around us and one by one, dropped to one knee. Then, each one raised a hand in the air, their fingers spread apart as they'd done in the past to Rainer, and later, as they'd done to me in the city.

I smirked sideways at Fisher, and her jaw hung loose.

First, we'd take down Hawkins; then, we'd save Murk.

PART FOUR

PART FOUR

PROLOGUE

I sucked in moist, salty air, feeling like I'd swallowed a glass of ocean water.

Where was I? By the water?

Why couldn't I remember anything? Where were my women? Coin? Hammer? Arenas? Johnson? Nearby, voices filled the air, but they were so faint they sounded like flies hovering around a dead carcass.

I tried to open my eyes, but they were sealed shut—literally. At first, I thought I'd been kidnapped in my sleep, only to be tied up and tortured by Rainer. Maybe they'd sewn my eyelids shut, and I was finally getting punished for my big mouth.

But then, rationality kicked in—it was nothing more than crust. I hadn't had this problem since I was a kid; it was terrifying, and every time, I'd scream for my mom. She'd come running into my room with a hot cloth to wipe the hardened gunk from my lids.

That was a long time ago, so why was it happening now? Had I cried in my sleep? God, I hoped not.

Any minute now, Alice Number Two would come pouring a bucket of rainwater on me, urging me to get up. She'd tell me I'd slept in long enough, accuse me of being useless, and force me to get my *lazy ass* over to the Food Station.

But there was no cold water, no shouting, nothing.

Why wasn't she coming? My heart raced—I hated the unknown. It made me feel vulnerable and, in a sense, weak. I needed to know what was happening at all times if I hoped to offer courage and guidance to the women around me.

I needed to be in control.

The air around me changed as if a thermostat controlled the outdoor air. It became cool and damp, rather than hot and sticky as it always was in the Northers' city.

Where was I? Something was wrong.

I fought against my eyelids, trying hard to pry my eyes open, but it was impossible, as though they'd been superglued shut. The texture over my lids was hard and crusty, and no matter how much I rubbed, all it did was allow a few flakes to fall.

A firm hand suddenly landed on my forearm and I flinched.

Without thinking, I snapped my arm out straight ahead and grabbed the woman, whoever she was, by the throat. Had I slept with a shiv—which I didn't as it was forbidden in the city—I'd have held it up to her throat. My own women knew not to startle me like that.

She pried at my arm and through broken speech, said, "B-B-Brone. It's... It's me."

I immediately let go. "Ellie?"

Ellie.

The Cove.

It was all coming back to me now.

"Oh God," I said. "I'm so sorry."

She brushed delicate fingers against my cheek and it was like an angel's wing against my skin. What a corny thought, but I couldn't help it. There was something so soothing about her touch.

I couldn't see her, but I heard her smile—the sound of lips unsticking from teeth and saliva popping.

"Good morning to you too, sunshine," she said.

I beamed, though the thought of having laid a hand on her made me wince. I hadn't meant to. It was instinctive—a reaction the island had created in me.

Was I prone to violence, now?

"Hold still," she said, and something warm and wet slid over my eyes and across my cheeks. She rubbed gently, and bit by bit, light filtered through the cracks of my sealed eyelids.

At last, I saw her.

She sat at my side, legs wrapped in a beige

cotton dress, giving her the appearance of a mermaid. And she looked like one, too—a soft, silky complexion, long wavy brown hair, penetrating eyes that seemed capable of reading minds, and a smile that made me want to do anything she asked of me.

She caught me staring and the corner of her lip curved up playfully. Shifting, she put the weight of her upper body on one arm. In the other, she gripped what seemed like a basic handcloth you'd find in a dollar store, but upon closer inspection, it was a clump of bunched seaweed she'd used to clean my face.

I cringed, knowing I'd have to get used to seaweed around here; in sixth grade, we became sworn enemies. I'd been swimming in a lake at an isolated cottage my mom's friend insisted we use for the weekend when something cold and slimy wrapped itself around my ankle and held me down beneath the surface of the water.

Thankfully, my mom was attentive when it came to keeping a close eye on me. She must have seen my arms flapping around in the water. The next thing I knew, she held me in her arms, her hot breath colliding with my face. "It's okay, baby, I've got you," she'd said over, and over again.

"Hey," Ellie said so lovingly that I wanted to pull her tight against me and go back to sleep.

Was I truly here? Was this the Universe's way of

giving back? Of rewarding me for all the torment I'd endured? This life—a life on the beach with Ellie by my side—was like something out of a romance movie.

I parted my lips to say something cheesy, like, *I could stay here forever*—even though I'd have never said that in a million years before meeting Ellie and the thought of it made me feel stupid—but I didn't have time.

Outside of our rocky shelter came a horrifying scream that caused the hairs on the back of my neck to stand up. Suddenly, Ellie and I were back to being two murderous convicts on Kormace Island, and my fantasy dissipated instantly. I recognized that sound—it was a cry of panic and sheer agony.

Were we being attacked? Had Zsasz found us at last?

I grabbed my bow and threw my quiver over my shoulder, its arrows rocking hard from side to side.

My feet slapped through the mixture of cool sand and stone as I ran toward the morning light, but I didn't even have to make it out of our cavern to know what was going on.

The terrorized shout that followed left no doubt as to what was happening.

"Shark!"

CHAPTER 1

It looked like someone had dumped a truckload of red food coloring in the water.

I didn't understand how that much blood could have come out of one person. Women gathered from every direction, forming a circle around something in the sand.

Had they killed the shark? Was that what they were looking at?

I ran toward them, the morning sun warming my back.

"Oh my God, oh my God, oh my God," one woman ranted, pacing back and forth, running her hands across her shaved head over and over again. Her mouth hung open so wide that had I not been standing beside her, I'd have thought she was yelling. "It's... it's my fault," she continued. "I didn't think anything would happen. We were... we were..."

Then, she dropped into the sand and quickly crawled like a crab toward the women forming a circle.

"Fuck, fuck, fuck," she continued, but I couldn't

see her. She'd disappeared behind dozens of legs. "Jovana..." Then, she coughed, and it sounded like snot bubbles had popped under her nose.

Elbows sticking out, I shoved my way through the crowd. Not willing to stand around, I needed to know what was going on. Yet the moment my foot broke through the dozens of legs—the moment I laid eyes on what could only be described as a senseless bloodbath—I wished I'd stayed at the back of the Cove.

A woman, assumedly Jovana, lay in the sand, her face whiter than a marshmallow and her arms spread out crookedly on either side of her body. Underneath her, the sand had turned a dark brown, but it was the bottom half of her body that caused me to keep staring: part of it was missing.

Her right leg was nothing more than a bloody stump with a protruding femur bone, torn muscles, and hanging ligaments. I sealed my lips tight together and averted my gaze, my surroundings spinning. I'd seen violence and gore before, but this was so fresh, and what bothered me most was that she was still alive.

"The fuck happened?" someone snapped.

The injured woman didn't move. Her breathing was rapid, and every few seconds, her body twitched. She'd probably passed out from the pain.

Any moment now, she'd wake up and see what remained of her leg.

"What were you guys doing out there?" someone else shouted.

They all sounded so angry, but it was probably the fear and anxiety creating tension.

"You know damn well we don't go in the water in the mornings or the evenings," someone growled.

It sounded like they were scolding the woman— the one with the shaved head sitting in the sand, prodding and pulling at her best friend or lover.

But she didn't answer anyone. Instead, she kept babbling, "Jovana..."

Someone scoffed, which surprised me so much that I pushed a woman out of my way to see who it was.

"Shouldn't'a been havin' sex in the fuckin' water, eh Sofia? That's what you get for bein' a fuckin' dyke."

The woman, a middle-aged bag of bones with skin so damaged it might as well have been melting off her, offered the grieving woman a rotten grin. She seemed proud of the heinous comment she'd made.

"You fu—" said Sofia, the grieving woman. Without finishing her sentence, she lunged straight at the bag of bones and they both fell onto the sand.

"What'd you say?" Sofia shouted, her voice breaking. She didn't let the older woman respond.

Instead, she bashed her fist into her face. A loud cracking sound prompted everyone to step back.

The hateful woman smiled up at her, blood spilling through the cracks of her teeth. Humping upward, she caused Sofia to shift from side to side and made a revolting moaning sound. "Yeah, ya like that? That what it felt like before that shark came at ya? Was it worth it?"

"Guys, stop!" someone shouted.

Sofia swung another tight fist right at the woman's nose, and blood splattered over her lips and chin.

She wasn't smiling anymore. She reached for her nose, which was no doubt broken, and winced.

Someone grabbed Sofia and dragged her off the woman. She didn't seem to mind that the fight had stopped. Immediately, she rushed back to Jovana and lay her head on her chest.

It was apparent, now—the love. She brushed her fingers along Jovana's forehead, then reached down and kissed it.

I swallowed past a lump in my throat.

I couldn't even imagine how she was feeling.

Had that been Ellie... I wasn't sure what I'd have done.

"Guys, give her some space," someone said.

"Space?" came another voice. "She needs help. Now. Where's that Proximity woman? The one who helped Fisher?"

"Proxy?"

"Yeah, her."

"She ain't no doctor, and ain't no way is she gonna help us."

Us? Were these Hawkins's women? The ones Fisher had warned me about?

"We gotta do—" but then, everyone stopped bickering.

They stepped aside as a tall woman came forward. It was like seeing the real-life version of a story I was taught as a kid—the story of Moses. The only difference was, this woman wasn't splitting water apart. She'd somehow managed to split the entire crowd in two without saying a word.

"What's going on, here?"

Her voice was deep, which suited her height. Her dirty-blond hair was tied back into a tight bun at the base of her skull. She had shoulders as broad as a man's, and a stance that exuberated confidence and fearlessness. At first, I'd thought her eyes were black but realized it was the way she bowed her head forward.

"Shark attack," someone said, sounding like a soldier on duty.

She raised her head, revealing strange gray eyes—not light but not dark, either. Her neck bore a green tattoo, which was likely once black but looked so weathered that the ink had lost most of its color. I had to stare at it for a few seconds to finally realize what it was—a sea trident with dozens of skulls floating in the background. The ink took up half her neck on the right side and continued down under her shirt, which was mostly an entanglement of seaweed and a poorly carved wooden chest plate. It made her look even bigger than she was.

She squinted at the bloody body in the sand, which meant she probably used to wear glasses. I wasn't all that surprised seeing as the woman looked to be in her forties or early fifties.

"What was she doing out in the ocean at this time?" she asked.

Although it seemed like she was talking to everyone at once, no one was brave enough to step forward and speak up. Finally, someone inched their way through the sand to approach the woman, head bowed. "Um, well, Sofia was with her."

The woman's creepy eyes rolled toward Sofia. "Is this true?"

Sofia didn't say anything. Instead, she pulled Jovana's body closer to hers and kissed her pale forehead again.

Without expressing an ounce of sympathy, the tall woman extracted from her belt a small, curved shiv made of either stone or a large seashell.

Sofia looked up when the woman's body cast a long shadow over her.

"Hawk, no, please," she begged.

Hawkins.

I should have known.

Hawkins knelt on one knee and pressed a delicate hand against Sofia's face. She offered a consoling smile, though from where I was standing, it didn't look sincere at all. It was as though her cheeks were being forced apart by invisible strings.

"You know it's better we help her before she wakes up," Hawkins said.

Sofia started babbling, saliva spilling from her slobbery lips. "P-p-please, don't do it. Maybe... Maybe she can survive this."

A woman behind Sofia crossed her flabby arms over her bare chest, pressing her sagging breasts flat against her belly. "Ain't no way, Sof. Look at all the blood she's lost."

"Please," Sofia begged, but then Hawkins looked up behind her and gave a quick nod.

At once, two women grabbed Sofia underneath her arms and dragged her away from Jovana's body.

"Let me go!" Sofia shrieked.

She kicked the air, pieces of sand and seashells making their way toward Hawkins and the crowd of women.

"Don't do it, please!" she cried.

Although I felt terrible for Sofia and knew I was

supposed to hate Hawkins without even knowing her, she was doing what was necessary. That was something I admired. Had I been in her shoes, I wouldn't have been able to do the same.

In one quick motion, and without even blinking, she sliced her shiv along Jovana's throat. Blood came spilling out, but not as aggressively as I'd have imagined. It happened so smoothly I blinked only a few times and Jovana was dead.

Hawkins wiped her shiv against Jovana's shirt and laid a hand over her face to close her eyelids. She bowed her head, offering a respectful moment of silence, then stood up and clicked her fingers.

"Get this cleaned up."

CHAPTER 2

"I don't get it," I said, "she doesn't seem all that bad."

Fisher scoffed. "All that bad? She killed one of her own. Isn't that what you told me?"

Fisher hadn't followed me to the bloody scene, but I'd told her everything.

"She didn't *kill*," I said, "she ended her misery."

Why was I defending Hawkins, anyways? I was supposed to hate her. Wasn't that what Fisher taught me? That Hawkins was the reason the Cove was falling apart?

Fisher's mouth dropped open, and she averted her gaze to Biggie, Flander, and Rocket, then back to me as if trying to put puzzle pieces together.

"I think Brone's right," Johnson said.

Fisher glowered at her as though ready to flatten her nose. "Nobody asked you."

Apparently, she didn't care what my women's opinions were since they hadn't spent the last few months alongside Hawkins.

Johnson looked at me as if to say, *Are you going to tolerate Fisher's attitude?*

After everything Johnson had seen me accomplish over the last few months, no doubt she felt it unfathomable for anyone to talk to me so rudely. But Fisher hadn't been part of any of that, and truthfully, Fisher would always be Fisher—she was fierce, bold, and unapologetic, and I loved her for it.

So, yes, I would tolerate her attitude.

"Bring it in!" someone shouted.

I looked up toward the shouter.

Around her, a crowd of women had gathered, their curious heads swaying back and forth. Clad in seaweed clothing and pieces of wood fastened around their wrists, shins, and on some, their chests, they appeared to be Hawkins's women. What were they doing? Jovana's dead body had been lying there only minutes ago.

Then, out of the water came two women pulling a giant mesh net. At first, it looked like they were dragging it through the sand by holding ropes over their shoulders, but it quickly became apparent that they'd caught something.

And it wasn't something small, either.

"What is that?" Rocket asked, glaring out toward shore.

Fisher shrugged. "Does it matter? Not like they're gonna share it."

Then, I caught a glimpse of its fin. It was gray and more massive than anything I'd seen on a sea creature before. Hawkins's women rolled it into the sand, and its white belly went faceup.

"Holy shit," I said. "Is that a shark? Is that *the* shark?"

Though women circled it like a bunch of hungry pigeons, blocking my view, I caught a glimpse of it every few seconds. It was huge—at least ten or fifteen feet long. It wasn't a great white by any means, but it was big enough to grab someone and pull them back into the water; it was big enough to tear someone's leg off.

In its side were two long spears, wiggling from side to side as the women continued to drag the dead creature up onshore. Had they attacked it as it was attacking Jovana? They must have.

"That thing's huge." I angled my head toward it. "Why wouldn't they share some of it?" I asked. "What happens if you ask? We need to eat, too. Why are they being so selfish about it?"

This time, Johnson laughed. "Wow, Brone, you've never been in a real prison, have you?"

I averted my gaze.

How was I supposed to answer that? Wasn't this technically prison? Or was she referring to being behind bars?

No, I'd never been held prisoner in an actual prison, aside from the few nights I'd spent waiting to be transported here.

"Ain't nothin' like here," Biggie said, plopping

herself down in the sand.

It felt like the ground shook, but it most likely was a gust of wind that swept out from underneath her.

"Yeah, well," Flander said, coming out from the cliff's cavern. She rubbed her entire face with her forearm as if she'd recently woken up. "Call me crazy, but I'd pick this island over prison any damn day."

"Ditto," Johnson said.

"What're you getting at?" I asked. "You made it sound like prison's worse, so wouldn't it stand to reason that the women on this island would behave better?"

Fisher let out a forced snicker. "You don't get it, Brone. You act like you live on some paradise of an island—"

I stuck a stiff finger in her face. How dare she say that? After everything I'd seen, everything I'd done, and everything I'd suffered through. "I don't fucking think that—"

"Relax," she breathed, patting me on the thigh. "I get it, okay? This place is a shithole. All I'm saying is you expect peace too often. We, everyone... We're all murderers. We're all criminals. We're not good people, Brone. There'll never be peace on this island. Ever. You have to stop chasing it."

"There was when Murk was in power," I muttered.

Everyone looked at me—half of them because they knew Murk was alive, and the others, because the sound of Murk's name seemed to dishearten them.

They didn't know.

Flander sat down and rested her head on Biggie's shoulder. "Murk made things better, yeah, but she din't get rid 'o all the hate, Brone. Women still fought. Only difference is, they didn't get caught."

I clenched my teeth. It didn't make sense to me. Weren't we all after the same thing? Survival?

Fisher let out a slow breath and ran both hands over her tightly tied hair. "People wanna be in charge. There's always someone who needs to prove they're bigger and *badder* than the next person."

"And that's Hawkins?" I asked, gazing out in her direction.

She was sitting on something, though it was impossible to tell what it was with all the women around her. She looked arrogant, too—legs spread wide apart, elbows on knees, and back hunched. She made jabbing motions toward the ground, and her lips kept flapping open and closed.

From here, it seemed like she was devising a plan of attack.

"What's she doing?" I asked.

"Who knows," Rocket said. "Probably planning

to kill us."

Fisher swung an open hand at Rocket's shin, but Rocket jumped back and let out a chuckle.

"Look, guys," I said. "We have to head back out. There are other women out there waiting for me. Quinn took them—"

"Who's Quinn?" Fisher asked.

"A friend," I said. My answer seemed enough for her and she didn't interrogate me on it. "She has a lot of women... A lot of people who ran away from the Northers like we did. If we can get them here—"

"And what?" Fisher interrupted. "Stand up to Hawkins? Is that your plan? What? You want to be the top dog, Brone? You want to take over the Cove and make everything better? Create your little paradise?"

"Jesus, Fisher, relax," I said. I wasn't sure where all this anger was coming from, but she had no right getting upset with me—not after what I'd done. Not after I'd basically saved her life.

She clenched her fist so tight that some of her knuckles cracked.

"What's your problem?" I asked.

"Nothing," she growled, but I didn't stop staring at her, and she let out a sharp sigh. "I'm sick of people dying, okay? Sick of all of this shit."

No one spoke, and a heavy silence filled the air. As the sun came up, more and more of my women started waking from sleep. I wasn't sure how long they'd slept, but I was certain it was longer than what they were used to. Finally, they were free; they were no longer prisoners to the Northers, which meant they didn't have to wake up to someone yelling at them.

"Hey," someone moaned with one eye open.

A few hellos were shared, and slowly, more and more women came out, yawning and stretching under the glow of the morning sun that crept its way up from behind the cliff. It reflected across the ocean water, creating a deep orange color across fluffy pink clouds. The ocean water turned a light purple, creating a scene that looked like cotton candy and making me want to dive right in. I couldn't remember the last time I'd seen the sunrise.

It was hard to imagine that only moments ago, someone's life had been taken here.

She couldn't see this sunrise, nor would she ever see any sunrise again, all because she'd wanted a few brief moments of privacy and pleasure with her partner. I understood now why Murk had enforced so many rules in her Village—why she'd forbidden anyone other than us, the Hunters, from venturing too far out into the jungle.

All she'd ever wanted was to protect us... to maintain a functional society with one goal in mind—our survival. Without her, women became primal, undoubtedly even more so than they'd been in the real world. There were no correctional officers, no laws, no basic human rights. In a sense, this island was a dreamland for anyone looking to commit more crime, making it dangerous without adequate order.

When Murk had been in charge, she'd made us feel like our crimes didn't define us. The past was the past, and what mattered above all else was how willing we were to contribute to a society looking to live a peaceful life—one that was as comfortable as possible given the circumstances.

I missed those days more than anything.

Sure, maybe they weren't perfect. I had, after all, been threatened at knifepoint and insulted time and time again by women across the Village and the Working Grounds. But at the end of the day, we had all been safe, warm, and fed.

We needed Murk.

"You ready, Brone?" came Jack's voice.

Why was she talking to me like we were best friends? I still didn't know how to feel about her. Had I not been so exhausted the night before, I'd probably have tried to sleep with my eyes open in fear of waking up with a knife pressed into my throat.

She was unpredictable, and it was only a matter of time before she killed someone.

For a moment, I entertained fantasies of

sending her after Hawkins, but if I did that, I'd get her killed. When those thoughts didn't sit well with me, I realized I still had a conscience. What a relief.

"Ready for what?" Fisher growled. She glared at me, then back up at Jack as if we'd spent all night conspiring against her.

"The plan," Jack said proudly. Had she been wearing overalls, she'd likely have snapped them with her thumbs.

"What *plan*?" Fisher said. "Is this about that Quinn girl?"

When she clenched her fists again, I laid a gentle hand on her forearm. I knew why she was angry—she was scared. If I left again, there was no guarantee I was coming back. Here was the Fisher I'd known since I'd met her. She reacted with anger when hurt emotionally, and her personality hadn't changed one bit since I'd last seen her.

I looked at her narrowed dark eyes, pasty white lips, high cheekbones, and defined jawline that looked even more defined now that she'd lost an unhealthy amount of weight. I couldn't help but smile—she seemed as pissed off as she was the first day I met her. When Rocket had introduced her, she'd given me a cursory look, opened her mouth, and said, "I don't like fishing."

"What's so funny?" she hissed.

Shaking my head, I said, "Nothing's funny, Fisher. I missed you."

Her furrowed eyebrows slowly spread apart a bit and she looked away.

"I'm coming back," I said. "I have to. After that, I'm going after the Northers."

The scowl on her face reappeared in one blink. "Are you fucking insane?"

"Hey," Jack said sternly the way a father would when scolding his disobedient child. She slapped two arms over her chest and took a step toward Fisher. "Watch how you talk to her!"

It was nice to know I had someone watching my back, but at the same time, Jack's words made me swallow harder than usual. Fisher wasn't the type to back down from confrontation. Any moment now, things would get heated.

But instead of shouting or pointing a finger at Jack, Fisher threw her head back and let out a laugh so loud I thought maybe she'd lost her mind. Why wasn't she flipping out? Name-calling? Telling Jack to go fuck herself?

Then, her cold glare turned on me.

"What? You're some big shot all of a sudden, Brone? You come back here with your fucking followers... Your puppets"—she gave Jack the most hateful up-and-down look I'd ever seen—"and you think you can change this place? You think you being here is gonna make any difference whatsoever about the way Hawkins is running shit? *Idiota*..."

Everyone circled us as if our argument was staged for their enjoyment. Was that what they wanted? A show? Although it pissed me off that no one was minding their own business, I wouldn't let it stop me from speaking my mind.

"It's not like that," I growled on the verge of yelling, but I kept my cool and told myself that Fisher was afraid and simply reacting in anger. "This isn't a life, Fisher. I spent the last God knows how long being held against my will and forced to work every single day no matter how I was feeling. I've been beaten, yelled at, starved, and sleep deprived." I waved my injured hand in front of her face, and although it was no longer broken, the skin was still discolored and I needed her to see it. "Had a bunch of my fingers broken, which was really fucking great. So no, I'm not some big shot. I only happened to have had enough of it all and managed to save some people from a shitty life. The reason I'm going to find Quinn is so we can build an army like Murk wanted—like she'd planned before all of this happened. I don't give a shit about Hawkins, okay? If she gets in my way, she'll be taken down."

Her eyes grew larger as I spoke, and I didn't blame her. Even I couldn't recognize myself as the words came out, but I couldn't hold them in.

"The Northers are never going to stop," I continued. "You're right, Fisher, we're not good people. We're a bunch of low-life criminals like you said. I'm not a good person. If I were, perhaps I'd have surrendered or submitted to Rainer and her people to avoid more death. To avoid all the lives that were taken when we tried to run the first time. Maybe I wouldn't fight. I wouldn't want violence. That's what a good person would do, right? I'm sorry, but fuck that." I wiped my lips when saliva came spraying out. "This is the only life we have, and no matter how crappy it is, it's still a life. I sure as hell am not going to sit around and let some monsters ruin it for all of us."

Fisher's lips trembled. Arching a brow, she said, "Maybe they won't find us—"

I cut her off before giving her the chance to embarrass herself. "Are you kidding me? They'll never stop. They burned our goddamn Village to the ground, Fisher. You know that. You know how the Northers are."

The women behind me cheered, and although they couldn't have known what I was talking about, given most had been imprisoned by the Northers far longer than I was, they clearly wanted revenge as much as I did.

"It's easy," I said, jabbing my finger in the sand at my feet. "We get more numbers, we train, and we attack."

"So more blood," Fisher said plainly.

"Some blood now to prevent more blood later,

yeah."

She shook her head and scratched hard at her eyebrow, evidently agreeing with everything I'd said but not wanting to admit it. "What happened to you?"

"Do you want Murk back, or not?"

"Murk?" she breathed.

"Yeah, she's alive. They have her tied up at the back of their city, and they let her hang there by her wrists. There are other women, too... some of our own. They're caged like a bunch of animals, Fisher. I can't sit around here and let—"

"I'm coming with you," Fisher said, and I shut my mouth.

It was as if I'd traveled back in time to when Fisher was filled with rage and an incessant desire to knock someone's teeth in. With shoulders drawn back, she leaned forward and balled a fist in the air as if to say, *You're right, let's do this.*

I nearly smiled, but then Aisha appeared, brows furrowed and lips forming a flat line above her small pointed chin.

The woman looked to be in her early twenties with muscles so lean it made her skin seem as soft as silk. I wasn't sure how she'd managed to maintain such a physique, being enslaved by the Beasts and all, but she'd succeeded in staying in shape. She could have been one of the women who jogged around the city every morning. They did it before anyone woke up and ran so often that they'd flattened the earth down to form a track around the tents.

Now, Aisha stared at us without saying a word. If there was one thing I'd lost patience for, it was being stared at.

"What?" I snapped.

"We can't go," she said so calmly it was as if her emotions had been sucked right out of her.

Fisher jumped up, at least as best as she could with her injured leg, and limped toward Aisha until they were nearly touching noses. "Why the fuck not?"

I planted a firm hand on Fisher's chest. "Relax."

"This isn't what Quinn wants," Aisha said. She sounded like a lawyer—straight to the point and dealing only with facts. "Quinn said we were to come get them only once we had safe land to live on." She swiveled the upper half of her body in the direction of Hawkins and her women. "This place isn't safe, so no... I'm sorry, Brone, but I can't take you to Quinn yet."

CHAPTER 3

"If Murk's out there," Fisher said, more so to Aisha than to me, "then we need to go get her. Now." Perhaps she was trying to make her feel guilty for not wanting to take us to Quinn.

But why was Fisher trying to convince Aisha of anything? Aisha didn't know Murk; she and Quinn came from a different clan on the island and had no attachment to Murk or to us. She didn't owe us anything. In fact, she was doing the same thing we were—remaining loyal to her leader.

I stared at the sand bunched up by my feet and in between the cracks of my toes. As much as I hated to admit it, Aisha was right—Quinn hadn't led all those surviving women to her old territory only for us to show up and demand they take part in a fight. None of those women wanted to fight— that was the whole reason they'd followed Quinn to begin with.

I was the one with the fighters. I couldn't possibly expect all those other survivors to arm up and face Hawkins and, ultimately, Rainer.

I needed someone else.

Someone who wanted to fight.

Pensively, I glanced toward shore, where Hawkins's women dragged the dead shark's carcass through the sand and toward the east side of the shore. The fin swayed from side to side as it moved, sending chills down my back. While I was glad the shark was dead, it was still frightening to see. The eyes, two black balls on either side of its face, remained open as the women pulled. Its mouth, too, remained open, revealing countless dagger-sharp teeth covered in blood. There was so much blood the shark's white belly looked pink.

At the far end of the beach, Hawkins sat comfortably in what appeared to be a chair built of wood and cotton cushions, waiting for her meal to arrive.

That was it.

Hawkins was the answer.

"Are you insane?" Fisher said.

I wasn't sure how to answer that. What else was I supposed to do? Could be the answer wasn't fighting Hawkins—it was befriending her. I'd spent the last months or even a year thinking of ways to solve our problems by killing the enemy.

Why did Hawkins have to be the enemy?

I turned to Fisher and gave her an uncertain shrug. "What else are we supposed to do? My original plan to get Quinn and the others is out the window. Face it, Fisher. Aisha's right... Even if we somehow find Quinn, those women won't fight. That's like asking a bunch of civilians to arm up and fight a military war. Hawkins, though..."

Fisher scoffed—the kind of reaction that made me feel insignificant or juvenile for even suggesting such an idea.

"Hawkins isn't some church lady with an attitude," Fisher said. "She's a cold-blooded killer. I see it in her eyes. You can't expect to walk up to her and have a civilized conversation."

"Has anyone even tried—" I started, but Fisher shook her head.

"You don't get it," she continued. She leaned in closer and glanced from side to side as if on the verge of telling me the world's biggest secret. "Rumor has it she killed three kids in a parking lot because they were standing too close to her car."

My eyes went big. I could understand murder driven by intense emotion—though there was never any excuse for murder—but kids? That was crossing a whole new line.

I didn't reflect on this too much. Deep down, I was only trying to make myself feel better by making Hawkins out to be some horrible monster who was worse than me.

"Yeah," Fisher went on, her horrified face matching mine. "The bitch is crazy. And it doesn't stop there. Apparently, she killed another three women in prison. It's like they kept her in gen pop to help control the population when she should have gone to the hole."

"I 'eard it was four women," Flander chimed in.

"Me too," came Biggie's deep voice.

"What hole?" I asked, and I felt stupid when Fisher's eyelids went flat.

"The SHU," she said.

What the hell was she talking about?

She smirked, and this time, it wasn't demeaning; she seemed amused.

"Sorry, Brone," she said. "I keep forgetting you never went to *real* prison."

I hated hearing that. Sure, I hadn't been surrounded by thick concrete walls, but I was trapped on an island surrounded by nothing but water. In my opinion, though my opinion didn't count, this was worse.

"It's seg, short for segregation unit," Fisher explained. "Some people call it solitary confinement. There's a ton of other names for it, but in short, you're stuck in a box without any human contact for God knows how long. And I'm not exaggerating, either. Twenty-three hours of your day are spent alone with your thoughts. You get fed through a hatch in a door. They're supposed to give you an hour of exercise time and fresh air every day, but we all know how corrupt prisons are." She let out a forced laugh as if I was supposed to know what she was talking about.

How could I? I was convicted at eighteen years old. I didn't know anything about prisons other than what I'd seen on television or read on the news. "You lose track of time," she continued. "It honestly makes you feel like you're going insane, but then you can't even be sure since no one's around. You don't even know what's normal and what isn't anymore."

She sucked in a long breath and looked away. It was evident that she'd experienced the *hole* before. She'd probably never talk about it, though. Fisher rarely ever opened up to anyone. Surprisingly, she'd once told me how she'd ended up here, on Kormace Island, which had been the result of her shooting a cop's kid for selling drugs on her gang's corner. In her defense, she hadn't known it was a cop's kid, but that didn't make the murder any less of a murder.

When she'd told me the story, I remembered not knowing whether to feel sorry for her or frightened by her. She hadn't seemed remorseful at all, which made me wonder what else she'd done in her past that she'd never talked about.

My eyes shifted toward shore at the shark. The women who were dragging it across the sand struggled, but surprisingly, with twelve of them holding on to whatever they could, they weren't having *that* hard of a time.

"What kind of shark is that?" I asked as if Fisher

were suddenly an ichthyologist.

She cocked an eyebrow at me, which translated to, *How the hell should I know?*

"Bull shark," came Proxy's voice. She stuck a bony finger in the air like she always did when she had some nerdy, though admittedly interesting comment to make. "Everyone's afraid of Great Whites, but in reality, bull sharks tend to be more dangerous. They have been nicknamed 'pit bull of the sea' due to their aggressive nature, which doesn't make all that much sense to me. Pit bulls aren't inherently aggressive... In the early twentieth century, pit bulls were revered as military heroes and family dogs. It isn't often they're used as guard dogs. They love people far too much for that." She rubbed her chin and stared at the sky. "I digress. Bull sharks. Their blood salt concentration sits at fifty percent, which means they're entirely capable of switching between salt water and fresh water. They've been seen in lakes and rivers many times before."

Johnson rolled her eyes as if to say, *Here we go again*, but no one interrupted Proxy—either because she was rambling too fast for anyone to get a word in or because what she was saying was actually interesting.

"Adults, which are fully mature at ten years of age, can measure up to eleven feet and can weigh as much as six hundred and sixty pounds. There's a lot of debate around the average lifespan, but one thing's certain: females typically outlive the males by several years."

Biggie slapped Flander's shoulder, and a loud crack resonated around us. She glowered at Biggie, her gray hair wiggling above her matching eyebrows, but all Biggie did was let out her usual deep belly laugh and say, "Makes sense to me! Women are smarter, so it'd make sense that they live longer!"

Johnson forced a laugh and shook her head. "That's completely sexist."

Biggie made a *pffft* sound with her thick lips and eyed Johnson from top to bottom. "Girl, whose side you on?"

"On the side that misses dick," Johnson said, smacking the insides of her thighs.

Hammer slapped herself on the forehead, obviously tired of penis jokes. "Well, you're better off becoming a lesbian since you won't be getting any of that anytime soon. Not unless you make your own with something around here..." She twirled her finger by her face.

"There are long rocks in the water," Rocket said, pointing a finger toward shore. She pulled on her wrist, holding it flat against her chest, and looked away as if she'd revealed a dirty secret.

This time, Flander was the one to swing her arm. The blow landed on Rocket's shoulder, and

Rocket let out a loud *oomph* sound.

"No need to be a perv about it," Flander said.

Rocket stared at her as though she were a high school kid staring at an overly strict teacher roaming the halls during break time; it was a look that said, *Why are you such a downer?*

"Will you guys shut up?" Fisher said. She plucked at a long, curling eyebrow over her right eye, examined it, then rubbed her fingers together until it disappeared in the wind.

"Oh God," Flander said, feeling along her neck under her chin. "What I wouldn't do for a pair o' tweezers..." She pinched at her skin over and over again but frowned every time she brought her fingers at eye level. "Can never get the stray bastards..."

"Tweezers?" Biggie blurted, spreading her legs apart. She pulled at some of the material over her groin area and peaked inside. "How 'bout a damn razor?"

Coin, who was sitting directly beside her, chuckled and revealed her golden tooth. "Girl, forget razors. I need a damn lawnmower."

Biggie burst out laughing so hard that my shoulders jerked forward. I hated when she did that, but at the same time, I loved it because every time she did, it made me want to laugh, too. Well, after my anxiety had passed. Her laugh was contagious, and I'd missed it even more than I'd remembered.

Coin, seemingly proud of her joke and happy at having made a new friend, elevated her chin and grinned from ear to ear.

"Speak for yourself, chicas," Arenas cut in. "I need me a fuckin' ridin' lawnmower." She clapped once and laughed out loud, but no one else joined in.

"That would kill you," Biggie said, matter-of-factly.

Arenas kept laughing, though it was obvious she was forcing it now.

I almost chuckled at how idiotic her joke had been when someone cleared their throat. It was as if the invisible bubble around us—around our familiar circle—suddenly popped, reminding us that we weren't alone. Masses of women sat nearby, some listening to our conversation, others relaxing in the sand.

Jack stood behind Arenas with two hands planted on her waist and a prideful look on her face—the one that said, *What's next and how can I help?*

I looked at her but didn't say anything until she must have realized I was waiting for her to talk.

"Er—sorry for interrupting." Her gaze shifted back and forth. "Was wonderin' if we were goin' to find that Quinn lady."

I was tempted to say, "Were you not paying

attention earlier?" but I kept my mouth shut. There was a good chance she hadn't overheard us when Aisha said she wasn't taking us anywhere—not until there was peace at the Cove.

"Sorry, Jack," I said. "We aren't going anywhere yet. Could be a few days."

She curled her upper lip over her rotten teeth. "What? A few days?"

"That's what she said." Fisher stuck her square chin out at Jack.

Jack's jaw muscles popped out and she glared down at Fisher, apparently ready to hold an aggressive staring contest. But it didn't seem to intimidate Fisher at all; she simply stared back, never blinking.

"Thanks for offering to help," I told Jack, and the grin on her face came back instantly. She gave me a brief bow of the head and walked away backward.

"You need to put a leash on that thing," Fisher said the moment Jack disappeared into the sea cave.

How was I supposed to respond to that? Jack was a loose cannon, but I had no idea what to do with her, and I was too worn down to figure it out.

"Hey," came Ellie's voice.

She walked through a circle of women tearing a fish apart—obviously a cherished prize they'd spent hours trying to catch in the ocean—and stood beside me.

"Hey," I breathed, admiring her beauty.

"You got a second?" she asked.

I jumped to my feet and moved away from the dozens of voices shouting over one another.

"What's going on?" I asked, reaching for her shoulder. "Is everything okay?"

She lit up, making me want to press my lips against hers.

"I wanna show you something," she said.

CHAPTER 4

Her laughter carried across the sea cave's walls, disappearing into the darkness up ahead.

How deep was this thing? A few women, some injured and others undoubtedly exhausted, lay on beds of leaves across the smooth rock platform. Farther ahead and past the cave's sleeping area, the platform narrowed along the water to expand across most of the cave.

When first being introduced to the sleeping area, I'd been a bit uneasy about the water beside me. It was a ten-foot drop alongside the sleeping area, and the water had appeared dark blue in the evening, which freaked me out—I didn't much appreciate water inside of caves.

Ever since I was a little girl, I believed that caves were where crocodiles lived. The fear was completely irrational, and I wasn't even certain how it had manifested, but I'd never gotten over it. Now that morning had come, the water was a clear turquoise, which came as a relief.

There were no crocodiles.

"Where are you taking me?" I asked, my voice

carrying down the cave.

Ellie turned around, smirked, and planted a silencing finger over her thick red lips. At the same time, someone rolled over in their bed of leaves and moaned, "Shut up."

The light from the cave's entrance seemed to diminish as we moved forward, but I could see as well as I had when I'd first entered the cave. This was in part due to the beige limestone walls surrounding us—the holey texture extended out from the water and all the way up to the ceiling, where it dripped downward, frozen in place. It looked as though a fire had caused the limestone to melt and then dry before dripping into the water.

It was the strangest thing I'd ever seen, but there was something so captivating about it.

"Come on," Ellie whispered, and we snuck around a bend, where the platform, now no wider than three feet, continued down the cave.

I kept my back to the wall and stared at the water below, which was slowly darkening as we moved deeper into the cave. The air, too, became cool and damp. I sucked in a deep breath, prepared to smell must or rot, given the look of the walls, but surprisingly, the air sliding through my nostrils was clean and crisp.

So clean, in fact, that I opened my mouth to take in another breath.

"How far are we going?" I asked.

She reached back and gently squeezed my wrist, no doubt sensing my anxiety.

"It'll be worth it," she said. "You'll see."

How was anything hidden within the depths of a dark cave *worth* seeing if you couldn't even see it? It was also hard to be optimistic about her surprise given that no one else was down here. Surely, there was a reason for that, but I didn't voice my concern. She looked so excited to be taking me to this secret place of hers that I didn't want to ruin it.

She suddenly stopped walking and I bumped into her.

"Whoa," I said, gripping two hands around her shoulders.

The last thing I wanted to do was knock her into the water. I glanced down again, swallowing hard. The clear turquoise water had turned a deep blue, and panic engulfed me.

She crouched down and reached for something in the water.

"What're you doing?" I hissed.

She swung her head around, pulled her hair from one shoulder to the other, and stared at me.

"You were held captive by the Northers and you survived. Why're you acting like such a little wimp?"

I bit my bottom lip. She was right, but phobias

weren't rational fears. How was I supposed to explain to her that all I kept envisioning was a crocodile lunging out from the murky water, its jaw wide open? And now that I'd seen it happen in real life, I was even more afraid. Crocodiles lived on the island.

"Look, can you tell me where you're taking me? I don't like..." I sighed and looked down at my toes. "I don't like dark cave water, okay?"

Without saying a word, she returned her attention to whatever she was reaching for.

"Get over here," she said playfully. I took a step forward but then realized she wasn't talking to me. "Gotcha!"

What was she doing?

Then, in one swift movement, she slid her legs out in front of her and jumped off the ledge.

"Ellie!" My voice echoed down the cave.

Her head popped back up. "Relax. The drop's only a few feet here." She beamed proudly. "Besides, I have a raft."

"A raft?"

Sticking my head out over the ledge, I noticed Ellie hadn't plunged herself into the water. Instead, she stood on a solid-looking raft with a paddle in her grip.

"You coming, or what?"

I nearly started ranting about how ridiculous this was, and how I had no interest in being taken down a poorly lit cave over dark water that looked like oil spilling through the cracks of her raft. But then, instead of looking at the water and instead of focusing on my fear of it, I stared at Ellie.

There was something so calming about her chocolate-colored eyes. She looked back at me, and without saying a word, tilted her head sideways as if to say, *Come on, Brone. I want to share something special with you. I wouldn't put you in harm's way.*

Swallowing my childish fear, I sat down and slid my butt close to the edge. She reached a firm arm out to help me down, and I instinctively let out a grunt when my bare toes touched the water.

"You're okay," she said, planting a firm kiss on my neck. "I've got you."

Despite the cool air around me, I immediately felt warm. How was it that I, fearless Hunter and savior to hundreds of women, cowered in the darkness? I felt stupid not only for being so anxious but also for having Ellie comfort *me*. I was supposed to be the one who protected *her*, wasn't I?

I let out a long breath, safe in her arms.

"You don't have to be so badass all the time," she said as if having entered my mind. "Remember when you first landed here? You were such a helpless little girl."

"I wasn't a little girl," I said, but I let out a soft

laugh. She was right, though I didn't want to admit it.

I'd been terrified beyond belief, weak, and vulnerable in every sense of the word. Although I wasn't Lydia anymore, I was still human—having doubts and fears were part of the package.

When her warm fingers came slipping through the cracks of mine, I softened even. She offered one last smile, and said, "Hang on," before grabbing the paddle and dipping it into the water.

It disappeared entirely from sight, and she pulled back, causing the raft to shift and float away from the safety of the platform I'd been standing on only seconds ago. The thought of jumping back to the platform became appealing, but instead, I focused on the hot skin of my fingers where she'd held on, and my nerves relaxed.

I could do this.

It wasn't that big of a deal.

"Close your eyes," she said.

I did the exact opposite and bulged them out at her. Was she insane?

She chuckled. "Close your eyes."

Inhaling a lungful of air, I carefully knelt on the platform, wetting my knees and shins, but I didn't care. I preferred not to be standing if I was going to become temporarily blind.

"Okay," I said, sealing them shut and planting both hands on the raft's wood for additional support.

She continued to paddle through the cave's water, one gentle stride at a time. Though it may have lasted all of two minutes, it seemed like an hour thanks to my overly imaginative brain picturing crocodiles circling the raft, the lumps on their heads and backs blending with the black water beneath us.

But then, behind closed eyelids, I saw light. At first, the skin of my lids appeared blue, then yellow, until I couldn't contain my curiosity. I shot my eyes open and stopped breathing.

The water, a rich turquoise-colored pool, took on the shape of a giant egg through the open space. Above us sat a large opening through which hundreds of vines decorated the hole's border and descended down its walls. They reached so far down that most of the limestone remained hidden behind thick greenery. I craned my neck even farther, spotting the bright blue sky. The sunlight beamed down through the opening, creating a yellow cylinder of brightness. It poured through the inside of the cave and all the way into the bottom of the water.

I stared, mesmerized by the sun's effect at the center of the pool; the water, a vivid green color, was like a sheet of crystal—blue and turquoise lines waved the surface, making me want to plunge right in.

"You can open your eyes," she said, staring at me with a grin on her face.

I parted my lips, but nothing came out.

For the first time in a long time, I was at peace. It was as if nothing beyond this miracle of a cave mattered—not the Northers, not Hawkins, nothing.

Then, without saying a word, Ellie slipped off her top, revealing perfectly shaped breasts and a flat stomach, across which ran a straight line between her abdominal muscles.

When she caught me staring, I averted my gaze, embarrassed for having looked in the first place.

"It's just skin," she said, slipping her bottoms off.

I cleared my throat and continued to stare at the water.

Suddenly, the raft shifted and water splashed on my face. I swung both arms in the air to maintain my balance before Ellie resurfaced, her dark wavy hair sticking to her bare shoulders. She blinked, spat out a mouthful of water, and smacked her lips together.

"You coming, or what?"

Without giving it too much though, I took off my clothes and dived in headfirst, the water so smooth it felt like therapeutic oil sliding on my skin. She spat out another mouthful, this time, directly at me.

"Hey!" I said.

"Hey, yourself."

I'd been about to scoop up water in my mouth to give her a taste of her own medicine when she grabbed my arm and pulled me toward her. The water between us parted as if by magic, and she pressed her body against mine.

She felt like silk—warm, freshly cleaned silk so soft I stopped treading water.

"Whoa," she said, catching me before my head dipped underwater.

She kicked harder to keep us both afloat until I started treading again, my thighs gliding against hers as we moved almost choreographically.

"Thanks for saving my life," she said, her breath perfume inside my nostrils.

"No problem, but you owe me," I said, and before she had the time to laugh at my response, I pulled her in even tighter against my body and kissed her hard.

CHAPTER 5

"Get the fuck up!" someone shouted from the other end of the Cove, making me wish I'd stayed a bit longer inside the sea cave with Ellie.

After the moment I'd shared with Ellie, all I wanted to do was sit by her side and bask in the warmth of the afternoon sun like a lustful character out of a cheesy romance story.

Women scrambled from left to right as two from Hawkins's group came marching through a crowd. It was easy to tell they were her people: shoulders drawn back with pride, hunting spears strapped to their backs, and wooden plates worn around their wrists and shins. The sight was enough to make me roll my eyes.

These two, unlike Hawkins, weren't wearing a chest plate. Assumedly, those were reserved for Hawkins and a few of her elites only.

"What're you doing?" someone shouted.

"Lacy here lost her necklace," said the thicker of the two, sticking a thumb out at her sidekick. She leaned forward and glowered at the woman who'd confronted her. "That means one of you bitches stole it."

Were these bullies Murk's women? If so, how'd they turn out so awful? Murk had always encouraged peace and collaboration. I supposed it was like a teenager turning to drugs and cigarettes despite their parents being overly kind, honest, religious folk.

The two bullies towered over their victims— three young Caucasian women sitting in a circle, sewing cotton or hemp together to form clothing and blankets. They kicked sand into the air and raised threatening fists, while the three women lifted their arms above their heads, trying to dodge any physical violence.

"We didn't take anything!" the youngest looking of the three shouted. She raised her hands even higher, prepared to take a blow for having talked back to Hawkins's women.

The thicker and more aggressive of the two bullies didn't seem to care what this woman had to say. She ignored her and started rummaging through crates made of thin wood and piles of freshly sewn blankets.

A loud cracking noise filled the air when she kicked two crates, sending them flying through the air and against the hard surface of the cliff's rocky wall.

"Hey!"

"Stop it!"

When the bullies realized they weren't finding what they were looking for, they went on to the next group of nearby women—six Asian women of different ages gathered in a circle, heads bowed, backs rounded, and brows furrowed in concentration. At first glance, it appeared they were playing with their own fingers, but then one of them reached into a wooden crate beside her thigh, extracted dry leaves, then opened a small sachet. Were they making tea bags?

The thick bully came in without warning and kicked her booted foot straight at the crate full of loose tea. It rolled several times, and dry leaves flew everywhere, landing sporadically in the sand.

"The fuck!" said one of the Asian women. She hopped to her feet, her stick legs looking like nothing more than toothpicks under her waist. Though she was incredibly small, she didn't seem intimidated by the bully.

The women sitting directly next to her, however, continued sprinkling tea leaves into a sachet, clearly wanting nothing to do with the altercation. She appeared older than the rest of them, perhaps in her late sixties, and it appeared she was the one teaching everyone else how to bag tea.

"Sit down," snarled the bully. She shoved the confrontational Asian woman so hard she fell back onto her friends and onto the elderly woman who squinted so hard in pain, her eyes seemed to disappear from her face.

I couldn't sit around and watch this. Why wasn't anyone else doing something? Dozens upon dozens of women stared silently from their posts like a bunch of spineless cowards.

Fisher placed a firm hand on my knee. Most likely she'd felt me tense up. "Don't. It isn't your business."

"You're gonna let them do whatever they want?" I asked. "They're bullies."

Biggie leaned back against the cliff wall and several pieces of rebel rolled off her shoulder. "Yeah, Brone. Better get used to it. They're always like that."

Was I in some sort of twilight zone? The idea that people could go around hurting others without any form of consequence was absurd. Weren't the women of the Cove growing tired of being treated like second-class citizens? No one deserved to be treated like an inferior being—not even these criminals.

They were *always* like that, I repeated in my mind. That wasn't a reason to allow it to continue. Could I be the one to put an end to it, or was I delusional? Probably delusional.

Escaping the Northers was likely getting to my head. I'd done something no one had managed to do in years, if at all.

Did that make me special? In a sense it did, though at the same time, it didn't. I wasn't invincible; it was only a matter of time before my luck ran out.

But I realized something else: had I been complacent when enslaved by the Northers, I wouldn't have ended up here at the Cove. Despite everything telling me to shut my mouth and keep my head low, I hadn't been able to sit around and do nothing.

Though I fought with myself to dismiss the subtle arrogance growing within me, I couldn't help but feel stronger and more capable than several of these women combined.

I talked back to Zsasz even though I knew it could have gotten me killed.

I didn't bow when Rainer stepped out into the city.

I somehow got out of a death battle more than once.

I was stronger than I gave myself credit for, and if I didn't use this strength, then I was no better than all these women staring mindlessly at the altercation before them.

As I glared toward the Hawkins women, I wanted nothing more than to launch two arrows into their chests. It was nothing more than a hateful fantasy. In reality, I'd never do that. I wasn't like Hawkins, a cold-blooded murderer. I'd do what I had to protect myself and my friends, but I wouldn't take someone's life simply because of interpersonal conflict.

Shoving Fisher's hand off my knee, I jumped up, my toes sliding in the cool sand.

"Brone?" came Ellie's voice. She was emerging from the sea cave, a crate of freshly cut fruit in her arms.

I glanced back at her as sweetly as possible. She hated it when I put myself in danger, but I'd be fine. I bent down and plucked my bow and quiver full of arrows out from underneath Johnson's legs. She tried to say something along the lines of "What're you doing?" but I didn't stick around long enough to hear the full sentence.

Voices erupted around me—from the shoreline, by the cliff wall, and from the center of the Cove, where handfuls of women continued to sit in the sand, working with building material and attempting to crack nuts.

The two bullies went on to make their way to the next group—eight black women, most with hair as poufy as their heads and bodies of different shapes, sizes, and skin tones. One of them was nearly as large as Biggie, and the smallest of them even shorter than Rocket. It looked like they were carving fishing spears, though I couldn't be sure. The moment they saw Hawkins's women approach, they tapped each other's shoulders and pointed in their direction.

"Look who's comin'," one of them said.

All at once, the eight women got up so slowly they looked irritated at being forced to stand their ground. Shoulders drawn back, they faced their bullies.

"What's this bullshit about Lacy losin' somethin'?" asked the woman standing in the middle. Her skin was as black as night, and it glistened under the sun like dark-stained wood coated with a high-gloss finish.

"Don't make this harder than it has to be," said the smaller of Hawkins's women. She hadn't said a word up until then, and it was apparent that she was at least as feisty as her thicker counterpart. She reminded me of a neo-Nazi: her head was shaved, and though I couldn't know for sure, something about her arrogant stance and condescending scowl made her look racist. She stared at the group of black women as if they were nothing more than fish carcasses left to rot on the shore.

"What's going on here?" I asked, finally reaching the crowd.

The black woman at the farthest right of the group—the one I was now standing directly beside—examined me closely and sucked on her upper teeth. "What you want, white girl?"

"White girl?" I said, fighting the urge to get

375

defensive. "I'm on your side."

"Yo, fuck off," said another woman.

What was going on? I was trying to help, and now, they were turning against me.

"Think you can come here with all your white bitches and take over? That it?" asked the tallest of the group. She stomped toward me, and I suddenly wished I had Biggie by my side.

Why was there so much racism at the Cove? How had this happened? How had all these women turned on each other because of something like skin color? It was so archaic, and there was no need for it. God, I missed Murk. She hadn't tolerated racial segregation.

"Look," I said, sticking to open palms on either side of my face. "I thought you guys were in trouble, and I was coming to help. That's it."

One of them made her eyes go huge and swayed her head from side to side. "Does it look like we need your help?"

"I'm not saying you do—" I tried.

"So mind your own fuckin' business," growled another.

What the hell was this? They were all turning on me, and Hawkins's women stood behind them, smirking smugly.

"All right," I said, and although I should have turned around and walked away without saying a word, I was too angry to keep my mouth shut. "Be a bunch of fucking animals for all I care. People like you are the reason this place is so goddamn miserable. We'll never survive like this."

I swung around and started marching back, fuming inside.

Who did they think they were? God, I hated women like that. Why couldn't they be civilized?

"People like you?" came a slow, calculated voice—I couldn't see who'd spoken, but if I'd had to guess what sort of face she was making, it would have been one with a forehead full of frown rolls, narrow eyes, and lips curled up as if preparing to let out a snarl.

Shit.

I hadn't meant it as a racist comment, but I realized then how it could be perceived. Before I could turn around to apologize and explain myself, something hard knocked me in the side of the head. I fell to the sand, my ears ringing, and when I looked up, a dark foot came straight at my face.

Something cracked, and my vision went blurry. Fortunately, the sand provided some cushion to the back of my head, but my face hadn't been so lucky.

"Hey!" someone shouted in the distance.

Someone kicked me in the stomach, knocking the wind right out of me.

"Hey!" the voice shouted again.

This time, several voices joined in, and the

sound of footsteps began storming across the shore. I rolled to my side, away from my attacker, and the first face I saw was Jack's. She came running at full speed with a huge rock in her right hand. Her short, gray-striped hair went flat on her head as she ran through the wind, and her rotten teeth were like century-old river stones covered in moss.

"Fucking bitches!" she shouted, sand kicking up higher than her scabby knees.

Behind her, dozens of women came stampeding along with her like Romans in an ancient war, but they weren't the ones who scared me; Jack was. Her lumpy brows and demonic features made it seem as though she was ready to smash in as many heads as necessary to protect me.

CHAPTER 6

Bone colliding with bone—a sound I'd become all too familiar with—resonated around me. I couldn't tell where the blows were coming from. Closed fists flew and neither side was backing down.

"You motherfucker!" came Jack's voice.

I rolled sideways once more, grains of sand sticking to the inside of my bottom lip, and got up with a grunt. The taste of blood lingered in my mouth, though I couldn't determine the source of it. I licked the smooth inside of my cheeks, my teeth, and even the roof of my mouth. The pain followed with every movement I made, which meant I'd bitten my tongue on my way down.

"Stop it. You're killing her!" someone shouted.

Jack.

Straddled on top of one of the black women, she swung both fists as hard as she could, the sound of cartilage clicking and crunching with every hit. The woman beneath her lay motionless in a lumpy bed of bloody sand, her body jerking with every blow.

But Jack wasn't stopping. Her face was so red

and her eyes so big that she didn't appear human anymore. She had the appearance of an extraterrestrial being wearing its victim's skin to pass for a human: jiggling skin, an upside-down grimace that took up half her face, an expression that made me fear for my own life even though she was actually defending it.

"Whoa, whoa," came Biggie's voice. She rushed behind Jack, looking three times her size, and waving in a panic grabbed her from underneath her arms.

"You mother fuckin' piece o' shit sugar stick fuckin' cock suckin'..." Jack shouted, still trying to take swings at the motionless woman in the sand. And it didn't stop there. She let out other disturbing curse words I'd never heard before, like dinosaur asshole, bile drinker, and beer bottle fucker.

Where did she come up with that?

Then, it was as if everyone had realized how bad the fight was getting and that sides didn't matter anymore. In the end, none of us wanted to die—not over something like this. Biggie wrapped one arm around Jack's neck and another behind her shoulders, something I'd seen Proxy do before to knock someone out.

"Piece o'... Fuck..." Jack tried, but her eyes rolled in the back of her head. She clawed at Biggie's arm, but Biggie wasn't budging and held on to Jack so tightly her knuckles turned a creamy white. Had Biggie not been twice the size of Jack, she could have pulled her down onto the sand and wrapped her legs around Jack's torso for maximum control.

And we all stared, waiting for Jack to pass out. Some women held others by the collars of their shirts, but no one swung any closed fists. It was as if someone had pressed pause on everything.

Biggie's chokehold may have lasted a total of five to ten seconds, but it felt like forever. Finally, Jack went limp and Biggie slowly placed her onto the sand.

"That your girl?" shouted one of the black women, her glare landing on me.

Then, as if someone hit the play button, everyone started yelling at each other again.

Jack wasn't out for long. Slowly, she turned to her side, scratched the top of her head, and sat upright in the middle of the argument. She wiped dark beige sand from her cheek and looked up at me as if trying to understand what had happened.

But I didn't have the time to explain to her that she'd only needed a time-out.

The one who'd yelled at me—a slender black woman with cornrows, plush pink lips, and perfectly shaped eyebrows, dropped to her knees beside her friend and began gently tapping her on the cheek.

"Dez, come on girl, wake up," she said. She was so thin that the vertebrae of her spine protruded from her rounded back, and her shoulder blades resembled wiggling baby bird wings as she tried to wake her friend. "Come on, wake up."

No one moved, and we all stood in a circle, waiting to see what would happen with Dez.

When nothing happened, the slender woman's menacing glare turned on us as if an evil force possessed her. Her thick bottom lip drooped, saliva collecting along its edge, and her eyes were so bloodshot it was difficult to differentiate the iris from the whites of her eyes.

"You," she snarled, her gaze now shifting to Jack.

Jack rubbed the back of her head, then twirled twice on the spot while slapping her hair. Bits of sand sprinkled onto her shoulders, and she smacked it off, too. When she realized we were all staring at her, she stiffened up and glanced back and forth. "What?" she said. "What're you all lookin' at? Is it that bad? Is there more?" She twirled again and again and went on to slap her lower back and her thighs so aggressively I wondered if she thought sand carried disease-causing bacteria.

Did she not remember what she'd done? Had she blacked out? Though it frightened me to know we had a woman among us capable of murdering someone and not even remembering it, a part of me felt bad for her. She was utterly clueless and confused as to why our enemies were staring at her with such hate.

Then, it was like a second personality took her over. Her curly-haired brows came together and she stomped her way over to me in the sand. "Did I miss something, Brone? Are these women givin' you a hard time?" She swung her head at our enemies. "'Cause if they are, I swear to God, I'll fuckin' slice 'em up—"

"No," I said, not wanting to aggravate the situation any further. "It's fine, Jack. We were just leaving."

The slender black woman stood up, her birdlike shoulders drawn back in an attempt to make herself look bigger, though it didn't work. "Leaving?" she repeated. "You think you're off the hook?"

"Girl, calm your damn pom-pom," Biggie said. This time, she was the one to come stomping toward me, the dozens of silver loops on her ears dancing with her movements. Biggie was the most smiley of the group, but right then, even I felt intimidated by her. She was scowling so hard that little bumps formed on her chin and thick rolls formed on her forehead. "Your girl ain't dead— she's unconscious." She pointed at the woman who lay still on the sand. "I can see her damn chest movin' up and down."

The slender woman didn't seem too impressed by Biggie's sense of observation. "Well, she isn't moving!"

Beside her, a short, stubby-limbed woman with fuzzy hair and skin as black as night stepped out like a bulldog, chest heaving and wide lower jaw pulled out farther than her upper teeth. She looked like a complete moron, but I supposed the anger had gotten the best of her, and she wasn't thinking about the face she was making.

"She ain't movin'!" said the bulldog-looking one. "And it's your fault!" she jabbed a fat finger toward Jack.

"My fault?" Jack pointed at herself. But then she caught a glimpse of something on her hand and looked down where rust-colored blood coated her pointed knuckles. "Oh," she said casually.

All at once, the entire group of black women started moving forward, fists clenched and eyes that stuck out so much they looked like wet, oversized cotton balls.

Despite having an entire crew of angry women coming toward us, I couldn't help but look over the slender one's shoulder and back at Hawkins's women. They stood with arms crossed loosely over their chests and smirks on their ugly faces. They were loving this. And why wouldn't they be? We'd taken the heat off them, and now, they were enjoying the show.

"Maybe you should be focusing on the real problem," I said, pointing an accusatory finger at the two bullies.

The slender woman, apparently the leader of the gang, curled her lip over her yellow upper teeth. If there hadn't been so many voices erupting around me, I might have heard a hiss escape her mouth. But despite her probable desire to murder me, my words seemed to resonate. She glanced back at Hawkins's women and then at me.

"I came here to help you," I said. "We have nothing against you. This whole thing's a complete misunderstanding."

They weren't buying it. Most offered looks full of attitude—ones that said, *Bitch, please*—while the others glared at me as if I were the reason they'd ended up on this island to begin with.

I couldn't understand why they held on to so much hatred. Though it frustrated me beyond belief, no doubt there was a reason for it.

"Look," I added. "I'm not asking you guys to be our best friends. You can go on living however it is you're living here. But I don't understand why these two idiots"—I pointed an open hand at the bullies behind them, whose grins suddenly vanished from their faces—"can go around accusing people of stealing their things. They're causing unnecessary conflict. We don't all have to be friends. There's nothing wrong with that. But do you enjoy living in a place where people are always trying to cause fights?"

Several exchanged glances, the hardness on their faces disappearing. Was I getting through to them? Was my reasoning sinking in?

"Stupid girl is right," said the slender one. She stood up, her head sticking up higher than anyone else's, and played with the red beaded necklace she wore. It appeared constructed of painted wood carved into small balls. That's when I noticed that most of them wore wooden jewelry of sorts— beaded bracelets, large gauge earrings, and even cylinder-shaped bits dangling from their woolly braided hair.

I wasn't sure where they were obtaining the color to decorate the wood, but it wasn't the first time I'd seen painted wood on Kormace Island. I looked to the back of the Cove and at the base of the cliff, where partially built cabins sat in the sand reminding me of a construction site. Planks of weathered wood, obviously taken from fallen trees, were laid out in a perfect square. The cabin on the far right had one wall up, but that was it. I hadn't seen anyone work on them since we'd arrived, most likely because they didn't have adequate resources or the required expertise.

In front of these partial cabins were wooden stakes jabbed into little hills of sand. They were painted yellow and stood out against the dark gray wood. Flags of cotton hung loosely at the wood's highest point. Did this represent something? Perhaps it was one's way of claiming the territory.

"You," said the slender woman, and I refocused my attention toward where she was pointing—at the two bullies. "Get out of here before this ends badly."

The taller bully scoffed and planted a white-knuckled fist on her waist. Her lips, which had once formed a contemptuous smile, now drooped upside down as if the result of severe nausea.

"You think you're getting away with theft?" Her shoulders expanded with every breath. She was apparently the type who wasn't afraid to fight or take a beating for that matter—like she'd been through hundreds of fights before, which she probably had. One of her front teeth was chipped and her left ear, which I assumed was once decorated by a looped earing, had a long scar on the lobe most likely the result of tearing. It had surely once hung in two parts but over the years had fused itself back together.

Lacy, the shorter of the two bullies, pulled her hair back behind her neck, giving off the appearance of a mullet—something Mom said made a reappearance in the 2040s—and sucked on her teeth. She reached behind her belt and extracted a blade so short it was a wonder how she even held on to it.

"We can go the easy way or the hard way," she said, her foul smile returning.

All at once, voices exploded around me, and I couldn't tell who was shouting at who. Part of me wanted to throw both arms in the air as a way of saying, *Forget this*, but the other part felt responsible for the fight. Maybe if I'd minded my own business, things wouldn't have escalated this far.

"Thought ya said she was dead!" shouted Jack, pointing a stubby finger at Dez.

Dez slowly sat up in a daze. Her nose, now a flat mess of black and red, barely resembled a nose at all. There was no doubt Jack had broken it in more than one spot. Two of her top teeth were missing, which was probably the reason Jack's knuckles were so bloody, and her right eye was swelling so fast it was taking over half her face.

Poor woman.

I swallowed past a lump in my throat. How awful—not only because of her pain but also the disfigurement Jack had caused.

It was my fault.

Lacy, the short bully with the tiny shiv in her hand, leaped forward with her teeth clenched so tight that her overbite caused her bottom lip to disappear. But she didn't have the time to swing her weapons at anyone.

Out of nowhere, a stern, authoritative voice

carried over all of us. "Enough!"

It was so confident, so bold, that even I found myself curiously searching for the source. Everyone split apart, feet dragging in the sand. Behind them, Hawkins stood tall, the afternoon sun landing at the top of her head and making part of her already light hair look white.

"What the hell's going on here?" she said.

She reminded me of a strict, over-the-top mother who often found herself scolding not only her own kids, but all the kids in the neighborhood. Yet Hawkins was far more terrifying than a mother; a mother wouldn't kill you where you stood, whereas Hawkins would, undoubtedly, cut you to pieces without ever batting an eyelash.

And like an overbearing mother, she appeared inherently tired. The bags that sat underneath her eyes looked like they'd been there all her life, as did the few wrinkles forming on her temples. She still had a mesmerizing beauty about her, only, in a mature way.

A streak of blood stained her right forearm, reminding me of the life she'd taken only hours ago onshore.

The women bowed their heads and stepped back even farther. Their scowling faces indicated they weren't doing it out of respect but rather to avoid pissing her off.

So, this was the Cove's wannabe leader, I

thought.

CHAPTER 7

"What's the problem, Granger?" Hawkins asked, glancing sideways at the taller of her two bullies.

Dozens of her followers observed from a distance, weapons in hand as if prepared to attack with a click of Hawkins's fingers. Granger stuck a thumb out at her sidekick, Lacy. "Lacy here lost her necklace, and I reckon one of these bitches took it."

"You *reckon*, do you?" Hawkins asked, an eyebrow arching high on her forehead.

Granger cleared her throat and her face reddened. "We think it was them, Hawk."

Hawkins, now resembling a mediator, crossed her wood-plated arms over her belly. "Do you have proof?" She turned sideways to stare at Granger, the sound of wood rubbing against wood reminding me of an amateur version of the Northers' armor. Was that what it was? Armor? Why did she need armor if we were all meant to coexist here? As she turned, the sea trident tattoo on her neck stretched with her skin, and I couldn't help but get lost in the skull designs extending along with it.

Granger, apparently stunned by Hawkins's disapproving demeanor, stammered a few times before finally saying, "W-we don't know for sure, Hawk, but I mean, come on. Who else would it be?"

One of the black women raised a tight fist by her face, nostrils wide and shoulders pulled back. "The fuck is that supposed to mean?"

"Back off, dipshit," Lacy growled. She reminded me of someone too weak to fight her own battles—someone who always found a way to remain safe alongside a stronger ally. Every time she'd opened her mouth to insult someone, she had side-glanced Granger, and now, her gaze kept darting toward Hawkins.

"There was no reason for this," I said, and my face warmed the moment the words came out, but I couldn't make my mouth stop. "These ladies were minding their business"—I pointed at the group of black women who seemed a bit surprised that I was standing up for them against Hawkins—"and these two goofs decided to start trouble."

Why couldn't I shut up? God, what was wrong with me? I'd done the same thing when imprisoned by the Northers. Where had my filter gone?

Everyone went quiet, undoubtedly shocked by my forwardness with Hawkins. I bit down on my teeth, prepared to get the shit kicked out of me again, when Hawkins let out a laugh. It was rough sounding, like a smoker's laugh, but it seemed genuine.

She turned sideways again toward Granger and Lacy, her lips pressed together for a moment. "Goofs?"

I wasn't sure how to respond to that. The word had just come out. I hadn't put any thought into it and tried to use the least offensive word I knew. When Hawkins looked at me again, however, I realized that *goof* meant something I wasn't familiar with. Her gaze narrowed, and she searched me as if trying to understand how some *newbie* like me had the courage to say something like that.

"Why don't you mind your own business, dipshit?" Granger said. "What was your stupid name again? Brone? You look like a fuckin' bone."

Hawkins's face changed so quickly it was as if a mask had fallen off. The skin of her temples tightened, and her hairline fell back. Her amusement only moments ago disappeared and was replaced by a bite of her bottom lip. Why was she looking at me like that?

"Brone?" Hawkins said as if she'd spoken my name countless times before.

Although I didn't know her, I couldn't help but feel like she knew me.

She wiggled her fingers in the air, and without even looking at Granger or Lacy, she said, "You two, fuck off."

They both glowered at me but did as they were told, storming off in the sand like children, their shoulders slouched, spitting sharp words between them.

Hawkins stared at me, wincing. Was I in trouble, or was she simply interested in meeting me for the first time? Was this Rocket's doing? I'd seen the way her women had stared at me—almost starstruck. Had Hawkins also heard about what I'd done and everything I'd gone through?

"You're the heroic Archer," she said, and I nearly laughed in her face. I held it back, though; considering the way she stared at me, never blinking, she clearly believed it.

Heroic was a bit of an overstatement, and to be honest, I didn't like the sound of it. I'd killed my mom's boyfriend with a cast iron frying pan, ended up on some remote island, and now had become a cold-blooded killer only to stay alive.

That didn't merit the title of *hero*.

She must have sensed my unwillingness to agree with her because she straightened her stance and elevated her chin, the bun of her hair touching her upper back. "Come with me."

CHAPTER 8

"Brone, don't do it," Biggie hissed.

The way she leaned forward, the entire upper half of her body towering over the shorter women around her, she reminded me of a giraffe. They, too, seemed to agree that following Hawkins was a bad idea.

Hawkins turned her head sideways, having apparently heard Biggie, and smirked—a smile that most likely translated to, *You can either mind your own business or things are going to get really ugly, really fast.*

Despite Biggie's warning, and Jack's—who rushed up to me, the hairs of her head wiggling in every direction as she tried to convince me not to follow Hawkins—I couldn't deny my incessant need to hear what Hawkins had to say.

There was no arguing she was dangerous. I'd heard all the stories about how she'd killed women in prison and how she'd even killed women here. But so had I. That didn't make us equal, especially not on a moral level, but given she was asking to *talk* to me, it made her seem a bit less threatening.

Had Rainer been in her place, she'd have asked her cultist followers to tie me up somewhere.

Hawkins, however, seemed more rational than that even if she was incredibly dangerous.

I followed her as she led me away from the women at the center of the Cove and to the other side of the beach, glancing back only once to spot Ellie standing beside Proxy, a hand over her mouth.

Poor Ellie.

Hopefully, she didn't think I was purposely trying to put myself in harm's way. It wasn't fair to put her through this stress—not knowing when she might see me for the last time—but if I hoped to reunite the women of the Cove, I had to hear Hawkins out and try to reason with her.

Hawkins's women, most of them identifiable by their wooden accessories, didn't seem all that impressed when they saw me approach. Most of them glared at me, and not because of the morning sun, but undoubtedly because they didn't understand why Hawkins was bringing someone from the *outside* into her group.

"What's this?" asked one of her women, throwing her chin out at me.

Hawkins stuck a thumb out at me. "This is my ticket to this Rainer bitch everyone keeps talking about."

Hawkins made me feel like I was in an actual penitentiary—at least, the kind that everyone kept describing to me. I'd never spent much time in a real prison other than the few nights before my conviction, and even then, I was entirely isolated.

She was intimidating but not so much in a fear-for-my-life kind of way—not the way Rainer had made me feel. Maybe that would change as I got to know her, but from where I was standing, all I saw was a dangerous criminal—not a barbaric woman who'd spent the last twenty years of her life on Kormace Island.

When I first arrived on the island, Hawkins would have likely terrified me. But after everything I'd seen—the ruthless killings, the torturous sacrificial altars, Rainer's army—Hawkins seemed a bit amateur to me.

I'd never voice this aloud, however; surely, she wouldn't hesitate to kill me where I stood. But if Hawkins thought she could take on Rainer, the wannabe leader had no idea what she was getting herself into.

"Is that her?" someone whispered, leaning into a woman with a shaved head and an AOP-looking tattoo on her shoulder—a black circle with a large X on the inside.

I cringed.

AOP stood for Age of Progression, and every time I saw the symbol on television, Mom would make some comment about history repeating itself and something to do with Nazis.

* * *

"Nah-what now?" Melody asked, leaning forward on the couch to grab another handful of ketchup chips from the coffee table.

My mom slapped her forehead. "What on Earth are they teaching you kids in school?"

She looked around as if afraid that questioning the education system, which was in a sense questioning the president himself, would somehow lead to severe consequences. It might— if she was caught. Ever since Bill-1203 was passed, it became illegal to talk against or even question President Seth.

I'd thought this to be ridiculous, but I couldn't say anything. I'd seen a few kids taken out of school for telling the teacher they thought President Seth was a *dictating piece of shit*.

It wasn't long before people stopped insulting him.

"They don't teach us much," Melody said, and she lit up when she looked at me.

I hated that next year, I wouldn't have Melody in any of my classes. She made everything about school a little less dull. I hoped that after high school was over, we'd stay friends.

"Nothing on the Second World War?" my mom asked. She then shook her head and laughed. "Of course not. Age of Progression... More like Age of Regression. God forbid anyone stands up and says it like it is"—her eyes shifted toward the holographic television and she lowered her voice— "that anyone compares President Seth to Hitler."

"Who's Hitler?" Melody asked, and my mom's jaw hung so low that her entire neck disappeared. She then got up with a swing of her upper body and limped her way into her bedroom.

"Where's your mom going?" Melody asked.

I shrugged, though I had an idea. She was retrieving her copy of *Evil on Earth*, a historical novel written by Professor Maverick Nicolson about the Second World War, or more precisely, a deep look into Hitler's past and how he managed to lead countless soldiers to murder millions of Jewish people.

When I'd first read the book, I'd cried for three nights straight. I couldn't believe anything like that had happened. Yet when President Seth came on the television, I understood why Mom was so adamant about teaching me everything she knew about World War II. The new history books, the ones about the previous wars, didn't mention Hitler at all, which infuriated my mom.

President Seth had ordered the destruction of any historic written word. And then, of course, with the government having their noses all over what was tolerated on the internet, you couldn't find it there either.

Mom often referred to President Seth as a

reincarnation of Hitler, and I believed her.

How could one human being ruin the lives of so many?

* * *

As I stared at Hawkins, I thought of everything my mom taught me, even though Hawkins didn't come close to comparing to Hitler or President Seth.

But still, she was a symbol of leadership, which meant she held the power to affect the lives of those around her. And she was doing exactly that— the women around her admired her, and it was clear they were willing to do anything she asked, even if there was no reason for it.

Then, the woman with the AOP tattoo, obviously a crazy white supremacist, locked eyes with me. Was she trying to intimidate me? I was sick and tired of women trying to act tough around here. There was no need for it.

Another woman, one with poorly maintained dreadlocks pulled back into a high ponytail, wrapped stringy material around carved seashells, fastening them to long, smooth-looking bamboo stems to create arrows. It was apparent that all these women wanted to do was fight. I recognized a few faces from the Working Grounds, but I didn't know their names.

After everything Murk had taught them, how could they turn around and follow some new drop like Hawkins?

Another woman who appeared to be sharpening shells against large rocks gave me a dirty look and kept carving away. How well could they even shoot those things? Had they received proper training? I glanced back toward the Asian group, searching for Pin and Hamu—Murk's two other Archers who had trained by my side in the Working Grounds. Although I didn't expect to find them here, it still saddened me to think that they'd most likely perished in the Village flames.

"How's she going to help?" asked the woman with the AOP tattoo.

I hated her for even having it, but I'd have been stupid to vocalize it. For all I knew, Hawkins had a similar tattoo underneath her wooden armor.

"Have a seat," Hawkins suddenly said. Her voice was rough, yet oddly soothing at the same time. It was like she was trying to sound gentle for my sake, but it didn't come naturally to her. She pointed an open palm at a tree stump beside the AOP-tattooed woman.

Figuring it would be rude to decline the invitation, I sat down, feeling the AOP-tattooed woman's hatred seeping through her skin. She stared at me, but I didn't stare back—I wasn't in the mood for another altercation after what had happened.

"So, you're Brone," Hawkins said, nodding slowly with slits for eyes.

I cleared my throat. "Um, yeah, that's me."

She let out a forced laugh and patted me on the knee as if capable of reading my mind. It felt strained and awkward, especially since the women around her were still glaring at me. They reminded me of cranky old dogs around a new puppy. Hawkins was showing interest in me, and they hated it.

"We all know who you are, kid," she said.

Kid? Was that how she viewed me? Instantly, I felt inferior.

She leaned forward, her face alight with intrigue. "So, you survived Rainer. Also heard you sacrificed yourself to save your women. That takes balls, kid."

I winced on the inside.

What was she getting at? What did she want? I rubbed my palms together, not knowing what else to do with myself and shifted on my tree stump of a chair.

Then, she leaned back in her wooden chair, arms resting on what appeared to be armrests made of softwood and moist, intertwined branches. Someone had constructed a throne-like chair for her, and she was proud of it. It made her sit taller than all of us and was likely the sturdiest piece of furniture on the Cove.

"What?" she said, catching me eyeing her throne. "You like it? You want it?"

Was this some game? I knew what Hawkins was capable of. Despite her friendly attitude toward me at that moment, if I didn't give her what she wanted, she wouldn't hesitate to cut me down— literally.

I cleared my throat again. "No, thank you. I'm okay here."

She patted me hard on the knee and this time I flinched. "Come on, now. We're all friends. Ain't that right, ladies?"

She turned from side to side, the blond bun at the back of her head following along, and her women nodded.

"I like to share," she said, leaning back. She rubbed her chin and pointed her fingers toward the sky. "I believe in... What do you call it? Fairness? Equality? You scratch my back, I scratch yours?"

Although it was tempting to say, "Spit it out already," I needed to be patient. What did she want from me?

She crossed one leg over her knee and let her head rest against the back of her chair. "What's the matter, Brone? Cat got your tongue?"

"No," I said plainly. "I just I don't understand what I'm doing here."

Her laugh was so loud that my shoulders jerked forward. "Oh, she's funny." She pointed right at me. Her women smirked, but they appeared as confused as me. Then, Hawkins's smile disappeared, and she leaned closer, her feet slapping down on the sand in front of her. "You're a fuckin' murderer, Brone. That's why you're here. 'Cause you fuckin' killed someone."

Her dark gray eyes looked black underneath the shadows of her brows, and she stared at me as if she'd been possessed by something—as if some other soul had entered her body.

Was this the Hawkins Fisher had warned me about? The unpredictable, dangerous woman who reminded me of Jack in a sense, only, without any good intentions whatsoever?

"Collins," she said, still staring at me. She clicked her fingers without saying a word, and the woman with the AOP tattoo—Collins, I assumed—got up and disappeared behind a flimsy-looking curtain. It hung from a branch that stuck straight out from the cliff's wall as if it had grown that way for the sole purpose of providing shelter for someone.

Collins came back out with a fist held tight by Hawkins's face. Hawkins opened a hand, gesturing her to drop it, and Collins let go of whatever she was holding. Hawkins scratched at her palm, then in a rapid motion that would have been undetectable had I not been paying attention, she placed a finger under her nostril and sucked hard.

She let out a forced breath, pupils dilated, and

her flat lips stretched into a devilish grin.

She stuck her open palm out at me. "Want some?"

At the center of it sat a green pouch, something that resembled a flower's head or a leaf glued to itself to create a bowl-like shape, and inside of it was a brown and white powder. It reminded me of salt and pepper, only, much lighter.

Although I didn't know what it was, it didn't take a genius to figure out that it was a drug.

"I'm okay, thank you."

Without answering, she dipped another finger into it and brought it straight for her nostril again. After the loud sucking of air, she shook her head. "Your loss, kid."

She gave Collins the pouch back, and Collins returned it to its safe spot.

"What do you want?" she suddenly asked.

Taken by surprise, I hesitated. Wasn't she the one who'd asked me to come here? Were the drugs affecting her memory?

"Most of all," she continued. "What do you want on this hellhole of an island?"

The answer should have been obvious, but she was still staring at me, so I shrugged and said, "To get off."

This time, she laughed so hard that thick red tonsils appeared at the back of her throat. Midlaugh, she stuck her thumb out at Collins.

"Collins here can arrange that."

Collins smirked and revealed a set of yellowing teeth, then made her tongue flap up and down rapidly.

I felt violated.

"Off the island," I corrected.

As the words came out of my mouth, it was as if I'd conjured magic—the clouds overhead suddenly seemed to stop moving as the wind disappeared. I wasn't an idiot; time hadn't stopped, but the silence that surrounded me became so disturbing I was forced to look away.

Hawkins spread her legs apart and rested both elbows on her knees, back hunched and shoulders curved forward. "Isn't that what we all want?"

How was I supposed to respond to that?

"What if I told you that isn't what I want?" she asked.

Now she had my interest. I had no idea where she was going with this, but her tone indicated she was about to reveal something important, so I paid close attention.

"How about I tell you what I want?" she asked.

Figuring she'd keep talking anyway, I kept my mouth shut.

"I want Rainer," she said. "I want her people. I want this whole fucking island."

I stared at her—at her dry, pale lips; her broad shoulders that seemed to form balls on either side of her neck; her trident tattoo; her damaged hands that looked like they'd experienced several lifetimes; her blond, slightly orange, uncombed eyebrows; her odd gray eyes that were like nothing I'd seen before; and her tangled hair that looked as though it had been tied in a bun and left to dry since she'd landed on Kormace Island.

She let out a breath through flared, pointed nostrils and gazed into nothingness, most likely fantasizing about taking down Rainer and ruling over all of Kormace Island.

"Let's make a deal," she said, her focus returning to me. "You bring me to Rainer, and I get you off this island."

I held back my laughter. Was she *that* high? We were most likely days away from any civilization. How the hell did she expect to get us off the island?

"What're you talking about?" I said, a sly smirk on my face. I hadn't meant to sound condescending—to make it seem like she was crazy—but I couldn't hold it back. "You gonna build me a boat? How far do you think that's going to take me? To take us? Because I'm not leaving without my friends."

"Whoa." She flicked her wrist in the air. "Relax, kid. I'm not a fuckin' amateur. If all it took was building a boat, I'd have started that the second I landed on this godforsaken place." She reached down beside her chair and slid a slab of wood out of the way. Underneath it was a hole—something they had evidently dug up—and inside of it, a wooden box. She reached even deeper into the hole, her ribs pressing against her armrest, and extracted something that could have been plucked out of a science fiction movie.

It looked like a communication device.

CHAPTER 9

My heart pounded. "What is that?"

She lowered her head and smirked. "This, my friend, is a C-42 Transponder."

I inched toward the edge of my tree stump. Technology? How did she have technology on the island? It couldn't be possible. The correctional officers in the helicopter would have never allowed it. And even if she'd somehow snuck it onto the island, how had it survived the water? How would it even survive the island? It would run out of power if it hadn't already.

She must have been watching me ponder to myself, because her smirk stretched into a proud smile and she leaned back again, chin elevated and skin pulled back on her face. She placed the gadget to her lips, pressed a button, and said, "Ace, Hawk in the sky, over."

A staticky sound came out of the machine's small speaker, and a man's voice echoed, "Ace in place, over."

She pressed the button one last time, creating a clicking noise, but didn't speak into it again. What had been said? Was it some sort of code language? Were they simply confirming their line of communication was still open? She tilted her head sideways, looking amused. Were my eyes bulging out that badly?

"You look surprised," she said. "It's military grade. Waterproof, blast proof, solar-powered. Basically, this motherfucker ain't goin' anywhere, and it can reach distances you'd never dream of."

"Wh-who was that?" I asked, my throat making a sticking sound as I swallowed.

Head still tilted to one side like a cat observing a mouse, she said, "A friend."

Was she really in communication with someone from the *outside*?

"You underestimate me, Brone," she said plainly.

I rubbed the back of my neck, feeling like an idiot.

She must have sensed that I presumed her to be less dangerous than Rainer, but I was beginning to realize that although she didn't possess survival skills needed for this island yet, she had other strengths—strengths that would probably prove themselves deadlier than survival skills.

"I have a lot of friends on the outside," she added, "and I always get what I want."

"And you want Rainer," I said.

She crossed her fingers together over her lap.

"I want this fuckin' island."

"Rainer controls it," I said, and this seemed to piss her off even more.

Her face went beet red as though she was holding it all in—saving the anger for when she would actually need it, which I assumed would be when she'd come head-to-head with Rainer. Yet she didn't say a word.

"I'll take you to her," I said.

She stiffened.

"I'll also tell you everything I know."

What Hawkins didn't realize was that I also wanted Rainer dead. If Rainer was dead, it meant I'd get Murk out of there, and it also meant peace for my women and me—at least until we got off the island as promised by Hawkins. What she didn't know was that she was about to fight my battle for me.

"I'll tell you what weapons they use, how many of them there are, and how they protect their territory," I continued. "But in exchange, I get what I want, too."

"You want off the island," she said.

"Me and all my women," I clarified.

She stared at me the way a mentor would their mentee—full of egotistical pride as if I were capable of becoming like her. The fact that I'd been brave enough to make such a demand without so much as blinking seemed to satisfy her.

As I sat quietly, staring back into her wild eyes and refusing to back down, the sound of Ellie's sweet voice slipped into my mind. She was far away, repeating the same word over and over again: *Hope*.

That word, having once been powerful enough to pull me from a spiraling depression, lingered only for a moment before I pushed it away.

I was done *hoping*.

If I wanted a real chance at life—if I wanted to get off this island—I'd have to fight for it.

Hawkins fell back into her chair, making a plopping noise upon impact, and crossed her arms over her wooden chest plate. "All right. Take me to Rainer, and I'll get you all off this island."

Visit **shadeowens.com** for more works by Shade Owens.

Made in the USA
Las Vegas, NV
01 April 2022

46715303R00246